Amor

in the 305

SHELLY CRUZ

eBook ISBN: 978-1-7358437-2-8
Print ISBN: 978-1-7358437-3-5

Visit my website at www.shellycruz.com

Cover Designer: Murphy Rae
Editor: Virginia Tesi Carey
Interior Designer/Formatting: Uplifting Author Services
Proofreaders: Courtney DeLollis and Amy Briggs

Amor in the 305

Fate had other plans...

♡ Shelly

ALSO BY SHELLY CRUZ

Nine Years Gone

Para todos los balseros cubanos quien arriesgaron sus vidas en busca de la libertad.

For all the Cuban rafters who risked their lives in search of freedom.

CONTENT WARNING

This book discusses domestic abuse. If this topic is a trigger for you, you may want to read with caution or choose to not continue reading.

PROLOGUE

Soledad

ONE YEAR AGO

The old analog digital clock on the TV stand reads 3:34 a.m. I shift and look over, he's sleeping on his back, his head hanging over the pillow underneath his neck. The subtle rise and fall of his chest are in sync with his snores, which are a loud rumble reverberating in the otherwise silent room. I can hear the dull buzzing of the exterior lights outside our bedroom window.

I push the blanket and sheets back then glance to see if he's moved. He remains in the same position. I rise from the bed and tiptoe toward the living room where I left my sneakers, phone charging, and purse. After slipping my shoes on and tying them, I stand in place. I can still hear the grumble of his snores. I grab my coat, phone, charger, and pockabook, and ease the front door open, pulling it closed behind me while holding the doorknob turned, to silently close the latch.

Last night when I returned home from work, I left the driver's side door unlocked so I wouldn't have to use the key fob to open it, allowing me to silently enter my car. Once inside, I push the key into the ignition, put the car in drive and take off toward my best friend's house, leaving behind everything I've ever owned except my phone and what's inside my purse.

CHAPTER ONE

Soledad

Today is the last day we have to soak up the sun before flying home to Boston tomorrow. We've been in Miami for three days for a much-needed girls' trip. Melida, Jestine, Krissa, and I have been friends for most of our lives and we're celebrating Jestine's twenty-ninth birthday, which is next week. Besides, after the awful winter we had, I was feening to feel the sun warm my skin and the sand between my toes.

"Will you pass the sunscreen?" I ask Mel.

Melida is beautiful with fair skin and silky dark brown hair resting right below her shoulders. Her brown eyes have flecks of golden yellow, making them shine bright. She's obsessed with wearing lipstick and I think her obsession rubbed off on me because I am also obsessed with it. Even now as she's lounging by the pool, her lips are lathered in a deep orange hue, accentuating their fullness, and matching her one-piece bathing suit and large brimmed hat.

"Heads up," Melida shouts as she's tossing me the sunscreen. Jestine is napping in the chaise next to mine and Krissa is in the pool cooling off, sipping on a fruity cocktail, and chatting with some guy.

We're staying at the historic Betsy Hotel at the quiet end of Ocean Drive—if you can even call it that. Maybe less rowdy is a better way to describe it. This way, we can relax at the hotel yet still be at the center of all the action in Miami Beach. The rooftop pool is what enticed us to stay here—that and because Krissa is friends with the hotel manager who hooked us up with a great price for the suite we're staying in. Krissa is the manager at one of the waterfront hotels in Boston and they met at some work event she attended.

The Betsy is a boutique hotel located inside a restored 1940s Georgian revival building, a classical building marked by an understated elegance with its symmetrical lines, terrazzo floors, lots of natural light, and an incredible lobby bar touting some of the best drinks in South Beach. After Krissa befriended the

Betsy's hotel manager, we started planning a trip to Miami. None of us had ever been here and it's the perfect getaway to escape the brutal weather.

"Thanks," I tell her. "What time should we leave tonight?"

"I made us dinner reservations for eight thirty, that way we can get to the club around eleven thirty. The restaurant is several blocks away so we can leave at eight," Melida responds.

"Where we having dinner?" mumbles Jestine as she stirs awake.

"Prime 112," I respond.

"Sol, did you get us a cab?" Krissa asks. Krissa and I became friends in the fourth grade after she and I got into a fight during recess at one of those old school metal merry-go-rounds. Our teacher punished us by making us have lunch together in the school's office every day for a week. It's a story we often share and laugh about because had it not been for her wanting to beat me up on the playground, we probably never would've been friends.

Standing at five feet eight, Krissa is tall, although she always complains about feeling short next to me.

Her light brown hair is shoulder length and freckles spread across her cheeks and nose. Her most striking feature is her light brown eyes, bordering on green, with naturally long eyelashes we all envy.

"Yeah, I just did. ETA is twelve minutes. Once I finish putting lipstick on, we can go."

"Hurry up," says Melida. "If we're more than fifteen minutes late for our reservation, we'll lose our table."

"Let's go, I'm done," I say.

As we approach the restaurant, I notice it's not typical South Beach architecture. This structure looks like it belongs on a beach in New England rather than amongst the Art Deco styled buildings of Ocean Drive.

Prime 112 is a steakhouse the hotel concierge recommended for dinner. He told us it was one of the best in Miami—a place where people go to be seen and hope for a celebrity sighting. As we wait in the crowded bar area to be taken to our table, I can't help but notice the patrons are all dressed to the nines in what seems to be typical Miami style—chic, short skirts, plunging necklines, and vibrant colors. Women wear beautiful halter dresses, both long and short, and men have dress shirts on, with open collars and shiny necklaces. Everyone has just the right shade of sun-kissed skin.

We follow the hostess toward our table, and I can't

few days. I'll have to look into the logistics and stuff but it's the first time I've been serious about making a change. If I'm being honest, I'm kinda excited about it, even if I'll miss you bitches."

"Even more reason to party tonight," Jestine says, raising her glass. We all raise our glasses, meeting them in the center of the table. In typical Jestine style, she's the first to accept without reservations and attempts to placate the situation.

"This conversation isn't over. I need all the details, Sol," Melida adds, before sipping her drink again.

"You know when I have them, I'll share," I reply.

"So, this club we're going to later, what kind of music is it?" Jestine inquires, always right on cue to change the subject when we need it most.

Although the four of us are all the same age, I didn't become friends with Jestine and Krissa until the fourth grade when the four of us were in the same class together. Krissa and Jestine were already friends and after the playground incident between Krissa and me, her and Jestine started sitting with Melida and me at lunch. We've been a tight circle since, even if I'm closest to Melida, and Jestine and Krissa are inseparable. Remnants from when we were kids, I suppose.

"It's Latin music. I read positive things about it online so hopefully it's good," I respond.

"Yeah, because I dance so well," Krissa says, sipping her wine.

"None of us know how to salsa but who cares. We're in Miami and we don't have many clubs like this at home. Supposedly it's one of the best dance clubs in Miami," I add.

"Maybe there will be some sexy as fuck Latin men who will teach us how to dance," Melida chimes in.

"We can only hope," adds Jestine. "They're scarce in Boston, so if we can't find them in Miami, we're fucked."

"I'll drink to that," I say, raising my glass again.

The cab pulls up to the club and the area is desolate.

"Um, there's no one here. Are you sure we're in the right place?" Melida asks.

"This is the address I found." The building displays the number of the address I have written down, but the lights are dark and there are zero people in front of the door or at the neighboring establishments.

I ask the cab driver if this is the correct place, which he confirms it is. Before getting out of the car, I ask him to wait a few minutes while we check the club because we don't want to be stuck in this unknown lips hovering at his ear.

"It's okay. Follow me," he responds, his breath tickling my ear as he speaks. I drop my eyes to watch his feet and try to mimic him to follow along, but it just causes me to get tangled up with myself.

"No look at your feet, *tienes que sentir la música,*" he adds, his voice deep and husky. Sure, letting the music guide me is easy for him to say since he knows what he's doing.

Growing up, I never learned how to dance salsa or any other type of Caribbean music, which means I have two left feet when it comes to dancing. My mother is from Argentina, and she mostly listened to tango or old folklore songs—neither of which calls for swaying of the hips the way the salsa music does. My mother isn't much into dancing and our family parties usually consisted of tango music rather than Caribbean beats like salsa and merengue, hence my hesitance.

Our bodies sway with the music, and I may have stepped on his feet a few times, but I feel the music and my body is tingling while in close proximity to him. His grasp tightens and he pulls me closer. He's wearing cologne, but I can still smell his unique scent, spicy and masculine mixed with sweat. It makes my skin prickle and my belly stir. Mr. Handsome is taller than me, but not by much considering I'm six feet and wearing low heels.

"Your hands, *están hirviendo*," he says, while stepping to the rhythm of the music and guiding me to follow. My hands don't feel hot, but I know when I'm attracted to someone, my internal temperature rises, and I radiate heat. My left hand rests on his upper back, just below his shoulder, my right at his trim waist, and I let him lead, allow his gentle nudges together with the music to guide my movements.

After dancing two songs, the band announces they're taking a short break and reggaeton music starts streaming through the speakers. The thumping of the urban music beats coupled with the fast-rhyming lyrics has people bumping and grinding on the dance floor, and leaves me in awe of the way the couples move with such fluidity. As I watch in wonder, I feel a tug and he says, "*Ven*," grabbing my hand and pulling me toward the bar to our left. I glance around, searching for the girls and catch sight of Melida on the dance floor while Jestine and Krissa are off to the side sipping drinks.

"*¿Cómo te llamas*?" he asks, leaning into my ear when we stop at the crowded bar.

"Soledad. And you, what's your name?"

"Amaury. I never see you at this club before, your first time?"

"Yes, it's our first time," I say, nodding. "We're

"Sure. Let's go." I nudge Amaury so he can move and let me out. Once standing I turn to him and say, "It was really nice to meet you. Thank you for the drink, and the dances."

"*¿Donde es tu hotel*? I can drive you," he says, stepping into me while caressing my arm. The contrast of his rough fingers along my soft skin causes my skin to prickle.

"We're staying in Miami Beach," I respond.

"*Yo te llevo,* I'm going to the beach," he says, reaching for my hand again.

I glance over at Melida. "He's offering to drive us because he's going to Miami Beach," I tell her. She purses her lips and gives a quick nod.

"What about your friend, are you gonna leave him here?" I ask him.

"He has his car. I'll text him. *Vámonos*." Mr. Handsome turns toward the door and reaches for my hand but instead I grasp onto my purse straps.

As we walk down *Calle Ocho,* I notice vibrantly painted ceramic roosters in front of many shop windows. "What's with all the roosters?" asks Melida.

"Roosters are part of the Cuban culture, *el folklore cubano*, and they represent strength and power," Amaury replies, looking at Melida.

A few blocks later, we stop at a black Chevy Tahoe,

which Amaury just unlocked. It smells like the black tree shaped air freshener hanging from the rearview mirror filling the air with a musky like masculine scent of woods and citrus. He opens the passenger side door for me and then the back door for the girls before walking around to climb into the driver's seat. After pulling his phone from his pocket, he sends out a text message and tosses the phone in the center console. When he starts the engine, a guitar riff starts blaring from the speakers and I look over to him with a raised eyebrow.

"Metallica? Not a band I pictured you listening to," I say.

"Rock. It's the music *que más me gusta*," he responds, his smile stretching across his beautiful face. "Rock music *me hace sentir vivo*. Makes me feel alive," he translates, while turning to the girls in the back seat.

"By the way, we're staying at the Betsy Hotel on Ocean Drive. Do you know where it is?" I ask him.

"*Claro que sí*," he responds, and flashes a crooked smile.

Amaury parks a few blocks from The Betsy. After exiting the car, he searches for my hand, both of which are wrapped around my purse straps. He stuffs his hands in his pockets and marches quietly alongside me toward the hotel entrance. When there, I turn to him and say, "Thank you for driving us, that was nice of you."

"*Quédate conmigo* for a little while. Let's sit on that bench—" he points across the street "—*para hablar un ratico*."

I glance at the bench and back at my friends. "Girls, I'll meet you inside in a little while. I have my key. I'm gonna sit and chat with him over there." I turn and point to the bench across the street.

"Do you have your phone?" Melida asks me.

"Yes." I stick my hand in my pockabook and pull it out, showing her my phone, then toss it back into my bag.

Melida nods and meets Amaury's gaze. "Thank you for driving us. Goodnight," she says.

"Thank you," both Krissa & Jestine echo.

With my hand firmly in Amaury's grip, we cross Ocean Drive and sit on the bench overlooking The Betsy and the neighboring hotels. The night is warm and there's a light breeze coming off the ocean cooling the air. I'm dreading going home tomorrow to the cold weather after spending the past few days in the sun.

Ocean Drive is lit up with its famous neon lights—greens, blues, pinks, and oranges—amidst the palm fronds blowing in the wind. You can hear the dull sound of music drifting through the air. The night is still young in Miami since it's not even two in the morning yet. People fill the sidewalks and boardwalk behind us, some carrying their drinks, most women scantily dressed for a night of partying.

"So, where are you from?" I ask.

"Cuba."

I purse my lips. "I've always wanted to visit Cuba. I hear it's beautiful there."

"It used to be beautiful. Not anymore. No visit now *que te hace llorar*."

"Why would visiting Cuba make me cry?"

"*Porque el gobierno* ruined it," he says matter-of-factly.

I'm not sure I understand. "What do you mean, the government ruined it?"

"Everything is old and broken. Nothing is fixed. *Pero* enough of Cuba," he says, wrapping my hand with both of his. "Let's talk of something else. You have fun dancing?" He shifts his body to face me and sweeps his right leg under his left, resting it on the bench.

"Yes, even if I don't know how to dance. I loved watching the others dance, especially the group of people dancing in a circle."

"What people?"

"I'm not sure. There was a small group of maybe

eight people, they danced with partners but in a circle and it seemed synchronized."

"Ah, sí, eso es una Rueda de Casino."

"It was impressive. I've never seen anything like it."

"*Muy típico cubano. En Cuba* many people *bailan Rueda*. It's very popular," he explains of the traditional Cuban style of dancing.

"Do you dance *Rueda*?" I ask.

"I can, but no usually."

"Why?" I inquire, in hopes of learning a little more about Mr. Handsome.

"Rock *es mi música* and I only listen to *música Latina* when I'm at parties or clubs and I'm no controlling the music. It's no really…how you say, *mi onda*?"

"Not your thing," I respond.

"Yes, that." He lifts his shoulder. "I like guitar solos or heavy drums more than the Caribbean beats."

"It definitely surprised me to hear Metallica in your car. I just assumed Latino music was your thing. Goes to show we shouldn't assume things about people." His lips curl upward.

"My friends, we are all *rockeros*, rockers who love rock music. We are *Los Frikis*," he tells me.

I lift my eyes to his. "Frikis? Like freaks? Why?"

"Because in Cuba everyone called us anti-social for

the music we listened to, and people called us Frikis."

"Anti-social? What does that mean?"

"Against the government." Amaury shifts in his seat again as he's speaking, releasing my hand. I'm not fully understanding what he means, but he doesn't seem to like to discuss Cuba much, so I won't push it.

"Tell me, *te gusta Miami*?" he asks, pushing the curls behind my ears, changing the subject he's reluctant to continue discussing.

"I love it here," I respond, a grin spreading across my face. "Of course, the weather is perfect but what I like the most is everywhere we went, there was a Latin flare. It's so different than Boston. In most places, people speak Spanish and there's almost always Latin or Caribbean music playing. And of course, the beach, I could live on the beach listening to the ocean waves crash."

He takes one of my curls in his fingers and begins twirling and wrapping it around his finger. "*Sí*. In many ways, Miami reminds me of Cuba."

"How so?"

"The people. *El mar*. Being so close to the water. It's why I live in Miami Beach." He gives me a lopsided grin.

"Do you live close by?"

His head shakes. "No too far from here."

When we pull into Melida's driveway, I see it. My car's tires are flat. All four of them, which only means they've been slashed, again. It's now the fourth time he's done it and why I left my car at Melida's house while we were in Miami, in hopes of this not happening. *Motherfucker*!

"I can't believe he did this again," I say, defeat overpowering me as I slump in my seat.

"What an asshole! And he knows we can't prove it's him, so he keeps getting away with it," Melida adds.

"I can't keep on like this. It's exhausting, and expensive. This is exactly why I want to move!" I sigh, and lay my head back into my seat, squeezing my eyes to fight back the tears threatening to let free.

"Spend the night here and we'll deal with this in the morning," Melida suggests.

Melida's dad sent a tow truck to pick up my car and take it back to his shop. I guess I should consider myself lucky he's a mechanic and owns his own place, at least it saves me some money on labor. After I watch my car drive off on a flatbed tow truck, Melida drops me at home.

The good energy and relaxation I had achieved the past few days in Miami evaporated in minutes when I saw my car last night. Once inside, I deadbolt both locks, kick my boots off, and roll my suitcase into my bedroom. I pad my way to the kitchen and put on the kettle to drink *Yerba Mate*, or *Mate* as it's more commonly known, and scoop the tea leaves into the gourd. *Yerba Mate* is an herbal tea made from twigs and leaves and drank from a gourd and *bombilla*, a special straw to filter the leaves. This is yet another tradition I learned with my mother, as drinking *Mate* is traditional in Argentina and throughout South America. It's my caffeine beverage of choice and I often drink it throughout the day for a pick-me-up.

After placing the gourd, kettle, and trivet on my coffee table, I plop onto the couch. I decide to call my mother because I need to break the news to her.

"*Hola*," she says.

"Hi, Ma. I'm home."

"Why do you sound like that? *¿Qué pasó*?"

"Yesterday when we got to Melida's house, my tires were slashed, again," I groan. I'm so defeated by this continually happening I'm past being angry about it.

"*¿Otra vez*? Did you call the police?"

"Yes, again, and no, I didn't. Last time I called them

all they did was write a report. They already told me there's nothing they can do if I don't have any proof it's him."

"*Entonces*, what will you do?"

I take a deep breath, inhaling through my nose in an attempt to ground myself. She's not going to like what I have to say. "I'm moving."

"Moving? *¿A donde*?" she asks, raising her tone.

I shift my body, bringing my legs up onto the couch, and crossing them. She's gonna flip out, no matter how I tell her where I'm moving to. May as well rip the Band-Aid off.

"Miami."

"¿Qué?" she shrieks. *"¿Pero por qué tan lejos?"*

Her reaction is exactly what I expected—she isn't happy with what I told her. I take another deep breath to calm my voice. I'm frustrated but don't want to take it out on her. "Ma, Miami isn't that far, just a three-hour flight away. Besides, I don't feel safe here anymore." Part of the reason my mother doesn't understand my wanting to move is because she doesn't know the truth about Carmine, only bits and pieces of what truly happened. I never wanted to share any of it with her—still don't.

"I can never walk anywhere alone, and no matter what I try, my tires keep getting slashed. What if he tries something worse next time? If I move to a new city I can start over and keep a low profile. Eventually he has to move on, right?"

"*Pero Soli*, how drastic!" she exclaims, yet I can still detect the tremor in her voice.

"What choice do I have?"

"*No se*. We can think of something, *estoy segura!*"

"No Ma, we can't, and there's no way you can be sure of anything. It's been nearly a year, and nothing has changed. How many times do we need to have the same conversation? I'm done waiting for the next thing to happen. I have to make a change!"

"If you leave, *me quedo sola*," she whispers, her voice cracking. This is how my mom is. She wants the best for me yet has no issues with laying the guilt on thick in hopes it'll persuade me to do what she wants.

"You won't be alone. You have your sisters, and brother. You're with one of them most of the time anyway."

My mother moved to Boston in the sixties after one of her brothers had visited family and decided to stay, because the opportunities were better in Boston than in Balcarce, the small town she grew up in in the province of Buenos Aires. Once my uncle established himself in the states, set up with a job and a place to live, he had my mother and aunt join him. My Tio Carlo, Tia Flora, and Tia Olga all live within minutes from my mom's house. The four of them are inseparable. My mother is also extremely close to Tio Carlos' wife, and many nights they all meet up to play Canasta gathered around someone's table until the wee hours of the morning. Her other brothers and sisters, all eight of them, still live in Argentina and she goes to visit often.

"*No es lo mismo*, you know that" she says in a softer tone.

"Ma, I know it's not the same, but after coming home to four slashed tires, my decision is made," I say, my voice getting louder as I speak. "Returning home from a relaxing vacation to find my tires slashed again! It ruined everything, and I can't do it anymore! Please, just support me. I'm gonna do it anyway; it'll be easier if you don't fight me on it." My raised voice coupled with the strong tone of my words is the only way I'll get through to my mother. The only way I can get her to end the guilt trip and really listen to what I'm saying.

There's silence on her end of the phone, but I can hear her heavy breaths as she's contemplating my words and letting the idea of my move settle in.

"*Bueno hijita mía*," she whispers, the words of endearment barely audible. "You know I love you and support you. *¿No me gusta* but what choice do I have?"

My lips curl upward, happy she gave in quickly this time.

"I know you don't like it, but you'll see it's what's best for me. Everything will work out fine. Thank you, Ma. I love you."

"Okay, *Soli*. I only want what's best for you but I'm selfish too and I'll miss you."

"Why don't you come over later around five, *para que me cocines*? You can make a *pastel de papa*. I haven't had it in a while and it's a perfect day for it." My mother's favorite thing to cook is shepherd's pie and with it being a cold day, it's the perfect meal.

FIVE MONTHS LATER

I invited Melida, Jestine, and Krissa over to help me pack and hang out. I'm going to miss them so much. Although they planned a going away get-together for me next weekend, this is the last time just the four of us will be together. It'll be the first time in our lives we're separated for an extended period. Thinking about it too much hurts my chest but I know I have to do it.

After we got back from Miami and I broke the news to my mom, I began planning for this move by searching for apartments, neighborhoods, and price ranges. I needed to budget for the move and searching for apartments would help me know what I was getting myself into. Krissa's friend, the manager at the Betsy Hotel, has been helpful with answering questions about neighborhoods and even hooked me up with a realtor to help me find an apartment when the time comes. It's made getting ready for my move south easier now that I'll have someone in Miami helping me.

"Are you taking these?" Krissa asks, holding up a set of candlestick holders that were displayed on the fireplace mantle. I can still vividly see the day we got into an argument, and he hurled one of them at me. It was the first time I decided to tell the girls about the real Carmine.

"No. Carmine's sister gave those to us, and I don't want anything that reminds me of him," I respond. "I can't believe I still have them."

I sit on the floor, rest my back against the wall. "Do you girls remember the night I told you I had finally decided to leave him?"

We had attended a concert in the city and then decided to stay out. It was a rare night out with my friends, since we barely saw each other anymore. I wasn't ready to go back to my house and it was one of those warm spring days and the evening was too beautiful to be home. With a bottle of wine and plastic cups, we found some benches in the Boston Common and popped the cork. As we were drinking, I suddenly blurted out, "I've decided I'm leaving Carmine." Krissa almost choked on her wine.

"What? When? How?" Melida asked. The shock on their faces is an image ingrained in my memories. Up until that night, they knew very little, only what I had selectively shared. I was always worried about sharing too much, worried about their judgment. That they'd think I was weak. But that night I shared everything. Once I started talking, I couldn't stop, and the girls proved me wrong. They cried with me and for me as I told them the stories about Carmine's behavior, the way he took pride in belittling me, and the look of satisfaction he had after he slapped me. I wished I had told them sooner. I explained I didn't have a plan yet and the only thing I knew was I was leaving.

"It's a night I'll never forget. I don't think any of us will," Jestine says. She stretches her hand out and rests it on my leg.

"Definitely not. When you told us about Carmine and how he'd been treating you, my perspective changed. I always knew he was a jerk, but I never would've imagined him hurling things at you or laying a hand on you," Melida says. "Whether you think you know someone or not, we never know what goes on behind closed doors."

"Anyway, if you weren't having a yard sale next week, I'd say let's have a bonfire and torch all this shit," Krissa adds, an evil laugh filling the air.

"That would be cathartic, but I'd rather get some extra cash for all this stuff. My mother loves having yard sales, so she's gathering stuff to sell too," I add.

"Did you give your notice already?" Jestine inquires.

"Yeah, last week," I respond, nodding.

"What did Mona say?" Jestine asks.

I attended UMass Boston. Despite being considered a full-time student, it took me five years to complete my degree because I only took four classes at a time since I had to work too. I double majored in Linguistics and Italian, with a minor in Spanish, and graduated with a bachelor's degree. In my final semester, I was required to do an internship and landed one at Every Word Counts Translations in the city, where Mona is the owner. After graduation, she hired me full-time as an interpreter and translator. Much of the work we do relates to court proceedings or documents used in lawsuits, so most of the clients we have are attorneys who need translations or interpreting for their clients. I spend most of my days translating documents from

Spanish or Italian to English or interpreting for people during in-court hearings. I really enjoy being in the courtroom, but only because I'm there to assist and not part of the proceedings.

"She cried when I told her. I've been working with her since my last year at UMass. It's the longest I've ever worked anywhere."

"After Mona got over the initial shock of me leaving, she offered to help me find a job in Miami because she has several connections. In fact, she even brought up the idea of a business opportunity—opening an Every Word Counts office in Miami and being her business partner, with me running the Miami office."

"What? That's incredible!" says Jestine.

"It's an amazing opportunity but I turned it down. I told her for the time being it would be too much for me to take on with a new city, a new move, and a new business. We decided to table the idea for the time being and revisit it once I get settled in Miami."

"Aw, how sweet. I'm sure she's gonna miss you. You basically ran that place for her," Krissa adds.

"She did help me find a job though. I mean, I'm not officially hired yet, and have an interview when I'm in Miami. But Mona assured me the job is pretty much mine and the interview is a formality."

"Do you have anything else lined up, in case the

overlook Biscayne Bay. You can see part of the Miami skyline, the cruise ships docked, and the causeway stretching across the water crossing over to Miami Beach. Breathtaking!

"Hello, Soledad," Lily says, as she circles her desk to greet me. "Mona has told me so much about you, I feel like I already know you."

Lily has curves in all the right places and the deep pink dress she's wearing hugs her figure to accentuate them. It falls just below her knees, paired perfectly with patent leather platform heels, and silver chandelier earrings hang from her ears. Her silky, smooth dark blonde hair falls over her shoulders and down her back.

I extend my hand to hers, and she pulls me to her, kissing me on the cheek. "Hello Ms. Bermudez, it's a pleasure to meet you," I say, a little taken aback by the greeting. Although I'm accustomed to the cheek-kiss when attending events with friends or family, I've never had someone do it in a formal setting. Maybe it's because Mona sent me? Or is it a Miami thing?

"Please, call me Lily. My mother is Ms. Bermudez, and I still feel like a young woman," she asserts, throwing her head back in laughter.

"Nice to meet you, Lily," I say and stand next to the chair but don't sit.

"You know, Mona told me you'd be a little serious. Don't worry, that will change soon enough. Here in Miami, we're more relaxed, laid-back. Please sit, I won't bite." She chuckles.

Lily offered me the job within minutes of being inside her office. Even so, we chatted about the work I did in Boston, Mona, and living in Miami. She was excited because she doesn't have any Italian language translators and had to refer those jobs out to another firm. Now that I'll be working with her, it'll no longer be necessary.

"Is it okay if I start next week? I just arrived last night, and I don't even have an apartment yet," I tell her. "I plan on seeing some over the next day or two. Hopefully I'll fall in love with one of them."

"Of course. Also, here's my mobile number," she says, writing it down on a sticky note. "Call me if you don't find a place, I can make a few calls for you and see what we can find."

"Thank you, Lily. I appreciate it."

"Mona spoke about you like you're the daughter she never had. That speaks volumes because she doesn't like anyone," she states, chuckling as she says the words.

"So kind. I love Mona and am gonna miss her, a lot! We've worked together since I was in college, and I've learned so much from her."

"Mona and I met in college many moons ago and despite the distance, we've remained close friends. I'm happy to have you join us here at Miami Language Solutions."

Lily and I walk toward the front together and see Dayren as we approach the reception area. "Dayi, Soledad will be starting next week and will make a great addition to the family. She's gonna fit right in."

"Great, welcome," says Dayi.

"Thank you. There's much to be excited about. New job, new city. So many great things happening," I exclaim, excited thinking about what's ahead.

"Sol, can I call you that?" asks Dayi, her eyebrow slightly raised.

"Yes, of course."

"Good," she says. "Here's my cell phone number—" she hands me a sticky note "—call me, we can meet up for dinner or drinks whenever."

"I'd love that. My mother is here for the next week or so and then it's a date!"

The realtor wasn't able to get any appointments to view apartments for after my interview yesterday but scheduled three for today. We've already seen one and I wasn't a fan. It was very small and in a high-rise building. I wasn't sure how I felt about living in a high-rise but after going through the hassle of getting there, parking, and busy elevators, I've decided it's not for me. The only positive of the high-rise apartment is the unit had a partial ocean view from the balcony, but the unit was on the twenty-second floor and the height kind of freaked me out.

This apartment we're about to see is a small two-story art deco building with only four units, two on each floor. This is more my style since I would have a private entry and only three neighbors. The building has no parking, which is a negative but there is a pool and in-unit laundry. If I want to live in Miami Beach, apartments with parking are the most difficult thing to find so I may have to compromise. Hopefully, once I get a resident's sticker for my car, parking won't be awful.

We climb the stairs to the second floor, which are located inside the building but visible from the street through an arched entryway. The unit is located on the left side of the building overlooking the pool and patio area, offering some privacy. The door is dark wood, rounded, and has a textured glass panel with bars over it near the top. When the realtor swings open the door, it opens into a large open space, a living room, dining room, and kitchen with dark hardwood floors. Along the left wall there are two large windows looking out to the street and the several trees surrounding the building, providing much needed natural light yet also enough shade from the sun. The kitchen on the far end has a counter to separate the living space from the cooking area. Along the back wall there's an electric stove, with the counter to the right and wrapping along the right wall, with a sink in the middle and dishwasher to the far right. A small window above the counter to the right of the stove brightens the kitchen making it appear bigger than it is. To the right of the entry is small hallway with a bathroom to the immediate left and two bedrooms just beyond. The washer and dryer are stacked inside a door within the bathroom and there is a tub where I plan on taking nice long baths. One of the bedrooms is large with a walk-in closet along the right wall. The picture window overlooks the patio and pool area. The second bedroom is smaller and perfect for me to use as an office and guest room.

"I'll take it," I tell the realtor. I love the layout, the space, the lighting, and the location. It has good vibes.

"You like it? You don't want to see the last place?" the realtor inquires.

"No." I shake my head. "I like this one. The second you opened the door I immediately loved how bright and open it feels. It's perfect. The only negative is no parking, but I'll deal with it. And the next apartment we're scheduled to see has no in-unit laundry, this does. Let's do it."

"*A mí también me gusta,*" my mother adds, giving her approval of the apartment.

Melida's name flashes across the phone's screen and I scoop it up and press the green button to answer. "What's up, Mel?" I drag a stool out from underneath the kitchen's island.

"How are you settling in?"

"Well, the movers came yesterday just in time to move into my new apartment, which I got the keys to the day before."

"Nice. Speaking of, I turned in your keys to your apartment here. The landlord was nice. He said he'd mail you a check once you give him an address."

"Awesome, I opened a P.O. Box, so I'll reach out to him to give him the info."

"When I was inside the apartment waiting for him, I saw Carmine through the window but by the time I got outside that fucker was gone." My spine straightens.

"Do you think he knows it's empty, that I moved?" I ask, uncrossing my legs and pulling my knees up to my chest.

"I don't know, but your curtains and stuff are gone so I don't think it would be too hard for him to figure it out, especially if he's peering in the windows."

"Ugh, what a creepy stalker! Be careful, Melida. Make sure you're always aware of your surroundings and try not to walk alone."

"I'm not worried about him doing anything to me, he's obsessed with you, and I don't think he'd harm me. Anyway, let's not talk about that douche anymore, all he does is ruin everything. Tell me more about Miami and what you've done."

My lips curl up at Melida's change in conversation. "Well, I got the job with Mona's friend, as expected, and start next week. This way I'll have time to finish unpacking and setting up the apartment. I think we're about halfway done with the boxes."

"Where's your mom?"

"Taking a shower. We've been unpacking most of the day. She's gonna make us dinner when she's done."

"Mmm, your mom cooks so good!"

"I know. I'm gonna miss it. Miss her."

"I bet. When does she fly home?"

"Sunday."

"Does she like it there?"

"Yeah, at least the little she's seen since we've been here. Although, she's not used to everyone speaking Spanish around us. Neither am I. Today we were at the grocery store, and she was commenting on how people were dressed, you know she's super judgmental. Anyway, I had to remind her that people here understand when she's talking shit about them."

Melida is laughing. "Oh my God! What did she say?"

"She made some remark about a woman's short skirt and said the lady was too old to be wearing so little clothes. The lady gave my mother a dirty look and walked the other way with her head held high."

Melida's laugh turns into a cackle and I can picture her throwing her head back in laughter as she so often does. "That's frigging hysterical! I can totally see your mom and the face she made."

"Sure, now that I'm telling you about what she did it is, but it wasn't while it was happening, I wanted to die," I say, chuckling. "When you're getting dirty looks from strangers because your mom is talking shit about them, there's not much to laugh about. I hope she learned her lesson and won't do it again."

"To be fair, it is Miami Beach. I remember the few days we spent there. People weren't wearing a heck of a lot of clothes."

"Not necessarily. I mean, here on the beach maybe. But when I was downtown the other day, people were professionally dressed so it's probably a good mix."

"Alright, Sol. Just wanted to check in. I gotta go to my parents' house but need to run to the store first. We'll talk soon."

"Okay. Love you, Mel," I exclaim, a smile spreading across my face.

"Love you more."

CHAPTER FIVE

Soledad

I've always wanted to own a Vespa scooter but it's too cold in Boston to use one most of the year. Now that I moved to Miami Beach, it's the first thing I'm going to buy. This way I won't have to drive as much. It'll be perfect to ride and get around locally since parking isn't easy. Besides, the weather calls for it.

The other day I saw a cute sign that read 305 Scoots, with a smiling sun donning sunglasses between the three and five. The uniqueness of the sign and name stuck out to me—using Miami's area code in the name to create a logo was clever! When I peeked through the window, I saw a showroom full of scooters.

After dropping my mother at the airport this morning, I decide to walk to the scooter shop since it's a short distance from my apartment. Although it's September, it's still hot outside—blue skies and a lot of sun—the exact type of weather I moved here for. After grabbing my pockabook and sunglasses, I head out toward the scooter shop.

Strolling along the sidewalk, I make a mental note to buy a large brim hat; the sun is pretty intense and hurts my eyes, regardless of the sunglasses. I take in the surroundings of my new neighborhood. Most of the buildings are art deco style and the streets are lined with bumper-to-bumper parked cars, which reminds me I have to get a resident's sticker for my vehicle.

There's a different vibe here than back in Boston. The people walking take their time as they stroll to their destination as opposed to back home where everyone always seems rushed and deliberate walking the city streets. Not to mention, many don beachwear and flip-flops. What's interesting and I hadn't noticed during my last visit with the girls is the sidewalks are red rather than the typical concrete color.

I've only walked a few blocks but I'm sweating so I grab the hair band around my wrist and pull my curls up into a messy bun. As I approach Alton Road, I see the 305 Scoots sign across the street and am excited.

I've ridden a scooter a few times in my life and finally getting one of my own is checking off a bucket list item.

Inside the shop is bigger than I expected, and rows of mopeds and scooters are displayed before me, with electric standing scooters lining the right side of the shop.

"Hello and welcome to 305 Scoots. I'm *Eduardo*. I can help you?" a man asks, in a thick accent.

I raise my head and wave at the tall man standing several feet to my left. "Hi. I'm interested in buying a Vespa scooter and want to see what you have."

"Sure, follow me," he says, turns, and strides toward the far left of the showroom. "These are the Vespas we have right now. It's our most popular scooter so there are not too many in stock." He's pointing at three scooters and there is one in the exact color I want. Vibrant red with a black leather seat.

"The red one. She's calling my name," I say, a smile spreading across my face as I approach the red Vespa. Once I reach it, I drag my hand along the black leather seat, the seat's stitching a deep red matching the scooter's color. "She's a beauty. Now I need to decide what I'll name her. Let's do this," I exclaim, turning to Eduardo, excitement coursing through my veins.

"She's beautiful, like you," he says. Heat rises to

my cheeks. "We only brought it onto the sales floor yesterday."

"Do you want to take her out?" he inquires, raising an eyebrow.

"Nope. She's exactly what I want." My smile stretches across my face.

"Okay. Let's go over to the desk and we can get the paperwork ready. I only need your license."

I find my wallet and take it out of my purse. As I try to pull my license out from where it's stuck to the clear plastic it's behind, I realize that's another thing I have to do, get a Florida license. "I don't have a Florida driver's license yet because I just moved here, is that gonna be a problem?" I ask.

"No problem. Just fill this out with your information," he says, sliding a blank form across the desk toward me. I complete the form, we discuss the details of the scooter, and I give him my ID.

While Eduardo begins the paperwork, I wander over to the accessories area to see what they have and begin browsing the helmets. I've seen people riding without a helmet but think I should wear one. I'm still new at this and can't be too safe. There are so many styles to choose from. I know I definitely don't want a full-face, it's too hot outside to wear one. There are two different open-face styles, need to see which I like more and fits more comfortably. I pull a solid black one off the shelf.

"¿Soledad, *eres tú*?" a man asks. When I raise my eyes to his, Amaury is standing beside me, the dark stubble giving him a dark and dangerous look.

"Hi," I say, pushing my curls behind my ears.

"You back in Miami for vacation again?" he asks, confusion spreading across his features. Or maybe disappointment because I haven't reached out to him. It's been months since I last saw him but he's as beautiful now as he was the night I met him—maybe more so now with the natural light accentuating his green eyes. The scar over his eye is a lot more visible now, the thick line running from his eyelid about an inch above the brow line.

"Actually, I decided to move here." I place the black helmet in my hands back onto the shelf.

"You live here now, very nice," he says, raising an eyebrow and crinkling his forehead.

"I've been here about a week, so far. I love it. Now that I live here, I'm buying a scooter. What about you, what are you doing here?" I ask, grabbing another helmet from the shelf in front of me, this one also black but with silver designs on it.

"This is my shop." He smiles now, a genuine grin reaching his eyes.

"Oh, well, even better then. I'm glad to know I'll be supporting someone I know."

He steps closer to me and with the back of his fingers grazes the skin on my upper arm. "You never called me."

His thick accent warms me from the inside, sending a chill up my spine and the helmet I'm holding drops to the floor, causing a loud thud. "I'm sorry."

"I got it." Amaury bends to pick up the helmet and places it back on the shelf, then turns to me. Standing before me his emerald eyes gaze into mine, and he grasps my fingers intertwining them with his, his proximity causing my breath to quicken. "I was thinking about you *todos los días* since I meet you," he whispers, bringing my hand up to his lips, dropping kisses along my fingers.

"I—"

"*Te extrañe*," he says. "We barely know each other but I missed you, *mucho*." His touch burns my skin and lights a fire within.

"I'd be lying if I said I didn't think about you too," I murmur. I can't believe I said that. It's like I don't know myself when he's near me. Thinking and feeling things I shouldn't, saying things I should keep to myself. His fiery touch mixed with his deep, sultry voice laced with a thick accent has me all worked up, intensifying the tingling between my legs.

"*¿Sí*? Good, it's decided then. We can see each other again and go out."

"Um." I draw my hand away from his, push my curls away from my face. "We can talk and then see about going out sometime."

"*Está bien.* I can be patient." He rewards me with a crooked smile.

"You choose a helmet?" I shake my head. "For you, *me gusta* this one—red with a black swirl design." He grabs a helmet from the bottom shelf and holds it out to me, tracing the design with his left fingers. It's an open face model covering the ears with a front visor.

I pull the elastic from my hair, letting my curls fall over my back and take the helmet from him, pushing it onto my head. "I like it and it fits good. Just need to figure out what to do with my hair when I ride," I say, staring at my reflection in the mirror to the right of the helmet shelf.

"You already choose a scooter?"

"Yes. The red Vespa over there," I say, pointing to where my new ride is on display. I remove the helmet and muss my hair a bit. "Eduardo is doing the paperwork."

"¡*Perfecto*! This helmet will match *tu nueva motoneta*," he says, grabbing the helmet from my hands.

"You decide what you will name her?"

I glance at him, a smile oozing from me. "I thought I was weird for naming my vehicles, but it turns out you do the same thing."

"Ah, yes. *Es muy importante* to give your new scooter the perfect name and it must be a woman's name because the Vespa *es clásica*. She's beautiful and has *curvas*. He drags the fingers of his right hand along my jawline, causing goosebumps to spread across my skin. "*Como tú*," he finishes.

I need to get control of myself. Mr. Handsome has barely spoken or touched me and I'm all flustered and out of sorts. I separate myself from him. "I haven't named her yet, I'll let you know when I do."

"*Ven*. Let's see if Eduardo is finished." He tucks the helmet under his left arm and then rests his hand on my waist, leading me toward the desk area.

"Eduardo, *te acuerdas* the woman *la noche en* Ball & Chain. This is her, Soledad."

"Ah, the mystery woman! I was starting to think she was only in your imagination. He's talked about you every day since that night. Today you have made him a happy man." Eduardo's words surprise me. Amaury and I spent less than two hours together, yet he's thought and talked about me for months.

The ringing of the front door's alert bell interrupts

us and Amaury tells Eduardo, "I finish helping Sol, you help him." He points to the man that just walked into the showroom.

"I've already finished the forms, she just needs to review and sign them," Eduardo says, then strides toward the gentleman perusing the scooters.

"You know how to ride this, or do you need lessons?" Amaury asks.

"I'm pretty sure I know how. I haven't ridden one in years but I'm sure it's like riding a bike," I respond, pulling a curl around my fingers. Nerves pool in my belly because what if I don't remember how to. Thankfully, my apartment is only a few blocks away so I should be okay.

The forms seem to be in order, and I sign them, pay for the helmet and scooter.

Amaury went to get a new helmet in the back. When he returns, he says, "*Vamos*, I bring it outside for you and get you ready to go, *sí*?"

Outside Amaury parked my new red beauty in the shade along the sidewalk.

"*Entonces* Sol, when I can see you?" he asks, stepping into me and caressing my jawline.

I lift my eyes to his. "I don't know. My cell phone number is on the forms inside. Call or text me and we can figure something out." I'm not ready to commit to anything just yet.

"Okay. *Hacemos las cosas a tu manera,*" he says, reluctantly agreeing to do things at my pace. "I want you to be ready *pa' lo que viene,*" he proclaims and presses his thumb to my lips, tracing them from left to right. I'm grateful he isn't pushing more. I'm into him but I'm nervous. A new relationship wouldn't be the worst thing, but regardless of what we do, I need to take it slow. I don't even know if I'm ready for a relationship again.

CHAPTER SIX

Amaury

I watch Soledad ride off on her new Vespa, my heart thrumming in my chest from spending the last thirty minutes with her. When we met and she didn't give me her number, I was sure it would be the last time I ever saw her. *Es nuestro destino* that she walked into my shop today. I've always been a big believer in destiny, and today's events show it's a good thing. When I can no longer see her or the Vespa, I turn on my heel and head back inside.

"Bro, *tremendo cañón*, you in love!" exclaims Eduardo as soon as I walk through the door.

"I know, she so beautiful! I no stop thinking about her since we met."

"In all the years I know you, I never see you act *así* with a woman," Eduardo says from where he's standing behind the desk.

Eduardo and I have been friends since we were young kids in Cuba. I'm a year older than him but we grew up on the same block, went to the same school, and had the same circle of friends. He didn't know I was leaving Cuba because it's one of those things you don't talk about, but he had the same plans as me and left about a week after I did. I'm glad he's here—him and several other friends from my childhood—since my brothers, sisters, and parents are still in Cuba and have no plans of leaving the island. Starting a new life as an adult in Miami was hard, especially by myself, but with friends like Eduardo, who is like a brother to me, it makes it much easier.

After being in Miami for a few years, I opened 305 Scoots with Eduardo. We were both mechanics back in Cuba so together we restore and fix old scooters. We decided to add rentals and sales to our shop here in Miami Beach. With it being a tourist destination all year round, it was an ideal business. Our first few years it went much better than expected and we decided to open a second location on Washington Avenue between Fifth and Sixth Streets. Although both locations are busy, the Washington Avenue location gets a lot busier with rentals since it's more central to the touristy area of South Beach.

"When I met her, something happened inside of me. When we danced the first night, our attraction was … *no se, inexplicable*," I recount, remembering the night I danced with Sol under the stars at Ball & Chain. I can't find the right words to explain what she makes me feel.

"*Pero*, she's no *cubana. ¿De dónde es?*" he asks, inquiring about Sol's origins.

"*Es Gringa* with Latino parents."

Sol wasn't a good dancer and stepped on my feet a few times, but she let me lead and carry us through the beat of the music. Her hands were on fire and she smelled like cinnamon. When I kissed her my body ignited from within, like fireworks. Then she went home never to be heard from again.

"So, when you seeing her again?" Eduardo asks, interrupting my memories.

I shrug. "She told me to call or text her so hopefully soon," I respond, searching for her paperwork so I can find and save her number to my phone.

I'm home and feel restless. I've put some groceries away, got my mail, watered my plants, and took a shower. Despite that, it feels like I still have unfinished business. Seeing Sol was unexpected yet the best thing that's happened all week. Her light brown eyes shone, and the lipstick she was wearing accentuated her full lips. I wanted to kiss her but had to restrain myself. There's something holding her back, keeping her from opening up to me. The night we met she didn't talk much and was quick to leave. Today as we talked about scooters and helmets, I could see her eyes wanted to tell me more. Whatever she was thinking or feeling, she kept to herself. I'll have to work on making her feel more comfortable around me. Get her to talk more.

Do I call her now or should I wait? Will she think I'm too pushy if I do? If I don't, will she think I'm not into her? I haven't dated in a while and don't know what's right or wrong anymore. Is there even a right and wrong?

Fuck it, I'm calling her. If I don't, I'm going to drive myself crazy. I grab my phone and pull up her name, hit send before I change my mind.

She answers on the second ring. "Hello."

"*Hola, Sol. Es Amaury*," I say, trying to keep my tone even to not sound too eager.

"Hi. I knew I'd hear from you tonight."

"Y eso?"

"You're not the type of guy to wait, when you want something, or in this case someone, you don't leave anything to chance." Her tone is playful and light, yet she's spot on. She has me pegged and we've spent a total of three hours together. Am I that transparent?

"What I can say? *Me gustas*, since the first night I met you. You got away last time and I no letting it happen again." Now that she opened the door to how I feel about her, I'm not letting the opportunity pass me by. She's silent at my confession, her breath even but loud in my ear.

Sol finally breaks the silence. "So, what do you have in mind?"

"*Hay un restaurante argentino en* North Beach. Dinner?" I know her mom is from Argentina, which is why I suggest dinner at an Argentine place.

"I'd like that. But, if it's okay with you, let's meet up later in the week," she says. Waiting isn't what I hoped for but she said yes, so I won't push my luck. I'm in for a long week waiting to see her again. "I'm still settling in, unpacking, and getting used to a new work schedule."

"*Está bien*. Any day *en particular*?" I ask, hoping she says Tuesday and not Friday.

"Let's do Thursday. Not sure what work will be like at my new job and if it's anything like the last place I worked, it'll be hectic."

Four days will feel like four weeks, but I haven't been this excited about anything in a long time.

"*Perfecto*," I say. "*¿Qué haces ahora*?" I ask, curious as to what she's doing.

"I'm getting my stuff ready for work. Tomorrow is my first day at my job and I want to leave everything ready for the morning."

"Where you will be working?"

"I'm an interpreter and translator. I'll be working for a company named Miami Language Solutions. The office is in Brickell."

"Wow. *Que* cool. *¿Para español*?"

"Yes, Spanish and Italian," she responds. I remember being at the courthouse a few years back and saw the interpreters working. It's difficult to listen and interpret simultaneously. I'm impressed.

"*¡Impresionante*!" I exclaim. "That's a great job."

"Thank you."

"I let you get back to what you are doing then. I wish Thursday to come soon."

"Me too. And Amaury?"

"*¿Sí*?"

"Thank you."

"Thank you *por qué*?"

"For knowing I wanted you to call without me actually saying it." My heart thunders at her confession.

"Good night, *muñeca*," I say, with a smile spread across my face.

"Buenas noches."

Hoy el tiempo no pasa. I spent the entire day looking at my watch and the minutes seemed like hours. Now outside the restaurant, I feel anxious and excited about seeing Sol. When I texted her yesterday, she asked if we could meet at the restaurant. I'm guessing it's her way of keeping her privacy until she feels safe with me. Understandable and smart.

I'm leaning against the wall, searching the area for Sol to make an appearance. A few minutes pass and I see her emerge from between two parked cars in the public lot across the street. I watch as she strolls to the corner and presses the button to wait for the light. She's such a rule follower. I would've crossed without waiting for the light. As she waits for the walk light, she's fidgeting, twirling her hair with her fingers. She hasn't noticed me watching her.

Sol is tall, not much shorter than me, and I'm six feet four. She's curvy with hips and an ass that drive me crazy, and legs for days. I hope I get the chance to wrap those legs around me. *Behave Amaury*, I can't be having a hard-on on my first date. She's already reserved, no need to give her a reason to run.

As she approaches me, her hand raises, waving. "Hi. Have you been waiting long?"

I shake my head. "No, just got here," I respond, and lean in to place a kiss on her cheeks. Her olive skin is warm and soft, the cinnamon scent invading my senses.

"Good. I hate making people wait."

"You could park your scooter here," I say, pointing to the motorcycle parking off to our right.

"I drove. I'm not comfortable enough to ride at night."

"Soon you will be a pro." I reach for her hand, but she wraps both hands around her purse straps.

We turn and walk to the entrance and the hostess seats us at a table by the window.

"Why'd you choose this place for dinner?" she asks me.

"I remember you said your mom *es de Argentina*."

"Funny, growing up we'd go to Argentina for two months in December to spend the summer with my mother's family in *Mar del Plata*. We'd always eat at the Manolo restaurant. I loved having meals there. When you suggested this place, I was surprised because I didn't know there was a Manolo's here and it brought back some good memories."

"*Acerté*," I say, and she graces me with a smile that reaches her eyes. A lucky guess on my part that she'd been to one of these in Argentina.

"Have you eaten here before?" she asks.

"Only the churros and the coffee. Not dinner," I respond, dropping my eyes to the menu. "There's a lot to choose from, *no se* what I want. You?"

"From what I remember there's a lot of similar menu items. I think I'm gonna get the Milanesa Full. It's what I used to get in *Mar del Plata*, and something *que mi mamá* made for dinner a lot." I peruse the menu in search of what she said she's ordering and find it. Breaded chicken or steak topped with two fried eggs and a side. Not something I would choose but sounds interesting.

"Funny, *nosotros los cubanos* call a milanesa—" I bring my eyes down and point at the menu "—a *bistec empanizado*. A breaded steak."

"That's one of the things I love about languages. We all speak Spanish, yet each country has different ways of identifying or saying things. Sometimes even within the same country there are varying dialects. I loved studying and learning about the linguistics of language." As she's talking about her studies, her lips curl up and her golden-brown eyes are bright.

"Why you decide to study that?"

"I grew up speaking Spanish with my mother. When I started kindergarten, I had to learn English and was the only kid who spoke Spanish. Then in junior high we had to take a language and I chose to study Italian because I already knew Spanish. Besides, that's where my grandfather is from, and it was either Italian or French. I learned quickly and studied all through high school. Also, I used to translate for my mother all the time. She speaks English but needed help to understand letters or if she was having a conversation with a doctor or lawyer. By the time I got to college, I loved languages and it was just part of my life, so I decided to major in linguistics and Italian, with a minor in Spanish." She shrugs as if studying languages is something easy.

"*Increíble!* Many people need translators to help. You will do good here in Miami with that job."

"I hope so because so far I really like living in Miami."

"So, which do you like more, speaking in English or *hablando en español*?"

"They both come naturally to me. I guess it depends on who I'm with. I mean, English is what I'm most used to but sometimes I think in Spanish too," she says, lifting her shoulder in uncertainty. "What about you, which do you prefer?"

"*Bueno*, it's easier to speak Spanish but English is better so I can practice. When I'm with someone who speaks both, I try to speak English. If I no speak it, I forget it and here in Miami it's easy to only speak Spanish."

"Makes sense. So, English it is, or at least for the most part because let's be honest, Spanglish is gonna happen." She chuckles.

The waiter arrives to take our order. "I'll take the *churrasco*, well done," I tell him when Sol finishes ordering.

"Well done?" Sol interrupts me, scrunches her face, and drops the menu on the table.

"*Sí*. Why?"

"My uncle would give you a lecture if he was here right now about eating meat, how to eat it, the proper way, blah blah. Then he would insist you order it medium, because that's the right way to eat steak—according to him, anyway."

"Really? *¿Y eso porqué?*" I ask, my eyebrow raising.

"He says it's the best temperature to get the true taste of the meat, to truly savor its flavors, especially since the Argentine's only use salt to season it.

My uncle is THE Grillmaster, grilling for us all year round—" her hands are animated as she's telling me about her uncle "—regardless of the freezing temperatures outside."

"Okay. I trust you. *Voy a probar* the steak like you suggest," I tell her, then turn to the waiter who is waiting for us to decide. I hope I don't regret trying it as she's suggested. "Medium, *como dijo la señorita*," I tell him.

"I agree with the lady. Medium is the best temperature to have your steak," the waiter chimes in.

"*Con papa fritas*," she adds, raising her eyes to the server. "Gotta have fries with your steak. It's the only way to have it," she says with a lopsided grin.

"*Me encantan las papitas*, good choice." She's right, fries are my go-to side dish when I have steak. Who knew talking about food would get Sol to open up, speak comfortably, and ease her nerves when speaking to me. We'll have to have more meals together so I can get her talking more freely.

When we finish ordering, I extend my hand across the table and place it near her to see if she'll extend hers to mine. She doesn't and instead tucks her hands under the table and away from me.

"So, steak is serious business?" I say, wanting to change the awkwardness I just caused by reaching across the table, and pull my hand back.

"Oh, not just steak. Eating in general is serious business. I'd say that eating, and cooking, are at the top of my list of favorite things to do."

"*Entonces, estamos hecho un pal'otro*," I respond, chuckling. "I love cooking and eating too. See, destiny! There's nothing like good food."

"What's your favorite thing to make?" she inquires, her eyes widening with enthusiasm.

"*Potajes*. Black beans, *chicharos, frijoles colorados*. Any type of beans."

"*Chicharos*. I don't think I'm familiar with those or ever had them. As for the other beans, I've probably only tried them once or twice and wasn't a fan. Beans aren't something my mother made because they're not a big part of the Argentinian diet."

"But your father, he's Puerto Rican, no?" I ask, curious as to how she's barely tried beans when they're a staple of the Puerto Rican diet.

She's twirling her curls with her right hand and staring out the window. "I remember very little about my father."

I don't want to pry too much because she is shifting in her seat as she stares out the window at the mention of her father. She's already tight-lipped, no need to help her with keeping quiet. "Hopefully you learn to like beans more. You no had them *bien hecho*, yet. How you make them makes a huge difference and many restaurants make theirs with canned beans."

"Well, you'll have to cook for me someday," she says with a lopsided grin, and meeting my eyes.

"*Cuando tú quieras* I cook for you." Maybe she'll take me up on my offer and allow me to cook for her soon. I take the opportunity and extend my hand across the table again, palm facing up, hoping she will meet me halfway—and she does, bringing her hand up from beneath the table and placing it in mine. I drag my fingers up and down the inside of her palm, letting her soft, warm skin graze my rough fingertips.

"I'd like that." She pulls her bottom lip between her teeth and licks her lips. *Dios mío*, her mouth is sensual and I'm thinking about all the things I'd like her to do to me with her mouth.

"So, Amaury. Can I ask how old you are?"

"Thirty-six. And you?"

"I guess it's only fair since I asked you." She grins. "I turned twenty-nine in July."

"What day?"

"The twenty-first. And you, when is your birthday?"

"July fourteen."

We exit the restaurant and stop at the corner. Before pressing the walk button, I ask, "*¿Quieres ir a la playa*, to sit *y escuchar el mar*? Look at the stars." Sitting on the beach to hear the sounds of the ocean is something I have to do regularly. She nods in agreement.

Even from here, two blocks from the shoreline, I can hear the ocean's roar; smell the salty air and as usual, my mind wanders back to Cuba and the nights I would spend along *El Malecon*, the waves crashing against the wall, drenching the sidewalk.

El Malecon is a five-mile stretch of seawall in Havana, often referred to as the soul of Havana. The promenade crosses through several city neighborhoods and shields the city from the ocean, which at times gets angry: the loud spray of the waves hitting the wall. It's like the city's outdoor lounge and along *El Malecon* you'll find tourists and locals, lovers strolling hand-in-hand or friends hanging out on hot days in hopes of the ocean spray cooling them off. Most days culminate with a sunset rivaled by no other. Although the beach here is not the same as back in Cuba, it connects me to my former home.

The night air is warm yet the steady breeze rolling

off the ocean cools the skin. I look over at Sol who is untying her cardigan from her waist and pushing her arms through the sleeves, wrapping the front closed. She's cold, even though it's not cold outside. I stretch my arm and wrap it around her, pulling her into me as we walk to my car. "This okay?" I ask. She nods and smiles, leaning into me as we continue to stroll down the sidewalk.

"Just need to grab the sheet from my truck for us to sit," I tell her as I open the trunk of the Tahoe.

"You didn't bring your scooter either," she says.

"No, I was in Broward today and came right here on my way back," I respond, tightening my arm around her as we continue toward the beach.

With the sheet in one hand and my other arm draped across Sol's shoulders, we cross the street and reach the sand. The moon is not quite full, a small sliver missing from the bottom rim, its reflection glaring off the dark ocean water, illuminating the night sky and the strip of water beneath it.

I spread the old, tattered sheet out and sit, leaning back on my elbows while I wait for Sol to join me.

"I've never been to the beach at night," Sol tells me, as she sits cross-legged to my left.

"*¿Nunca*?" I raise an eyebrow, taken aback that it's her first time visiting the beach at night.

"No. Growing up in Boston I'd go to the beach three or four times a week during the summer, but we'd leave early."

"*La playa de noche* is beautiful. I come for calm. For peace. A place for me and my thoughts. There's no one at the beach and you really listen to what's around you, and what's inside of you. *El silencio* is heavy but I always feel better. I like coming at night more than the day. *Es mí lugar favorito.* It's also the only place I feel connected to Cuba."

The beach has always been my favorite place, especially as a young boy in Cuba because it's the one place I felt carefree. Then as teens we'd spend so many days and nights there. The island of Cuba is surrounded by pristine blue waters and white sand beaches. A beauty I've yet to see anywhere else. After so much destruction of its cities, the beaches are the only beautiful thing left in Cuba.

"It's definitely different. So quiet, relaxing."

"*En Cuba* I would spend many nights at the beach, listening to the waves, have fires, be with friends, and even sleep there. Some of my best memories of Cuba are from the beach."

"How long have you been here?" she asks.

"Twelve years."

Sol lies back and props her head up with her right

hand. “Why did you leave Cuba?”

CHAPTER SEVEN

Soledad

For the past several days I'd been nervous about today. It would be the first time I was going on a date since the night I escaped from Carmine's clutches. Despite being excited because I am attracted to Amaury, I'm also scared because I have to trust a man again. My relationship history isn't great, and although I'm sure I'm partly to blame, my father abandoning me as a child doesn't help the situation. I know I can't punish Amaury for Carmine's actions, but it doesn't change the fact I'm anxious about it. There's something about him that makes me feel at ease, but I haven't spent enough time with him yet to know what it is. Besides, I had good feelings about Carmine the first time we went out and look how well our relationship ended. I already promised myself I would take it slow with him, which is why I chose to meet him at the restaurant. This way, if I get any weird vibes, I can thank him and drive home.

Last week when I saw him at the scooter shop it was a surprise, albeit a nice one. I had thought about calling him once I settled into my new apartment and job, but fate intervened for us. When he asked me out, I wanted to say yes, but my anxiety about moving too quickly took over and prevented me from it. A lot of good it did me considering he called me later that night and by the end of the conversation, I had agreed to have dinner with him.

"To live free," Amaury responds matter-of-factly.

"What do you mean?"

Amaury extends his legs out, in search of a comfortable position. "Cuba is a communist country and we Cubans can't live freely." Even though I'm Latina, I know very little of Cuba and its history. Growing up in the United States we didn't learn much about it in history classes, and I never took the time to learn about it.

"I know Cuba has a communist government but I'm ashamed to say I don't know much about what that means or how it affects people's lives. I remember hearing a little about it when President Clinton passed a law relating to Cubans, but the truth is I was young and didn't pay attention to any of it."

"It's not you, Sol. Most people *no saben* what it's like. Most people cannot even imagine it. *Es horrible*." I know him telling me most people don't know about Cuba or Cuban history is meant to make me feel better, but it doesn't.

"Tell me about it," I say, shifting my body toward his.

"I no fear death, I fear no living. If I stay *en Cuba*, that's no life, it's survival. That's why I left on a raft. It's better to die free in the ocean than live in Cuba."

My eyes widen, the shock of the words I just heard fall from Amaury's lips something I was not expecting. "Did you say a raft?"

"*Sí. Soy balsero*. A Cuban rafter."

I gasp. "Wait, what? How?"

"Desperation makes you do things you otherwise no have courage for, *mi bella* Sol." He caresses my jawline before looking out over the water. "One day twelve years ago, I went to see my mother, *Mima*, to eat lunch at her house. My best friend, Roberto, lived next door to her and I asked *Mima* if she know where Roberto is. When my mother say yes, she saw him earlier that day and he had left in a hurry to Miguel's house. I knew right away what Roberto and Miguel were doing."

"Who's Miguel?"

"A friend *de Cuba* who came on the raft with us."

Amaury is speaking, but his gaze is lost somewhere out at sea, as if the story he's sharing is taking him back to the moment it took place.

"Right away I stand up. *Mima, vuelvo enseguida*, I told her, even if I knew I no be coming back. I left my lunch half eaten and ran to Miguel's house, who lived near the beach. When I arrived, Roberto, Miguel, and five others were there. They were building a raft made of inner tubes and were almost finished. When I asked when they were leaving, they told me after sunset. I left with them; there was no other choice for me. I couldn't stay in Cuba."

"Just like that? Did you say goodbye to your mom, your family, or friends?"

"No," he says, shaking his head adamantly. "You cannot say anything about those things. Because if people know, they talk, and then we would be arrested."

"How old were you?"

"Twenty-four."

Goosebumps spread across my skin at his words. I cannot imagine what that must feel like. To feel so desperate in a situation you would risk your life on a homemade raft to cross the ocean. I grew up working class with a single mom and thought I didn't have much, but, after hearing him recount what desperation drove him to do, my upbringing pales in comparison. "What was it like when you left? Were you scared?"

He's nodding. "Yes, very scared. But I was more desperate than scared." A chill runs up my spine at his words and I lift my legs and sit up, bringing my knees to my chest to wrap my arms around them.

"There were eight of us on the raft. We took turns *remando*—" he motions his arms back and forth in a rowing motion "—two at a time. Most of us wore rain jackets to protect our skin from the sun. We had water, canned foods, and prepared sugar water."

"Sugar water? What's that for?"

"*Te mata el hambre*," he responds, my mouth agape at the story falling from his lips. "We had food, but being on a *balsa* in the open ocean, it's no easy to eat because you throw up. So, you drink sugar water. It's something we learned living in Cuba on days we didn't have food to eat. Sugar kills your hunger." He glances at me, his eyes soft and his lips slightly downturned.

"How long did it take you to get here?"

"Four days, four nights."

"Holy shit," I whisper. "How did you know where

to go?"

He points up at the night sky. "*Las estrellas*, *la luna*, *y el sol*," he responds, meeting my gaze while running the back of his hand down my cheek, causing my skin to prickle. A homemade raft being guided by the stars, the moon, and the sun—it's like a story ripped from the pages of a book, except it's his reality.

"What was it like, being out there—" I point to the ocean "—for four days and nights?"

"The first night when we left Miguel's house the moon was almost full and the ocean was, how you say *picado*?" he asks, shifting his eyes toward me.

"Choppy," I respond.

"*Bueno*, the ocean was choppy. After two hours it started raining, heavy rain and winds. We fight a lot because now we were in the ocean in the middle of a storm, *estábamos desesperados*, like maybe it was a mistake." As he talks about the feelings of desperation he felt the night they left, he pulls his knees up to his chest and wraps his arms around his legs.

"In that moment we no know if we make the right decision. The next day it was sunny, there was no more storm, and the ocean was calm. We started talking about past memories growing up, of concerts we saw, or things we did, all to try to make the time pass. With the sun it was very hot. *Pero* at night, *mucho frio*. We were freezing, and we could barely sleep." With his right hand he takes his shoelace between his fingers and starts rolling it back and forth.

"By the third night we started seeing things, we thought they were lights, or land. Of course, it was just, *alucinaciones*. *No se* how you say in English."

"Hallucinations," I add.

"Yes, that. We saw many other *balsas* too, some people alive, some dead. *Era triste*." His voice softens as he recalls the sadness of seeing dead Cubans floating on homemade rafts.

"Did you see a lot of them?"

"Yes." His head bobs up and down. "Too many." I cannot even imagine seeing the things he's telling me about, rafts full of people, both dead and alive in the middle of the open ocean.

"What happened when you saw them?"

"*Nada*. You no can get close. *Era muy peligroso*. We risk sinking. *Acuérdate*, all of us were very desperate to reach *la Yuma*."

"*La Yuma*? What's that?"

"*Nosotros los cubanos* call United States *La Yuma.*"

"Hmm, interesting."

I've never heard anything like what he's telling me. I'm fascinated and sad and cannot believe it's the first time I'm learning about any of this. Here I thought I was pretty educated. While I may be in my area of study, there's still so much to learn. I have so many questions about his trek to the United States.

"When you got here, where did you land?"

"Two miles from Miami. *La Guarda Costa*, found us. They put us on the ship while they look for other *balseros* to rescue," he says, describing the Coast Guard ship in Spanish. "I cried when I was on the boat with Americans. I was finally free. Then, they took us to a warship that carries airplanes for two days before they took us back to Cuba."

I'm confused at what he's explaining. "Why would they take you back to Cuba?"

"Refugee camp *en Guantánamo*."

"Did you have to stay there?"

"*Sí*." He nods in agreement. "I lived there for nine months until I came to Miami."

"Have you seen your mom or family since you left?"

He's shaking his head.

"Will you ever see them again?"

"I no think so. It's not easy to travel to Cuba, especially for someone like me. The government says I deserted my country, and in Cuba, that's criminal."

I'm still. Everything I've listened to is shocking to

me because I never could've, or would've, imagined anything like what he's shared existed.

"So will you ever return to Cuba?"

"No. I no want to go back there. United States is my home. This country gave me life."

"Do you talk to your family at all?"

"*Sí*. We can talk on the phone, *pero* very little. Not everyone in Cuba has phones, and it's expensive to call there. I have to call a neighbor in Cuba who then lets my family use the phone."

"Wow Amaury!" I extend my hand out to his arm, trace my fingers along his wrist up to his forearm and back down. "I've never heard anything like what you've told me. It all seems so surreal, like something I would read about in books or see in the movies."

"Because you were born and raised in a country that lets you live free. *Cosas así* no *pasan aquí*," he tells me, and pushes my curls behind my ear. Those things not existing in this country is precisely why I'd never imagine it could happen anywhere. Listening to Amaury's harrowing tale of how they risked their lives on the open ocean makes me realize I was lucky to have grown up how I did.

"Your story is incredible."

He shrugs. "I no really see it that way. It was what we needed to do." He starts toying with the ends of the shoelaces again, his brow furrowed, a sullen look across his face. He's probably lost in thought about his family in Cuba. I shouldn't have asked so many questions.

"Thank you for sharing," I say, extending my hand out to let my fingers skim the stubble growing along his jawline. "I can't imagine what you went through, or how hard it is to be here without your family."

"Some days are not so bad, other days I feel lonely *sin mi familia.* The friends from Cuba are like family, *pero no es lo mismo.*" I reach for his hand, intertwine my fingers with his and squeeze. He reciprocates.

"I had a great time tonight," I continue. "I'm glad I decided to come out."

"You no want to come tonight?"

"It's not that I didn't want to, I was hesitant."

"¿Por qué?"

Why? What a loaded question! Our night has been heavy already, no need to burden him with my baggage too. Isn't there some rule about not talking about exes when you're on a date? Well, I definitely don't want to talk about mine, primarily because I try to forget all the harm he caused me, and how I allowed myself to be manipulated. But also because I don't want Amaury to take pity on me.

I raise my shoulder in uncertainty. "I'm a bit shy."

"Shy?" He shakes his head. "You are not shy."

"Maybe shy isn't the right word," I say. "Once I know you, I'm not shy. Maybe introverted is a better way to describe myself."

"*Bueno*, I hope you open up with me. We can start by doing what I been dreaming about for months." He leans in, his lips hovering above mine. He hesitates, waiting for me to give him the green light. I lift my hand, rest it at the nape of his neck and pull him to me, letting our lips crash. The stubble along his jaw scratches at my skin, intensifying our make out session.

Our kisses are slow and intense, and I lie back, Amaury following my lead and extending himself to lie down next to me, all while not letting our lips separate. His large hand grips my hip and squeezes, shooting a tingling sensation through my body.

He takes my bottom lip between his teeth and begins softly sucking, savoring as he explores. His hand drops to my leg, his fingers tracing the seam along the side of the pant leg, slowly dragging them up and down.

My heart is thumping in my chest and heat is emanating from my core. I feel like ripping my clothes off but know I can't. For one, we're on a public beach. Besides, it's our first date and I promised myself I'd take it slow—it's a promise I'm keeping. We hear voices off in the distance and thoughts of Carmine flash through my mind, causing me to put space between us. He lifts his head to search the area before returning his penetrating gaze to mine, stoking the fire deep in my belly.

"*Eres única*," he whispers, before dropping kisses along my neck. Suddenly a phone starts vibrating and Amaury stuffs his hand in his pocket and silences it before dropping it onto the old sheet.

"What time is it?" I ask.

"Almost eleven," he responds, in his thick Cuban accent while looking at his watch.

"I think we should call it a night. I have to get up early for work," I tell him, somewhat reluctantly. It's my way of separating myself from him and keeping my promise to myself. I'm suddenly not in the same headspace anymore after Carmine creeped his way into my memories.

"*Está bien, muñeca.*" His lips cover mine and then he grazes my cheek before hopping to his feet.

We walk hand in hand to my car, Amaury's finger drawing circles on my palm, something he's done each time our hands are linked. I wonder if it's something he does without thinking.

"Why do you do that, draw circles on my palm?" I ask.

"Your skin feels so soft in my rough hands," he says. "*Y porque quiero devorarte.*"

I'd be lying if I said I don't want him to devour me, which is exactly why I need to leave.

"That's me, over there," I say, changing the subject and pointing to my car, a red MINI Cooper with a white top and sunroof. I've had Anja for three years. I love her but have been thinking about buying a new car. It's one of the last ties to my old life and if I'm starting anew, it makes sense to get rid of the old car as well. I need to do everything possible to ensure Carmine never finds me. Soon, I'll make it happen.

"Red car. Red scooter. Red sneakers. I imagine *que también tienes fuego en el corazón*," he tells me, before pulling me flush to him and crushing our lips together. I wouldn't say I have fire in my heart, but when I'm near him, my heart feels like it's on fire.

My hands rest on Amaury's chest and I put space between us, shifting my eyes up to meet his. His green eyes are dark tonight, I can see the lust burning at their rims. "I had a great time tonight, Amaury. Thank you for dinner, and for sharing so much about yourself."

"*Sí*, next time *te toca a ti*." He caresses my chin. "You have to tell me about you. You no tell me anything tonight." He smirks.

"I'll see what I can do," I tell him, licking my lips,

and wrapping a curl around my fingers. He leans in, brushing his lips to mine softly.

"You say you're not comfortable riding the scooter, you want me to help you learn more?" The tip of his nose grazes mine as he moves it in a back and forth motion.

My heart is racing. "I'd like that, yes."

"*Perfecto*. I'll call you *mañana*," he says, leaning into me.

I shift to avoid him, unlocking the driver's side door and climbing in. "Good night." I buckle my seat-belt and back out. Amaury stands and watches me drive off. When I'm at the red light, I stick my hand into my pockabook and grab my phone. Three missed calls. I punch in the unlock code and the missed calls are from an unknown number, causing a chill to snake its way up my spine.

CHAPTER EIGHT

Amaury

When driving I usually have the music loud, let the guitar riffs course through me as they fill the air around me. But not tonight. Tonight it's the sounds of the road and my thoughts.

It's been years since I've talked about my journey from Cuba and Sol asking so many questions flooded me with old memories and opened up old wounds. It's not that I don't like sharing my story, but it's also something I don't talk about too often. Some days I feel better about it than others. It's heavy and Sol's reaction was the reaction I'm used to, shock and awe. Unless the person on the receiving end of my story is Cuban or familiar with Cuban history and politics, they're always stunned to learn I risked my life on the ocean to live free. What shocks them more is I left my family, friends, and entire life, and never said a word of the journey we were about to take.

Don't get me wrong, Sol asking questions means she's interested in getting to know me better, which is what I want. Anything to get her talking more. I knew we'd have this conversation eventually, I just didn't expect it to be on our first date. It shouldn't surprise me, though. I'm a Cuban rafter and it's an integral part of the man I am.

When Sol asked about my leaving, I was transported back twelve years, sitting at my mother's table eating a plate of white rice, black beans, and *tostones*. I can still see the dull white plate, with several chips along the outer edges, the worn silver fork that was too small to eat with but the only ones my mother had. The faded floral print on the plastic tablecloth that's adorned the table since I was a child. It had started like every other day, but when my mother mentioned where Roberto was, I knew his plans. I knew the day would end like no other.

Roberto lived next door to me my entire life and we were like brothers, did everything together—walked to school, chased girls, went to rock concerts, did military duty, and even got locked up together for being "anti-social." My brothers and sisters in Cuba are all younger so having someone my age to cause mischief with was everything to me.

We both listened to all the rock music we could get our hands on from the tourists we'd meet at the beach. We'd often befriend the tourists at the beaches, and when the tourists learned we didn't have access to a lot of music in Cuba, they'd offer us their cassette tapes—probably because they felt pity for us. The beaches were the only place we'd run into tourists and have an opportunity to talk with them at length, and even that was scarce, as there were few places native Cubans and tourists could be found mingling. This was the only way for us to get the music from the American rock bands we wanted to listen to.

During our military tour, Roberto and I would often talk about coming to the United States to start a new life. Roberto was discharged from the military service months before I was and as soon as he was out, he started building rafts and trying to escape with a few mutual friends. The first few times they tried they were caught, because either they told too many people their plans or they left at the wrong times and were caught by the Cuban Coast Guard. Each time they'd get sent to jail until someone in the family could obtain their release—usually Roberto's father who was well connected with the Cuban government.

With each raft Roberto built, he improved, each one built sturdier and more reliable. By the time he built the raft we left on, it was solid. It was made with inner tubes from bikes and tires, tarps stolen from local shipping yards, empty rice sacks, and lots of rope. The raft never got damaged over the four-day journey and for that we were all thankful.

When I arrived at Roberto's, him and the other guys were putting the finishing touches on the raft—tightening knots, fortifying the inner tubes, filling jugs with sugar water, and securing the oars. When we were ready, we drove to another friend's house who lived by the point of departure. We remained hidden inside the house until darkness fell, seeking the cover of night to protect us from being caught. For a few weeks before leaving, Roberto had surveilled the Cuban Coast Guard and the times they'd patrol in that specific area. We knew we had a window of fifty-seven minutes to put the raft in the water, row away from the shoreline, and out of sight from their next patrol round. It would be tight, but we had no choice but to try.

As we waited for the time to pass, I was nervous, anxious, excited, and jumpy. Every noise around me enhanced by the tight knots in my stomach. That night

I didn't know all the other guys felt the same. We all kept those feelings to ourselves, too afraid to voice how scared we truly were for fear if one backed out, others would follow. It wasn't until months later while living at the refugee camp in *Guantánamo* that we all confessed our true feelings. Turns out each one of us was more scared than the next—afraid we would die in the ocean but willing to risk it for freedom, for the chance at living a life free from oppression and hunger.

A honk from the car behind mine startles me back to the here and now. I realize as I'm driving down Alton Road, I'm going twenty miles per hour, the whirring of the engine purring reminding me of where I am. I've been lost in a daze and don't recall driving from where I was parked to my current location. I missed my turn on Forty-seventh Street and need to make a U-turn to head back toward my house.

Once I get home, I kick my shoes off by the door and pull off my socks, dropping them onto the floor. I place my keys and wallet onto the counter and head straight to my backyard to lie by the pool under the moonlight, which illuminates the entire sky. This is my favorite spot at the house, my oasis. It's where I spend most of my time while home. A backyard surrounded in tall, lush greenery, the privacy from my neighbors something I craved after growing up in a place where everyone was up in your business.

I search for a playlist on my phone, music from the sixties reminiscent of the music I'd listen to with my father in Cuba on the nightly *Nocturno* show—the Beatles, Rita Pavone, Formula V, and Boney M, among others. Growing up we didn't have a television, so the radio was always on in our house. At night my father would turn on the *Nocturno* show, where the music would play for two hours. I would lie in bed listening to my father's music and dream about a life better than the one I was living. My father's love for music turned me on to rock music. Similar genre but different eras, different sounds.

My first few years in Miami I rented apartments, but I moved into this house a few years back when Eduardo's now ex-girlfriend encouraged me to buy a home instead of rent and pay someone else's mortgage. I was reluctant at first, unsure I'd be able to pay the mortgage and still afford the expenses that accompany homeownership, but the scooter business was doing well, and I wanted a place I could call home.

I miss Cuba terribly, not because I miss living under government oppression or the awful conditions, but because I miss my family. I was close to my parents and siblings but since the day I fled, the distance between us isn't only physical, but emotional too. The ability to communicate regularly with them is difficult because the calls are exorbitant in costs and my family didn't, and doesn't, have a phone at their house. We have to coordinate to speak by calling a neighbor's house. Although we have mobile phones here, in Cuba they're scarce and there is very little mobile phone service.

My mother was angry at me for years after leaving.

Angry because I left so suddenly.

Angry because she never knew of my plans.

Angry because I didn't bring her with me.

My siblings were less upset and understood my desire for a better life. But it was my father who surprised me the most. He was a military man his whole life. He fought alongside Fidel Castro during the Revolution all those years ago. My father truly believed the Revolution was for a better Cuba. But it wasn't until my early teen years when my father finally accepted he'd been deceived—him and an entire country.

When I first spoke to my father a year after leaving Cuba, I heard relief in his voice. He told me while the entire family was worried something had happened to me because no one knew of my whereabouts, he knew I had fled on a raft. He said he'd always known I wouldn't last long in Cuba because I was too wild to live under the watchful eye of the Cuban government.

With the departure of tens of thousands of Cubans by way of raft, my father was certain I'd risked my life on the open ocean.

During our call we cried—for all the division that was forced between us because of ideological beliefs. I hadn't spoken to my father, or any family, for over a year, but they knew I was safe. At some point during my stay at *Guantánamo*, the Miami Herald had released a comprehensive list of names of all the refugees housed at *Guantánamo*. That list somehow made its way back to Cuba and my father learned I was safe. His biggest fear had not come to fruition.

My phone dings, signaling an incoming text message and it brings me back to the calm night before me. It's not as windy now as it was earlier when we were sitting on the beach. I extend my hand to grab the phone next to my feet and slide the unlock feature. A smile spreads across my face when I see Sol's name on my screen.

Sol: *Gracias* for tonight. I had a great time.

My heartbeat quickens at the words in the text message. She's coming around and I'm ecstatic thinking about it. I've been here for twelve years and although I barely know her, Sol is the first woman to make me feel I want more. The first night I met her I was drawn to her, as if she had a rope tied around me and was pulling me toward her. After she left, I thought I'd never see her but couldn't stop thinking about her. I drove Eduardo crazy with all my talk of the mystery woman, as he started calling her.

Her texting me tonight is a big step for her considering she's been so reserved and reluctant to let me in. I know I can be imposing and have no filter when I speak, which could frighten her. I need to be cautious on how I approach her and how I get her to open up with me, to feel like she can trust me.

Our date tonight went too quickly, but I'm so happy she said yes. Turns out the Argentinian restaurant was a good choice. She was relaxed as soon as we sat and took the liberty to insist I eat my steak a certain way. Turns out I liked the steak as recommended. Who knew?

I thoroughly enjoyed watching Sol eat her meal. She truly savored her food as she consumed it. I like that she ate and wasn't shy about it. I've not been on a lot of dates but most of the time the girls I dated didn't eat much. I'm not sure if it's because they weren't hungry or if they didn't want to eat on a date, but either way, it was weird to me, especially since I love to eat.

There are so many things I want to text back to Sol but instead I keep it simple to let her know I hope we have a second date soon.

Amaury: *Gracias a ti. Que se repita pronto. =)*

CHAPTER NINE

Soledad

Melida answers on the third ring, which I'm thankful for. I want to tell her about my date with Amaury last night. I'm terrified of what I'm feeling and know she'll have sound advice for me.

"What's up Sol, I was just thinking about you. Your ears must've been ringing."

"Yeah, whatcha thinking about?" I ask, as I pour some water into the gourd.

"How much I miss you. Definitely not the same with you gone. The other day I wanted to go to your house to chill and couldn't. It felt so weird."

"I miss you too, especially since I have no friends

here yet. I mean, the office manager at work has invited me out and she seems nice. I'll probably finally have lunch with her this week once things have settled in at work and I've finished unpacking."

"How do you like Miami so far?"

"I'm liking it a lot, and it's always hot outside, which I love!"

"I like the warmth too but love my four seasons—even if I bitch about it half the winter." She huffs before laughing.

"How's the girls? I haven't talked to them." It's been a couple weeks since leaving and I've only spoke to Jestine once, and only texted with Krissa. I just left Boston and already communications are dwindling.

"They're good. I haven't seen either of them in over a week. Krissa has been working a lot of OT and Jestine met a guy right after you left so she's been out with him a couple of times. I probably won't see either of them until next week."

"Wow. I'll have to reach out and get all the details. If you talk to them, tell them I miss them!"

"I will."

"So, remember the guy from the club in April, the one who drove us home? Well, I ran into him last week and we went out last night."

"No suh! What are the odds? So, how'd it go? Tell

me everything!"

I update her on running into Amaury and everything that transpired on our date. "When I'm with him I feel comfortable, and that scares me. I've had such rotten luck with guys in the past, but you already know that." They've all been the ones to break up with me, except for Carmine, who is an aggressive asshole and stalker. I shift in my seat at the mere thought of his name.

"Speaking of your past, I saw Carmine the other day and I don't know if it was a coincidence or if he was stalking me to find you."

"Knowing him and his past behavior, it's the latter. He's probably freaking out now that my apartment is empty, and he doesn't know where I am. Did he say anything to you?"

"Yeah, he came up and said hi, had that smirk on his face. You know the one." Carmine's grin was sexy and enticing. His full lips would stretch across his beautiful face in a half grin. It's the first thing I noticed about him when we met, his panty melting smile. For the first several months of our relationship he was kind and hid his true nature. It wasn't until he'd wrapped me around his finger did his true colors start seeping. "I told him to fuck off, that I had nothing to say to him and walked away," she says.

"That's it? He didn't say anything else?" I ask, shifting on the stool. At first, he would get angry about me hanging out with my friends, said I spent too much time with them and not him. He became wary of me, started monitoring my phone, and would have jealous outbursts in public places. I made excuses for him, apologized for his behavior, which only made him worse. It was a mindfuck!

"As I walked away, he told me he'd be seeing me again soon," she replies, causing me to shiver. When controlling me wasn't enough, he started intimidating me through his insults and threats of harm to himself, and to me. After scaring the shit out of me, he'd apologize profusely and profess his love for me, promise it would be the last time he'd act that way. They were all lies. I was blinded and unable to see what was in plain sight.

"Mel, he's following you because he's looking for me. I'm freaking out just thinking about it." Eventually my friends caught on to his behaviors, but I covered for him.

Denied his behaviors.

Defended him.

Lied for him.

"I'll be careful Sol, I promise. I've known who Carmine is for a long time. Don't worry about me, okay?"

"How can I not? He terrorized me for over a year of our relationship plus a year after leaving him and ultimately drove me out of Boston. The guy's got issues!" I stand and pace over to the window, pull back the curtain to gaze out at the blue sky. I'm concerned for Melida's safety.

"He definitely does but you know I've been taking self-defense classes for years. I can't be certain, but I'm pretty sure he's following me because he wants to find you, not hurt me. He might have issues, but he's smart too. He knows not to fuck with me.""You're right, but it doesn't make me feel any better."

"Anyway, enough about that douche, tell me more about this guy. What scares you about him?"

"I wouldn't say it's him, per se. I think I'm just scared of a relationship in general. He's nice, talkative, attentive, maybe too much though. And as you saw the night at the club, he's not shy." I pad across the living room and sit on the couch again, crossing my legs.

"Well, it doesn't necessarily make him a bad guy. Does his behavior weird you out or make you feel uncomfortable?"

"No, nothing like that. It makes me feel at ease, oddly enough. I felt safe with him, but the fact I felt safe with him scares me because I don't know him enough to feel safe. Does that make sense?"

"I know what you're saying. Look, take it slow with him. Hang out, be cautious but don't let your past stand in the way of your future. Otherwise, you could ruin a good thing. Remember, this guy isn't Carmine. Lucky for you Carmine is a one-of-a-kind loser."

"True. Definitely need to get out of my own head and start trusting myself again."

"Sol, what happened with Carmine isn't your fault. You did nothing wrong. You need to remember, he's the asshole. He's the one who hurt you and caused all that shit."

I pull a curl between my fingers and twirl. "I know. I turned a blind eye and made excuses for him. I mean, you saw him for who he was and kept telling me, but I wouldn't listen. It wasn't until I left that everything he'd done to me became crystal clear."

"That happens in life though. Afterall, hindsight is twenty-twenty. When you're inside a situation, you want to see the best of it. I don't think it's because you're ignoring it or not seeing it, but I think it's because you genuinely care and want things to work out for the best. At the end of the day, we're all human and none of us are perfect. Sometimes, those imperfections are things we can look past and accept. Sometimes, in Carmine's case, they're not. The important part is you got out, you finally saw his true colors and left."

"I guess. Carmine fucked with my head and all the shit that went down made me not trust myself. I already have trust issues with guys, I don't need to have trust issues with myself."

"Whatever you do, don't punish the new guy. That doesn't mean you shouldn't be cautious but have fun. You deserve it."

"Thanks, Mel. I always feel better after talking to you. You know how I get, doubting and questioning myself and my abilities."

"It's because I love your ass, which I'm gonna see in a few weeks. I decided I'm coming to visit you for my birthday. Not sure if Jestine or Krissa can come but I'll go by myself if they can't."

"Oh my God!!! I'm wicked excited!" I squeal in excitement. "I have something to look forward to now!"

"Hey Dayi, you want to grab lunch?" I ask after returning from the courthouse where I spent the last few hours interpreting at a hearing.

Since starting work, I've been sent out on an assignment nearly every day, with most days being spent at one of the various courthouses in Miami. This week alone I was at the civil courthouse, the family courthouse, and the federal courthouse. I'm so grateful to Mona and Lily for setting up this opportunity for me. It's made my transition to Miami much easier because it's keeping me busy doing something I love.

"It's about time." She rolls her eyes before busting out in laughter.

"I can't believe how busy I've been in my first few weeks here," I tell her, dropping my pockabook onto the chair to my right.

"We're always this busy, so get used to it, *chica*."

"So, where should we have lunch? Any good seafood places?"

"Let's go to Garcia's. It's on the Miami River *y la comida es deliciosa*," she exclaims.

I've been craving seafood since being in Miami and hope the food at Garcia's is as good as Dayi believes it to be. There's nothing worse than craving a good meal and being disappointed.

We walk through the door and the scent of fried fish invades my senses. The front room has a lunch counter in front of the open kitchen, which is to the left of the fresh seafood market.

"Let's sit on the back patio, otherwise we'll smell like fried fish when we leave," Dayi says, walking toward the back of the restaurant.

After sitting and ordering our drinks, Dayi starts

asking me a million questions about my past and the reason I moved to Miami. I skip over the Carmine bit and tell her I moved here for the weather and the Latin flair, which is all true.

Dayi is Miami to the core. Born in Cuba, she came to Miami when she was two years old, the daughter of Cuban exiles, like so many living in South Florida. Her curls drape down her back, the dark locks a stark contrast to her pale skin and blazing green eyes. She's short, about five feet five, yet voluptuous, thick, curvy, and wears dresses that hug her in all the right places. Dayi is beautiful and she knows it.

"Tell me about you Dayi, what's your story?"

"I'm recently single and looking for an apartment. I'm finally moving out of my parents' house, which they're not happy about. I'm twenty-six and they're giving me a lot of shit for leaving."

"Really, why's that?"

"It's common for Cuban kids to live with their family for years into adulthood. They'd rather me be home, close to them."

"If my mom had a choice, I would live with her too. At some point we gotta do our own thing."

My phone vibrates and when I peer at it, I see a text message alert from Amaury.

Amaury: *Te extraño*, when can I see you again?

A smile spreads across my face as I read his words.

Sol: Actually, I want one of those cases for the back of my Vespa. Can I stop by the shop later?

Amaury: *Dale*, see you later.

I place the phone back on the table and lift my eyes to meet Dayi's. "Who you texting with that makes you light up?" she asks.

"A guy I met."

"Girl, spill. I need something juicy in my life."

I park the scooter in the shade outside of 305 Scoots and walk into the shop expecting to find Amaury in the showroom, but there's no one there. There's music coming from the back, so I cross the showroom floor to the door leading into the garage and peer around the corner.

Amaury's back is to me, and I decide to watch him. He has a mint-colored Vespa on a lift and is leaning in while doing something with the engine. His jeans are held up by a belt but his lower back peeks out. His white t-shirt is snug around his biceps, accentuating the corded muscles on his golden-brown arms. I can't wait to feel the strength of his arms around me, the sensation of his skin up against mine. Fuck me is this man sexy. Merely watching him sends a tingle through me. He shifts his body, but still doesn't see me. His long straight nose is dripping sweat and he's biting his lip in concentration. I'm so turned on just staring at him. The butterflies in my stomach flutter relentlessly. I know when we finally sleep together, I'm going to come undone.

"¡*Coño*!" he yells, dropping the wrench he was holding and starts shaking his right hand.

"Did you hurt yourself?" I ask, scurrying across the garage floor to get closer to him.

His head swiftly turns to me. "How long you been here?" He grabs a rag hanging from his back pocket and wipes his face with it.

"A few minutes. I was standing over by the door." I gesture my head toward the door behind me.

"Doing what?" He takes the last few steps, closing the gap between us.

"Sorry, I should've told you I was here." I pull a curl into my right hand and begin twirling it.

"You no have to say sorry. You can surprise me anytime you like. *Ahora* tell me, what were you doing?"

"Watching you." I lick my lips.

"*¿Qué viste*?" he asks, smirking. What did I see?

More like what was I dreaming about? I cannot tell him I was picturing his arms wrapped around me, as we both lay naked.

"White is a good color on you, you should wear it more often."

"That's it?" he says, pursing his lips and squinting.

I nod and smirk at the same time.

"*No te creo*," he whispers into my ear before scurrying across the floor and disappearing through the door I just came in. I wouldn't believe me either, I'm a terrible liar and have no game face.

When Amaury returns he crosses the garage to the far end where there's an office. "You coming?" he shouts. I stride across the open space and see Amaury washing his hands in a small bathroom.

"Is this your office?" The small room doesn't have much in it. There's a wooden desk in the middle and a closed laptop off to the side with papers strewn next to it. There's one bookshelf to my left stacked with catalogs from different vendors. On the wall hangs a large picture of a beach, slightly crooked. A peninsula with palm tree lined white sand and pristine turquoise water.

"*Sí*, but we no use it much since we have the computers out front."

"What beach is this?" I ask, pointing to the black framed picture and straightening it.

"*Varadero*. It was my favorite beach *en Cuba*."

"It looks amazing."

"*La foto no le hace justicia*," he says, staring intently at the image. Pictures rarely do anything justice so I can imagine how incredible the beach must be in real life if it's this beautiful in a picture.

"Must be gorgeous in person!"

"No beautiful like you." His lips press against mine, his arms wrapping around me, our bodies as one. He lifts me to sit on the desk as his onslaught of kisses intensifies, our tongues tangling.

The heat between my legs burns and I reach for the hem of my shirt. I separate from Amaury to pull my shirt off and quickly search for his lips. I tangle my fingers in his thick locks, massaging his scalp as I suck on his bottom lip.

Amaury's kisses stray from my mouth to my neck and make their way toward my breasts. He pulls back the bra and takes my breast in his mouth, rolling my nipple between his teeth causing me to squirm. I reach down for his belt and begin unbuckling when suddenly he stops and pulls away from me.

"*No muñeca*, stop. We can't." The lust burning from his eyes contradicts his words.

"What do you mean we can't, why not?" My rushed breathing matches my rapid heartrate. Shame creeps into me and I search for my shirt to put it back on, adjusting myself and hopping off the desk. What does he think of me if I'm the one who was willing to do this in his office?

"It's our first time. *Quiero hacerte el amor* and we no can do that here." The back of his hand caresses my cheek, his verdant green eyes searching mine.

I swallow the lump in my throat. He's telling me he wants to make love to me, and this isn't the right place, but it still feels like rejection. I should feel happy but instead my cheeks are burning, and I avert his gaze.

"I should go," I say, exiting the office and dashing across the garage.

CHAPTER TEN

Amaury

A few days ago, after I stopped us mid-make out session at the shop and Sol left, I wasn't sure if we were okay. I've tried calling her but got voicemail. The few times we've texted and I asked to see her she told me she's busy with work or ignores my request. It's been nearly a week and I'm starting to get worried. I didn't realize she was so upset. I decide to try and call her again now because she should be home from work.

"Hello," she says, answering after four rings. When she saw it was me, she probably wavered between answering or not. Besides, it's not her usual way of answering when I call. She usually says, "hey" or "what's up" but never "hello."

"*Hola, muñeca,* how are you?" I ask. I'm sitting on the couch and lean forward, rubbing the back of my neck with my free hand.

"Good. A little tired after another long day at work but can't complain."

"It's good to hear your voice." After the other day, I'm not sure where we stand. Not sure how much or little to say.

"Yours too." Silence hangs between us and I don't want to say the wrong thing, so I opt to not say anything at all, which is making it awkward. "Listen," she says, followed by a long sigh. "I know you've been trying to reach me. I've been busy at work and needed a few days to sort things out in my head, sorry."

I stand and begin pacing in my living room. "I understand," I say, even if I don't fully understand her or what goes through her mind. The silence on both ends continues, and I can hear her breathing.

"Look—"

"Muñeca—"

We speak simultaneously.

"You first," I tell her.

"I'm sorry about leaving the way I did the other day."

"You no have to say sorry. But we should talk

about it."

"I agree, but would rather discuss it when we see each other and not over the phone." Relief rushes through me and my legs feel shaky. If she wants to see me, then we have hope.

"*De acuerdo*." I agree with her, it's better we have this conversation face-to-face and not over the phone.

"Want to come over tomorrow? I can make us dinner, or we can order takeout." Her offer to make dinner is yet another sign we'll be okay, otherwise she wouldn't invite me to her place for dinner, especially since it'll be my first time there.

"Yes. What time?" A slow smile stretches across my face.

"I'll be working from home tomorrow so whenever you're done with work." If it were up to me, I'd show up first thing in the morning but that would probably freak her out.

When Sol answers the door, she's wearing a burgundy-colored dress that hugs her curves and falls at her knees layered with a red and white polka dotted apron over it. Red flip-flops on her feet. Her lips have a deep red color lathered over them and her curls are tied up and hanging loosely around her face. Dear God, she looks incredible and just the sight of her makes my dick twitch.

"Hi," she says, opening the door. A smile spreads across her gorgeous face, the lip stain complementing her olive skin.

"Hola, *muñeca*." Her lips are full, the cupid's bow defined with the red stain coloring them. She's covered in red, and it lures me to her like a bull to a bullfighter. I kiss her not caring I'll ruin her lipstick and be covered in it when I'm done. Sol lets me explore her mouth and as I suck on her bottom lip, I imagine the wonders her mouth can do exploring my body. My jeans tighten and I decide to pull away from her.

"Well, that's a nice hello." She gives me a crooked smile and rubs the skin around her lips, attempting to remove some of the color that's transferred.

"*El rojo*—" my fingers linger at her neckline "—makes me crazy *como un toro*."

"I like red too," she says, winking. "But I'm no bullfighter."

"I brought you these," I say, extending my hand holding a floral bouquet of mixed flowers.

"They're beautiful, thank you." She takes them and spins to cross the living room toward the kitchen and I stare at her ass as she sashays across the room.

Her apartment is cute, a large open living area with the kitchen on the far end. She has a framed picture hanging between the two windows along the left wall. It's of a couple dancing in the rain while a maid and butler hold umbrellas, the woman is wearing a red dress and gloves. Flanked on each side of the windows hang additional pictures—one is a sketch of a woman's silhouette, and the other is a drawing of a woman's face, half covered by her dark colored curls.

I follow her into the kitchen and sidle up to Sol who is chopping something. When I get closer, I see it's bacon.

"Bacon, what are you making?"

"Close, it's actually *guanciale*. It's similar to bacon, but a thousand times better. I'm making *Bucatini all'Amatriciana*, which is my favorite pasta dish, and a salad."

"Need help?"

"I'm good for now, thank you."

I grab a stool and sit at the counter so I can watch Sol doing her thing in the kitchen when her phone rings. She peeks at it and silences it, placing it facedown. I don't want to bring up what happened at my shop until she does because I'd rather discuss it on her terms.

"Amaury—" she turns and leans on the counter

next to the stove, locking her eyes with mine "—about the other night."

"I can say something first?" I feel bad about interrupting her, but it's important she hears what I have to say. She nods in agreement. "I no reject you, I respect you. *Es muy diferente.*" There's a huge difference and I hope she understands me.

"I understand, but in your office, it didn't feel that way and I felt ashamed."

"No feel ashamed, *muñeca*. You are special to me."

Abruptly, she turns and opens a cabinet, pulling out two wine glasses. "Can I get you some wine? I opened a bottle of Pinot Noir." She slides a wine glass across the counter for me.

"No *gracias*. I no drink."

Her eyes widen. "Oh. I'm sorry. I just assumed you did since you ordered us drinks at the club the night we met."

"Water, *por favor*," I tell her, a smile creeping across my face.

"I also have club soda or ginger ale."

"*Agua está bien*. With ice please." She spins, grabs another glass from the cabinet then extends the glass to the ice maker on the refrigerator door.

"One water on the rocks for the gentleman," she teases, sliding the tall glass across the counter.

"Thank you, *muñeca*." I bring the glass to my lips.

Sol leans onto the counter and I catch a glimpse of the swell of her breasts peeking out over the top of her dress. I glance up not wanting her to catch my wandering eyes. "Why don't you drink, if you don't mind me asking?" she asks.

I lick my lips and meet her light brown eyes. They have a golden ring encircling her pupil and are soft at the edges. One of the things I liked about her the first night is she wasn't wearing all that makeup around her eyes many women wear. Seems she may not wear it at all because I also haven't seen it on her the few times we've seen each other since.

"I no drink *en Cuba* because alcohol was homemade, *y no me gustaba* the taste of it. By the time I was in Miami, *ya no me interesaba*." I wasn't interested in drinking when still in Cuba because the homemade alcohol tasted like gasoline, and it burned the entire time I drank it. After trying it once, I never touched it again.

"Homemade?" She raises an eyebrow as she questions me.

"*Sí*. It tastes very strong, terrible. But it was the only thing available." Sol's lips part, as if she wants to say something but can't find the words. A common reaction to stories of my life in Cuba.

"No beer? Wine?"

I shake my head. "That stuff was only available for tourists, not Cubans. Since then, I only drink water when my friends drink." She nods in quiet contemplation and then sips her wine.

Another of the injustices I lived through in Cuba. It was difficult not having access to everyday necessities like toilet paper or toothpaste and luxuries like alcohol or beef. Yet, tourists visiting Cuba would have access to everything without question. The government does this so the tourists think Cubans live well. Like everything else, it's all a farce.

"What do you mean, only available for tourists?" she inquires, her right eyebrow lifting up.

"*En Cuba* tourists would experience a fake life. Nice hotels, good meals chosen from large menus. *Pero nosotros los cubanos* we no allowed to have those things and no allowed to go into tourist Cuba." Sol's eyes widen, incredulity spreading across her face as she listens to me talk about the disparity and how Cubans are treated.

"That's crazy. Each time you share about your life in Cuba I'm shocked at what you're telling me."

"*Lo se.*" I know when people hear of life on the island, they're in disbelief. Most people never hear or read about how Cubans truly live. Instead, people are fed lies to lead them to believe the narrative the

Cuban government is selling. Propaganda at its finest. "Enough about Cuba, talk to me about the other day when you came to see me."

She smirks, pulling a lock of hair and twisting it around her finger. "I'm not sure what overcame me, I'm not usually so forward. I'm sorry." She sips her wine again, her eyes searching mine. Her gaze is hypnotic.

"You no have to apologize for how you feel, Sol." My fingers caress her wrist that's resting on the counter.

"I just feel different around you and I don't know how to explain it."

Her confession makes my heart burst. I slide the stool back and circle around the counter so I can wrap my arms around her. "I liked it." My lips meet her neckline and I drop kisses, one above the next, as I approach her lips.

"You did?" She raises her chin, giving me access to her jawline.

"*Llévame a la cama*," she whispers. Her words send a shiver down my spine. I was not expecting her to ask me to take her to bed, at least not this early in the night. But I'd be a fool to reject her now, especially after the way things ended at my shop the other day.

"You sure?" I ask, pulling back from her to search

her eyes for any hint of reluctance.

She nods, grasps my hand, and I follow her across the living room.

Sol turns the lamp on the nightstand on and then leans against her bed. She's already untied the apron and tossed it on the floor. Her gaze meets mine and I'm at a loss for words, which is not common. Her movements are slow and deliberate. She kicks her flip-flops to the side then stands and turns. Peeking out from the top of her dress is black ink, what looks to be a tattoo.

I place my hands on her hips and pull her flush to me, whispering into her ear. "You have a tattoo?"

Her head turns and she bites her bottom lip. "Maybe. Why don't you take my dress off and see for yourself?" Good lord, this woman is going to drive me crazy. My right hand drifts to the zipper at the top and I begin to drag it down, exposing the letters inked onto her skin and her black bra. I slide one shoulder off, then the next and her dress drops to the floor, leaving her in only in her bra and purple underwear.

I begin tracing the black letters, written in script. *Alis volat propriis*, with wings jutting out to the left and right between the words *Alis* and *volat*. "What does this mean?" I ask, as I continue to trace my fingers along the ink.

"She flies with her own wings," she responds,

dropping her head. My lips find the ink and my tongue draws slow circles along the lines of the tattoo while my hands squeeze her curvy hips. My jeans tighten as I savor Sol's skin, the cinnamon scent at her neck invading my senses, her skin soft beneath my lips. I pull my shirt off then reach for my wallet to grab a condom, placing both onto the nightstand.

I take the opportunity and pull the clip from her hair, the curls cascading down her back. She climbs onto the bed and crawls across it, before turning and locking her eyes with mine. Her nipples are prominently visible beneath her bra. My hands reach for my belt to unbuckle it and I swiftly undo my jeans letting them fall to the floor, the tip of my erection peeking out of the top of my white briefs. Sol's eyes drop to my waistline, and she licks her lips as she stares at the protruding bulge.

"Tell me, Sol. *¿Qué quieres*?" I want her to tell me what she wants. To take the lead. To feel in control. Her eyes are wild, and I can see the hesitation in her thoughts as she wrestles with what she's feeling, and what to say.

"I—" She swallows words rather than letting them free.

"I can join you on the bed?" She nods and scoots back. I toss the condom to her left and remove my underwear, stroking myself as I climb onto the bed. Sol is gazing at me, lust burning at the rims of her tawny gaze.

Sol reaches for her panties and begins removing them. “Leave them,” I say. “I want you to wear them while I’m inside of you.” She swallows again, then reaches for the condom on the bed, handing it to me.

“You ready for me to put this on?” I ask, tearing the wrapper open and glancing up at her, locking my eyes with hers. Again, Sol nods and licks her lips as she watches me. She has no words but she’s speaking to me with each gesture, movement, and glance. After I sheath myself, I grasp onto her curvy hips and pull her close to me. She leans back onto her elbows and spreads her wings for me, inviting me into her sacred place. I slide the panties to the side and fill her, letting her grip me into oblivion.

CHAPTER ELEVEN

Soledad

I stir awake and when I stretch my arm across the bed to search for Amaury, I feel the cool sheets under my fingers, which causes me to quickly sit up. I glance over to the floor where he left his clothes last night and they're gone.

He's gone.

I should've known he'd sleep with me then disappear! I shove my face in my pillow and let out a muffled scream. *I'm so stupid.*

After throwing my robe on I make my way to the bathroom and stare at myself in the mirror. *What's wrong with you*? I whisper to myself. Why do I attract men like this who are only into themselves? Tears leak from my eyes, and I allow myself to feel somber. At least I learned what type of guy he is early on, saving me heartache down the line.

After a few minutes, I brush my teeth, splash some water on my face, and head to the kitchen. When I reach for the coffee machine, I catch a glimpse of a handwritten note.

Went running – see you later, besos – A.

I guess my meltdown was for nothing. I thought I had endured being humiliated and abandoned by yet another man. But for once, I was wrong. I smile, thinking about him and how good he made me feel. When I sit to have my coffee, and pick up my phone, I see a text message from him.

Amaury: *Muñeca*, you looked beautiful sleeping this morning & I no want to bother you. See you later?

His words cause my belly to stir. At first him calling me *muñeca*, or doll, felt weird and I wasn't sure how I felt about it but it's grown on me. Of course I want to see him.

Amaury called earlier asking if I wanted to go with him to his friend's house. They're having a get-together, which is something he told me they do at least once a month. Initially I wasn't sure but kept hearing Melida's voice telling me to not overthink it. As we're driving south on the Palmetto Expressway, Amaury rests his hand on my leg, rubbing his thumb and index fingers in a back-and-forth motion. "Let me warn you, my friend Alain *está siempre jodiendo*, he's the funny guy of the group. You're new so he'll make jokes about me, and maybe you too. But he's only playing, no listen to him."

Great. I'm already super nervous about meeting Amaury's circle. His family doesn't live here so his friends are the next best thing. For sure I'll turn beet red when Alain starts with the jokes. I'm not good at being on the spot, and don't like the attention on me, which tonight it will be since I'm the new girl infiltrating the group. Just remember to breathe, Sol.

"Okay. I'll keep that in mind *cuando estoy nerviosa*. I tend to get nervous in new situations around people I don't know," I say, twirling my hair as I stare out the window.

"I remember when we met, you were quiet. Now I know you, *y no tanto*," he adds, his smile stretching across his face.

"Is that your way of telling me I talk too much?" I ask, smacking his hand.

He shakes his head. "I love hearing you talk, your accent … *me calienta*," he confesses, pulling his bottom lip under his teeth. Knowing he gets turned on when I speak to him causes my belly to stir with desire.

"You're beautiful when you blush. It's the same face you had *cuando tuviste un orgasmo* last night." My heart thumps in my chest and my breath quickens as I think about last night's memories—him drawing my orgasm from me with his hands, his mouth, and his body. I peek at him briefly and smirk before turning to look out the window, twisting the curls in my fingers.

We park along the swale in front of the house and grab the beers and other groceries from the trunk. "*¿Estás lista?*" he asks.

"As ready as I'll ever be," I respond, forcing a smile. My belly is tight from the nerves twisting.

Instead of going through the front door, we walk around the side of the house and the backyard is full. There has to be at least twenty people back here. The rock music is blaring through the speakers. I still can't get used to the fact Amaury, and his friends, are into heavy metal and rock. I don't know why but it's not something I imagined, wrong as that may be. I assumed because they're Latino, they like Latino music like salsa or reggaeton. How wrong I was.

As we enter the yard, I see a full kitchen underneath an overhang and we drop the beer and groceries on the counter.

"*Oye mi hermano, qué vuelta*," says Alain. That's a greeting I'd never heard until moving to Miami, one used predominantly by Cubans. Funny how despite speaking the same language, we have so many differences between us.

"Esta es la jeva, Sol," Amaury says. *Jeva*? I think it means girlfriend but I'm not sure, I'll have to ask him.

"Hi. Nice to meet you," I say, extending my hand out.

"She's only with you because she didn't meet me first, we all know I'd be her number one choice," says Alain, chuckling as he pulls me into an embrace. I wasn't expecting a hug but try to make it as least awkward as possible and squeeze him back. When I step away from him, a short blonde woman is standing next to him.

"*Finalmente*, Amaury has a girlfriend. We thought he'd be alone forever!" she shouts. "I'm Zamira but call me Rubi—" she pulls a fist of blonde hair up, essentially telling me that's her nickname because she's blonde, or *rubia* as it's known in Spanish "*—la mujer de* Alain," she says, introducing herself as Alain's girl while gesturing to her right before pulling me into an embrace.

"It's nice to meet you," I respond, squeezing her back. I feel so welcome, and we just got here, which calms me a bit. Amaury had told me his friends would be like this, and they'd immediately make me feel part of the family. With each passing hello, the bundle of nerves in my tummy loosens.

"Hi Sol, good to see you again," Eduardo says, and places a kiss on my cheek.

"Good to see you too, Eduardo. Nice to see a familiar face," I tell him.

"*Quien sabe* what Sol sees in this guy, he's been single forever for a reason," Alain says, throwing his head back in laughter while smacking Amaury's shoulder. Amaury wasn't lying when he said his friend is a jokester.

"*Mala hoja*," shouts another guy sitting behind me. When I turn around, he's laughing as he's pulling his hair back into a ponytail. What the heck does that mean? I don't understand all the Cuban slang. I'll have to ask Amaury about that too.

"*Pregúntale a la socia si soy mala hoja*," says Amaury, then leans into me. Why is he telling them to ask me, I don't even know what they're talking about. "Tell them *muñeca*. Roberto seems to think *que soy mala hoja*?" he says, as he drops kisses along my temple and pulls me into a side hug while pointing to Roberto, whose hair is now in a low ponytail.

"Umm. I don't understand what he said. What's *mala hoja* mean?"

Amaury chuckles before whispering in my ear, "It means I suck in bed. But after last night, I think you know *que no es verdad*." I can feel my cheeks burning up as laughter fills the space around us. I'm going to have to get thicker skin to hang around this crew. "*Si tienes dudas*, I can refresh your memory a little later," he finishes and then nips my cheek with his teeth.

I have no doubts he rocked my world last night. I shake my head and peek up at Amaury, the flutters in my belly swirl in anticipation thinking about how incredible he made me feel. Since the moment we met I've felt this connection to him but kept it at bay because of my own insecurities over my past. It felt right and I knew asking him to take me to bed was the right decision.

He was gentle and worshipped my body as he slowly undressed me. Amaury's words and movements were assertive, yet he ensured I was the one making the decisions. His caresses and whispers calmed the freight train of thoughts running through my mind, allowing me to fully appreciate the emotions and feelings of having Amaury inside of me. As he thrusted in and out of me, my mind was clear and the uninhibited feeling of enjoying each other is one I hadn't ever felt. Watching goosebumps spread across Amaury's skin as he came undone was so satisfying. We barely slept last night as Amaury made love to me over and over. It's like we couldn't get enough of each other.

"*Dejen de molestar*," shouts Rubi. "Don't pay attention to these guys; they're never serious about anything." Her words intrude into my memories and I'm thankful she asked them to ease up on me.

"And *jeva*? Why did you call me that?" I whisper to Amaury.

"Girlfriend, my beautiful *muñeca*," he responds, pulling me closer to him, his lips landing on mine. I smirk underneath his kisses.

"I like it," I say, chastely kissing him before separating our bodies. He drifts off to join his buddies and I rest against the wall behind me, just watching everyone.

Off to the right there's a square table and four people are playing dominoes, slamming down their pieces and boisterous in their interactions. I've seen people play, but don't know how. I know playing dominoes is popular in the Caribbean islands, so it's no surprise to see a game going.

"You hungry?" asks Rubi. She turns toward the counter, and I push off the wall to follow. "There's *arroz moro* and *yuca. El Puerco* is still *en la caja china*," she says. The rice and beans look delicious, a blend of rice and black beans made all together. *Yuca* is something I tried for the first time in Miami, but it's growing on me. It's similar to potatoes, but tastes different, better. At the Cuban restaurant I ate at they make it with *mojo*, an oil-based marinade that's poured over the *yuca* after it's boiled.

"What's *la caja china*?" I ask. I know she said pork, but don't know what that box she mentioned is. She spins and grasps my hand in hers, dragging me toward the box. Across the front it says, "Roasting Box *La Caja China*."

"That." She points to the box. "It's where we cook the pig. It's delicious and is almost ready. When Alain takes it out, he'll put it on this table—" she gestures to the table on the left of the roasting box "—and everyone will flock here, *como las moscas*." She chuckles at her reference to everyone gathering around the roasted pig like flies.

After eating, most of us sit around the large table while a few continue to play dominoes. I've somewhat zoned out of the conversation because as they talk amongst each other, they're speaking in Cuban slang and very quickly—to the point I don't understand most of what they're saying. I grab my cell phone from my back pocket and see several missed calls from an unknown number. They've been coming in more regularly, and it's starting to make me nervous.

"What do you think, Sol?" Alain asks me, interrupting my thoughts.

"Uhh—" I slip my phone into my back pocket "—I'm not sure," I respond, shrugging as I avert Alain's gaze and glance at Amaury. "I don't understand what you guys are talking about."

"You no speak Spanish?" Alain asks, his eyes widening.

"Yeah, I do but I'm not familiar with Cuban slang and you guys are speaking so fast, so I don't understand what you're saying." My fingers begin twirling the curls hanging over my shoulder. I feel like an idiot telling them I have no idea what they're talking about. The few times Amaury and I have spoken Spanish, he doesn't speak as quickly to me as he does with his friends. Must be the familiarity they all have with each other.

I feel like all eyes have been on me since we've gotten here, especially after confessing I don't understand their conversation. In an attempt to shift those feelings, I ask Amaury, "So, how long have you all been friends?" I point left to right at his friends sitting around the table.

"*Toda la vida*," Amaury responds, a grin stretching across his face as he recounts that they've been friends their entire lives. "We all grew up in the same neighborhood in Cuba. Roberto was one of the guys on the raft with me. Eduardo and Alain came by raft too, but they left a few days after us. We all met up in *Guantánamo*."

"That's awesome you've all been friends for so long."

"Alain was close with my younger brother, *pero eramos un piquete*," Amaury says.

"*¿Piquete*?" I ask, confused by yet another word being used.

"Group of friends," Alain chimes in.

They start telling stories of their time in Guantanamo and I take the opportunity to go to the restroom. "Where's the bathroom?" I ask Amaury in a low voice.

He points to the door to our right. "Through there, first door on the left."

"*No tupas el inodoro*!" yells Alain as I rise from my seat, my eyes widening, causing everyone to erupt in laughter. I'm so embarrassed at his insinuation that I'm going to clog the toilet after using the bathroom. I can't even turn around to face everyone. My heart beats rapidly in my chest as I scurry toward the door and lock myself in the bathroom.

Once inside I lean onto the vanity and stare at my reflection—my cheeks are flush, a deep red. Amaury wasn't kidding when he said his friends are heavy on the sarcasm and jokes. Holy crap! I'm not used to anything like this but if our relationship continues, I'm going to have to learn to roll with it better. Hopefully once I get to know everyone better it'll get easier.

After quickly using the bathroom, I hear a knock as I'm washing my hands.

"Sol, it's me. You okay?" I use the towel to dry off my hands and crack open the door. He pushes the door open, steps in, and closes the door behind him.

"Hi. Yes, why wouldn't I be?"

"My friends are … *pesado*. Too much sometimes with their jokes. Want to make sure they no bother you too much." He pushes my hair behind my ears before nudging my chin up for my eyes to meet his. They're soft at the corners and his lips are slightly pursed.

"I like them, they're nice. But yeah, not used to it. I'll come around."

Amaury kisses me, his lips soft and warm, his stubble scratching at my skin. "*¿Nos vamos*?" he asks, his lips hovering over mine. "We can go to my house."

I nod, glad he asked if I want to leave, as I nibble and suck on his plump bottom lip.

"*Vámonos*," he says, pulling the door open and grasping my hand on the way out.

An hour later, we pull into the driveway in front of a garage at Amaury's house along Royal Palm Ave. We both live in Miami Beach but the area I live in is all small buildings whereas this area is a traditional neighborhood with standalone houses. It's a beautiful area.

Once Amaury opens the front door, it opens to a foyer, with stairs immediately to my right and three rooms separated by arched beams. The first a sitting room with all white couches, followed by a dining room with a long wooden table stretching the length of the room. Farther beyond is a Florida room with more couches overlooking his backyard. The Florida room is expansive, with skylights and more windows than wall space. To the right of the dining room and Florida room is a kitchen with a large island in the middle.

"Your house is beautiful," I say, as I'm taking in his home. The walls are adorned with artwork depicting different beaches, with one wall markedly different from the others with its pictures of old buildings and antique cars.

"I like it, but I'm lonely in this big house," he says, a bleak grin gracing his gorgeous face.

"You live by yourself?"

"Yes, with all of my plants and flowers." He signals to the plants placed around the rooms we just walked through. Plants at the foot of the steps, placed in the corners and underneath windows. Surprising, although not sure why. I mean, they're just plants.

"I love them. I kill everything so I'm impressed, especially considering I have a black thumb and am known for killing cactus." I shrug, while grazing the leaves of the plant in front of me.

"Black thumbs are a lie. You only need to learn, *muñeca. Ven*, I show you the backyard."

I follow him through the French doors in the Florida room and the yard is long and wide, with a shimmering, blue-lit pool in the middle, two lounge chairs at each of the pool corners closest to us. Along the perimeter of the rectangular yard are several palm trees with Ficus bushes lining the entire yard behind them. The palm fronds at the forefront of the night sky ablaze from the setting sun, a few cloud swirls in the fire lit heavens.

"*Mis orquídeas*," he says, as we approach the palm trees along the left side. He's pointing to a vivid pink orchid growing on the side of the palm tree, and then to the purple one growing on the palm tree next to it. It's then I notice each palm tree lining the yard has an orchid growing on it—red, yellow, blue, white, and orange.

"How do you get them to grow like this?" I'm fascinated by the vibrantly colored flowers growing on the tree trunks.

"I tie them on the trunk with a *trapo viejo*. *No se* the word *en inglés*."

"A rag. An old rag."

"Yes, that. It helps the orchid grow roots and eventually the orchid lives alone." I never would've thought about tying an orchid to a tree so it could grow. How interesting.

"I like that you're a plant lover."

"*Sí, por qué*?" he asks, turning toward me, with a lopsided grin. I should've known he'd want to know why.

"Because it shows you care for things, you're nurturing, loving, and have patience."

"*Bueno*, I no good with patience *pero sí me gusta cuidar las cosas que amo*," he proclaims, his words almost a whisper as he steps closer to me, dragging the back of his hand along my cheek. I swallow the lump in my throat, try to hide my surprise at him showing a softer side with his confession that he likes to care for the things he loves. When I think Amaury is going to kiss me, he steps back and pulls his shirt up and off.

"What are you doing?" I ask, looking around. He doesn't respond to my question. Instead, he meanders to the side of the pool and kicks off his shoes, then begins unbuckling his jeans, pulling them down and stepping out of them. My cheeks burn as I watch him peel his socks off, and lastly slip off his tighty-whities. I squeeze my legs, the tingling sensation spreading from my core. His golden-brown skin glows, even with the sky nearly dark.

Amaury jumps into the pool, emerging with water dripping from his dark locks, positioning himself along the wall opposite where I stand. He stretches his arms along the wall, his chest glistening from the water. "*Ven*," he says.

I swallow. "Um. You want me to swim naked?"

CHAPTER TWELVE

Amaury

"What if someone sees me? Sees us?" she inquires, searching the yard. She wraps her arms around her torso, as if she were already unclothed.

"No one will see," I tell her, licking my lips as my desire for her increases. I point to the Ficus hedges surrounding the yard and she looks up at the bushes encircling my property, which is thick and stands high, shielding the yard from everything surrounding it.

"*En Cuba*, everyone knows everything you do. There is no privacy," I say.

"No privacy?" she asks, wrinkling her nose.

I shake my head. "Every *barrio* had a *chivatón,*

someone who told the government everything we all did. The *chivatón* would get better treatment for being a government agent. Another method of control used by the Cuban government," I say. Her eyes widen, as they do each time I share a little bit of my life in Cuba. Disbelief is written all over her face. Having grown up here in the U.S. with the comforts this country offers, it's hard for her to understand, for anyone outside of Cuba, how we suffered and lived. "It was the neighborhood *chivatón* who told on us when we tried to leave on a raft before the time we left. We spent a few days in jail until Roberto's father got us out." It was misery at its finest.

"Wow." The words are barely audible.

"When I moved here, after freedom the only thing I wanted was privacy." The first thing I did after I bought this house was place Ficus around the perimeter of the property. Now the Ficus stand over ten feet tall and it's what I love the most about my yard—I'm shielded from the outside world.

"That makes sense," she whispers as her eyes scan the yard.

"*Dale*, the water is warm. I'm waiting for you." I splash at the surface of the water with my hands, calling for her to join me.

Sol searches the yard again, pursing her lips as she

does. She strides over to the lounge chair and drops her bag on it. When her eyes meet mine, she kicks off her sandals and unbuttons her jeans, letting them fall to the ground. She's wearing red panties and they're snug around her curvy hips. I watch as her hands reach for the hem of her shirt, pulling it up and over her long curls. She slides one strap off then the next, unclasping the beige bra at the front.

Her heavy breasts fall, the dark pink skin surrounding her nipples prickles and she shimmies her underwear over her thick thighs. I swallow, can feel my erection growing. I want to devour this woman; her curves drive me crazy. As she slowly approaches the water, I'm remembering the weight of her body on me last night as she rode me, drawing my orgasm from me. There's no sensation I love more than the weight of a woman on top of me as I fill her. I've never felt so alive as I did with her last night. The timid side of her was gone when we were alone and naked in her bed.

Between my memories of last night and the beautiful woman wading into the water, I'm hard as a rock and feel as if I'm about to explode. My insides are on fire, and I need her to douse the flames. When she's on the second step and the water reaches halfway up her calves she stops in place. I can hear the vibration of her phone and watch as her shoulders subtly stiffen. Why would her phone ringing cause her to freeze up? Her shoulders soften once the phone is no longer vibrating. She takes the remaining steps into the water and stops at the bottom, the water at the apex of her thighs. Her nipples are hard and the skin that's still not in the water is prickled from the cold she's feeling after immersing herself into the water.

I cross the pool to where my jeans are and pull a condom from the pocket. After wading over to the stairs, I sit on the top step. Sol turns to watch me as I tear open the small foil packet. She's gawking as I roll the condom on. "*Ven*," I say, calling her over to me. With her legs straddling me, she lowers herself until I'm filling her. Once I'm fully inside of her I grab the globes of her ass to hold onto her as the rhythm of our bodies move in unison.

We're stretched out on the lounge chairs, the music streaming through the speakers. I put music on earlier, Sol volunteering her playlist to play on shuffle. Right now, "She Will Be Loved" by Maroon 5 is playing. "I love this album," she says, turning toward me and tangling her legs with mine.

Sol is wearing my t-shirt, which hits the top of her

thighs. She went inside earlier to get a glass of water and I ogled her as she strode across the patio because I caught a glimpse of her red panties, and it makes me want to rip them off and fuck her again. After I made love to her, she told me there was no reason for her to get dressed again. There was no objection from me when she pulled my dark gray t-shirt over her head. Don't get me wrong, I love the way her jeans hug her ass, but I enjoy it more when her warm, radiant skin is exposed and ready for me.

"It's a good album," I say. Her feet rub against mine and she peeks up at me with a mischievous grin on her face.

"Did you have fun tonight?" she asks, before sipping on her water.

I nod. I was nervous taking her to my friend's house, although more for her than for me. I know how intense they can be when joking around, and I wasn't sure how Sol would handle it. She did well for the first time and I'm proud of her. Plus, my friends loved her, as I expected. "*Sí, mucho*! You?"

"I really like your friends," she says. Her toe is rubbing the underside of my foot in a slow up and down motion. "But you guys speak too fast when you're all together. Between that and your Cuban lingo, I didn't understand a lot of what you were talking about."

"You get used to it soon." I smirk, then kiss the tip of her nose and pull her bottom lip between mine.

She pulls away. "I'm hungry," she says. "Have anything we can eat?"

"Maybe, *no se*." I'm not sure what's in my kitchen. I haven't been food shopping in over a week.

She hops to her feet and skips toward the kitchen, and I follow, watching her ass bounce. I find some plantain chips and open the bag, pouring them into a bowl. Sol grabs a handful and begins crunching.

"I never ate these until I moved to Miami," she tells me.

"*Mariquitas* are my favorite. *En Cuba,* I made them at my house a lot because *plátanos* are something we ate a lot of."

"Meanwhile, I've barely eaten them, well at least until I moved here. Now I eat them a lot," she proclaims, and lifts herself up to sit on the counter. I gaze at her, her curls cascading around her squared jaw.

"*Muñeca, me tienes loco*," I mumble, grasping onto her curvy hips and pulling her into me, dropping kisses along her neck. She must know she's driving me crazy as she wraps her legs around me while practically naked.

Funny, in that moment "Brujeria" by El Gran Combo de Puerto Rico starts playing because the lyrics match my thoughts. What has this woman done to me? It feels like witchcraft. She has me feeling crazy and in love. “You have salsa music on your playlist?” I ask, trying to calm my erratic thoughts.

She nods and leaps off the counter. “I love it. I just wish I could dance it better.” She extends her hand out. “Come on, let’s dance now and you can teach me some of your moves.” She throws her head back in laughter.

“I no a good teacher. You have to feel the music, listen to the beats. *Cuenta* while you step. One, two, three, and then repeat.” I grasp onto her hip pulling her to me and envelop her right hand in mine. “Listen, count, and follow.”

As we move to the music Sol’s eyes watch her feet in concentration, not letting the music carry her, which confuses her.

“*Sol, deja que la música te lleve*,” I tell her. If she would let the music guide her, the beats tell your body how it should move. “You think too much. Let the music in, your body will follow.”

“Easy for you to say. You’re a natural at this,” she huffs, frustrated.

“Start the song again, *pero* this time, let me see your eyes while we dance.” Sol does as instructed and when she isn’t thinking about how to dance, she moves well and lets me lead her through the spins and twirls.

"Let me change the playlist, play only salsa music so we can dance some more," she says, scurrying across the room to grab her phone.

After a few songs of our bodies rubbing up against each other and her perk nipples visible under the soft cotton tee, I can't control the tightness in my jeans any longer. If I'm reading Sol's body language correctly, she's ready for me again too.

Sol strides toward the couch and sprawls herself across the white cushions, pulling my gray shirt up and off, leaving her naked except for the lacy red underwear stretching across her skin. "Amaury," she says, as she lifts her legs letting her hands drag along the inside of her thighs.

"*Dime, muñeca*," I need her to tell me what she wants from me but my words are barely a whisper as they fall from my lips. With each move she makes, each word that falls from her lips, I fall deeper under her spell.

CHAPTER THIRTEEN

Soledad

TWO MONTHS LATER

Today is my first day in the office after finishing a two-week jury trial where I was the primary interpreter for the defense. The jury verdict came back and the client was found not guilty. The case was centered around drug trafficking and the person on trial was facing life in prison. It's a big deal here in Miami as there were news cameras all over the place, including inside the courtroom.

I'm sitting in my office when Melida's name flashes across my phone.

"Hey Mel, what's up?"

"I just saw you on TV!" My back stiffens.

"What? Where?"

"On CNN. You were in the courtroom, and they were talking about the case where the guy was found not guilty. They kept showing the clip of you next to him." Panic creeps in as Melida tells me she saw me on CNN.

"This can't be happening. I cannot be on national TV." I slump in my chair. There were a lot of news networks there, but all of them were local. Never did I imagine it would make national news.

"It's fine. It's like a five second clip of you."

"Yeah, a five second clip that you said the network kept showing." My breath quickens as I begin to think of who could've seen it, primarily Carmine.

"Hey, Sol, you okay?"

"I'm freaking out, Mel. Not gonna lie. What if Carmine sees it?"

"You're freaking out for no reason. You're safe, you're not in Boston anymore and just because your face was on TV in a courtroom, doesn't mean he can find you. Breathe." She's right, but it doesn't make me feel any better.

"Sol. Stop. I already know what you're doing. Don't overthink it. Let's change the subject. Friday can't come soon enough. The next two days are gonna drag."

"I'm wicked excited to see you," I say, trying to convince myself. "Although I've made a friend, it's not the same without you."

"It doesn't matter how many friends you make, you'll always miss me because I'm me." She chuckles.

"You're definitely one of a kind, Mel."

"Anyway, my flight gets in Friday night at 5:45 p.m. Where are we going after you pick me up?" I know Mel means well, trying to change the subject but it's gonna take more than Mel's usual charm for my anxiety about Carmine to be silenced.

"Not sure but I'll have a few ideas for us when I pick you up."

After Mel and I finish the conversation, I decide I need to speak with Lily. I want to find out about doing less courtroom work for the next few weeks, if possible. When I reach Lily's office, her door is open, so I knock twice before entering.

"Hi, Sol. Our phones have been ringing all morning after our firm was identified in the paper." Great, now the name of the place I work at was made known too.

"That's precisely what I wanted to talk to you about," I say, my words not as firm as I want them to be. I'm nervous. I'm still new here and not sure how I should approach this subject with her. On the one hand, I know she's good friends with my last boss and probably the primary reason I've gotten so much work. But, on the other hand, Lily doesn't know me so I'm not sure how she'll receive the request for me to do less courtroom work because of personal drama. I stop behind the chair and lean against it.

"The client said you did an incredible job interpreting at that trial. She's already told me she would like to use you exclusively for all of her future hearings and case work." Great, I can't say anything now. I'll have to suck it up and deal. Be extra vigilant.

"Wow, that's really nice of the client. I'm so happy she's pleased with my work." I give her a smile that doesn't reach my eyes.

"Sol, you're excellent at what you do, of course she's pleased with you. All of the assignments I've given you have returned with incredible feedback about your interpreting skills. You're easily one of the best employees I've ever had." My smile lifts, reaching my eyes.

"Thank you, Lily. Coming from you, it means a lot."

"What is it you wanted to discuss?" she asks, leaning back in her chair.

I swallow the words sitting on my tongue. "Oh, I wanted to make sure you knew CNN picked up the coverage and showed a clip of me next to the defendant. I'm not sure if they gave the company name but my friend from Boston called to tell me she saw me." My smile no longer reaches my eyes, I hope Lily doesn't pick up on it.

"Excellent. More exposure for us ensures we have continued business."

"Anyway, I'm almost finished translating the contracts for the Neville case. I should have them by the end of the day." I spin to walk back to my office and I swallow the lump in my throat.

"Thank you, Soledad," Lily says.

The rest of the day at the office dragged by, despite me keeping busy with the contract translations. All I could think about was Melida's call and her seeing me on the news. I searched the internet for a little while to see what I could find. Some of the local Miami papers identified me as "an interpreter from Miami Language Solutions" but I haven't seen any with my name. Not that it makes a difference, you can clearly see my face and now everyone knows where I work. It was all starting to give me a headache, so I left early in search of sunshine and fresh air.

Yesterday Amaury and I made plans for him to come over after work. If I'm being honest, I don't feel like company because he's going to pick up on my mood, notice I'm not myself. Since hanging up with Melida I've been shaky and nervous. I'm also not ready to discuss Carmine with Amaury but if I cancel on him, he'll know something's up anyway. He's perceptive and reads me like an open book. I need to shake this off. Hopefully a nice glass of wine will help take the edge off.

On my way home I stopped by the liquor store to pick up a couple bottles of wine, even though Amaury doesn't drink, although I wish he did. Solo drinking when he's with me isn't as enjoyable and I've noticed I drink less. He pointed it out to me once and I wrote it off as I didn't feel like having anymore for the night, but that wasn't entirely true. The only reason I didn't feel like having any more is because he was with me. Anyway, maybe it's a good thing.

We decided to order sushi for dinner, which he's never tried. I'm not sure how that even happens but here we are. I hope he likes it. There's a sushi place a few blocks from my apartment that's quickly become a go-to for me. I probably order from them once a week because when I call to put in an order the woman who answers the phone recognizes me and knows my favorites.

The first thing I do when I get home is pour myself a glass of wine, a nice Riesling recommended by the woman working at the store. I hit shuffle on one of my playlists and stretch my legs to rest on the coffee table. My thoughts are racing with Carmine and the CNN clip. There's no way he won't find out. He knows everyone in Boston, and someone is bound to say something to him. I know he's the one making all those unknown calls to me and when he finds out I'm here, I don't know what he'll do. I'm not sure how to deal with it, especially since I'm here by myself.

The knock at my door pulls me back to the here and now. Before opening the door, I peek at myself in the mirror to the right of the front door and take a deep breath. I need to shake this feeling.

"Who is it?" I ask, even though I know it's him. The one thing I don't like about this apartment is there is no peephole on my door.

"Amaury," he responds, and I quickly pull the door open. His dark hair is growing long, the bangs hanging over his right eye.

"Hi," I say, pulling the door open.

"Hello, *muñeca*." He sweeps me in his arms, our

lips crashing, kicking the door shut behind him.

Deeply.

Passionately.

Fervently.

I reciprocate, each stroke of his tongue turning the heat up and igniting my desire for him. He stretches his arm to lock the door while his onslaught of kisses continues. Before I know it, we're in my bedroom and he's lifting me onto my bed.

When he's no longer kissing my mouth, his lips are dragging along my neck, over my breasts, along the skin he's exposed by lifting my dress, until he pulls the elastic of my underwear between his teeth. Amaury drops to his knees before me, and I adjust myself by leaning on my elbows. I'm about to lift myself to remove my underwear when he tears them off and tosses them to the side. His teeth nip at the inside of my thighs, the stubble growing on his face grates my skin and I squirm under his touch. As he explores, I tangle my fingers in his thick, silky mane.

His tongue makes circles as it approaches my apex and my heart races. Amaury is sucking, swirling, and licking. His fingers and tongue at odds with each other, both with the same goal. A moan slips from me and I pull at his locks in rhythm with him.

"Well, that's a nice greeting. Did you miss me?" I tease. I'm lying on my bed, engulfed in a passionate haze.

"I always miss you, *muñeca.*" He gives me a lop-sided grin.

"A girl can get used to greetings like that."

"I give you that every day, *si me dejas*," he exclaims before climbing onto the bed. His mouth is glistening but before I can say anything, his lips are on mine. I squirm away to separate myself from him.

"Yuck!"

"*Que* yuck *ni* yuck," he responds. "I love how you taste." His emerald gaze is intense as a smirk spreads across his beautiful face.

I find his t-shirt and throw it on, followed by a fresh pair of underwear and head toward the kitchen. "Let's eat, I'm starving," I say on my way out.

We're at the kitchen counter eating sushi and the look on Amaury's face tells me he's not into it. "You like it?"

He shrugs. "*No se.* It's new to me. I like seafood but never ate it like this. It's not bad." He pops another roll into his mouth, eating with his hands because he was frustrated with trying to use chopsticks. "I like the fried one best."

"Of course you do, everything tastes better fried." I chuckle.

"How was your day, *muñeca*?"

I lift my shoulder. "It was fine. Nothing exciting," I respond, averting his gaze in search of my next piece of sushi but I can feel his eyes on me.

Following.

Watching.

Analyzing.

"I no believe you," he blurts out. I'm transparent, I know I am. I've always been a terrible liar.

"Okay, but my answer isn't gonna change. It was just another day," I quip, and take a sip of wine.

"*Bueno*, if you say so." His hand stretches across the counter and our fingers interlock. Our eyes contemplating one another.

"How was your day?" I ask.

"Just another day," he says, then he gives me a fake smile, showing me all of his teeth.

"Ha, ha." I smack his arm.

"You no wanna talk today?"

"I'm talking."

"*Sí*, you talking but you no telling me anything." He dips a dragon roll into the soy sauce and takes a bite.

I purse my lips and shift in my seat. "What do you want to know?"

"Tell me about your father." My heart sinks. I knew this question would eventually come but I wasn't expecting it today. It's either talk about my father or talk about Carmine. My father is the easier of the two so father it is. Before I respond, I reach for the bottle of wine, pour, and pull from my glass.

"There isn't much to tell." I shrug, and sip from my wine glass again. "He left when I was five. I still remember the day he left. He was wearing a pale-yellow shirt, dark blue jeans, and black shoes. I watched him walk out the front door to his red car and never look back while I screamed for him. My mother held me and wouldn't let me run outside. It was the last time I saw him. He left me, left my mother, and disappeared."

I sip my wine again trying to calm the nerves fluttering in my belly, which appear each time the topic of my father comes up. It's been years and as much as I want to believe I'm over it, I'm not. I'm hurt he left me and wanted no part in my life. I'm hurt my mother refuses to discuss him with me. It's a permanent thorn in my side.

"*Perdóname Sol*, I no mean to upset you." He extends his hand once more, palm facing up, waiting for me to extend mine as well.

"It's fine. I'm used to it after all these years."

"You are? When I mentioned your father on our first date and again now, you change. *Te pones seria.*" He's perceptive, nothing gets by him. My demeanor definitely changes when the topic comes up. I can't hide it.

"I guess what I mean is, I've accepted my father doesn't love me and wants nothing to do with me. He left me at five years old and never once cared enough to call or visit." I pull from my glass once more. "It will always hurt to think my father is the kind of man that could give up his child when all I wanted was for him to love me. The worst part is I'll never be able to ask him about it. I don't even know his name." A tear escapes and glides down my cheek.

"And your mother, what does she say?" he inquires. He swipes his thumb across my cheek, wiping away the tear.

"My mother doesn't talk about it either. I haven't asked her in a long time but before I would try and ask questions and she'd get mad, end up yelling at me to stop asking questions. Eventually I stopped." Tears begin streaming down my cheeks and my gaze drifts off to the side. "What I haven't told my mother is that her unwillingness to tell me why he left hurts nearly as much as my father leaving."

Amaury leaps to his feet and circles the counter to wrap me in his arms. His hands roam my lower back in an effort to console me. I try to hide the whimpers, but I haven't talked about this with anyone in a long time and it feels good to let it out. Amaury puts some space between us and cups my face in his hands, wiping the tears away with the pads of his thumbs. "*No me gusta ver esos ojos tan lindos triste*," he tells me, kissing my cheeks between words. I feel like saying, believe me Amaury, I don't like having sad eyes either, but I'm done holding it in.

"I'm sorry, I no should've asked you about your father. I make you upset." I shake my head then drape my arms over his shoulders, my fingers tickling the nape of his neck. My lips crush his and I explore his mouth with my tongue. I want to get lost in him, try to forget the melancholy feeling talking about my father brought layered on top of the day I've had.

I whisper in his ear, "Make me forget."

CHAPTER FOURTEEN

Amaury

Tonight I'm taking Soledad to a Carlos Varela concert. Varela is a Cuban artist who sings about the political situation in Cuba, but his songs are hauntingly beautiful metaphors for what's happening to our country, to our people, and to our freedoms. He rose to popularity when I was still living there, and his music represents a part of my life where I struggled with my identity and how it clashed with the politics we were surrounded by, what I wanted, and learning how to be myself while living under a tyrannical rule. When his first album came out, I was nineteen, in the military, hating my oppressed life yet incapable of making any changes. I felt trapped and his music resonated with me. Resonated with so many Cubans, which is why he became so popular.

With such a big Cuban exile community in Miami, it's only normal he's now playing in concert here. It's the first time I'll be seeing him live in concert and I'm stoked. I'm even more excited Sol will be experiencing this with me. I hope she enjoys the show. I've played some of his songs for her so she can familiarize herself with the music and she's told me she likes it, has even learned the words to some of my favorite songs.

I pick Sol up at her house and as she walks toward my car, I can't help but stare. She's wearing a vibrant red wrap dress with quarter sleeves and a deep v-neck. Her breasts spill over the top and it hugs all of those curves but it's too long, falling below her knees. I've noticed all the dresses she wears are longer in length. Don't get me wrong, she looks incredible in it no matter what, but I would love to see a little more of those thick thighs.

"Hola, *muñeca*," I say as she climbs into the Tahoe.

She closes the door and leans over, her lips gently brushing mine.

"That's it? That's my kiss?" I ask, pursing my lips and feigning disbelief.

"I don't want to mess up my lipstick, so yes. Especially knowing the way you kiss me." She sticks her tongue out then buckles her seatbelt.

Before heading to the show, we decide to have an early dinner at La Locanda here on the beach. The show starts at eight thirty, which is my usual dinnertime, so dinner at six fifteen is not something I'm used to. I'll probably be hungry after the show too. Sol chose this place for dinner because she came for lunch with some of the people from the office and said the pasta was delicious. Said it was so good it reminded her of restaurants in Boston.

We have a table inside because it's too hot to eat outside. We're sitting along the banquette in the back corner, the wall decorated with art, mirrors, and flowers. It's early so we're the only ones in here, which is kind of nice. Seems late dining is a Miami thing. Nearly all the restaurants in the neighborhood have very few diners at this time.

Sol orders a glass of white wine and I'm drinking sparkling water. She enjoys the bubbly water and she got me into drinking it as well. I order chicken marsala and Sol a *Spaghetti alla Carbonara*. I don't think I've ever met someone who loves pasta as much as she does. Before meeting her I rarely ate pasta, I'm more of a rice and beans with steak kinda guy. It's growing on me, although I can't eat it more than once a week.

"So, I've been meaning to ask you," Sol says, as she pushes her hair behind her ears.

"You can ask me anything." I grasp her hand in mine, draw circles on her palm.

"How'd you get that scar on your eyebrow?" She stretches her hand across the table, her fingers gently caressing the scar over my left eye.

"In the orange grove."

After taking a sip of wine, she asks, "What do you mean?"

"I worked with my father every morning when I no have school. We picked oranges for the owner who sold them. One day I fell from the tree and—" I pause, trying to think of the word in English "—how you say, *rama*?"

"Tree branch," she chimes in.

"The tree branch cut my face. We saw a doctor but there was little supplies. That's why the scar *es tan feo* and why you can see the marks from when they sewed it."

For years I was self-conscious about the scar and how ugly it looks, the markings prominent in the absence of my eyebrow. The older I got, the more I realized my physical appearance was the last thing I should worry about, especially since I had so many other things to stress about. During my years in the military, I got the nickname, "*el Ceja*," because the scar left only a small part of my left eyebrow—a sliver on each end—giving the appearance I only have one eyebrow. My commanding officers called me *the eyebrow* as an insult. Glad it never stuck outside of my time in the Army.

"Stitches, the marks from the stitches." Her hand squeezes mine. "That must've been scary."

I lift my shoulder. "I no scared. My father was more scared because there was a lot of blood."

"How old were you?"

"Fourteen." Her eyes widen.

"Did your father let you stop working after you fell?"

My head shakes. "No, *muñeca*. I have to always work to help the family. My father told me if I can walk then I be okay."

As the oldest of five kids, it was my responsibility to work with my father to help the family. When I turned thirteen, I offered to stop going to school so I can work with my father all year round, but my father wouldn't allow it. He told me working to help the family was important, but I had to go to school to make sure I had the education to make something of myself.

Something else he told me is, "*Cuba took everything from us, I won't take your childhood away too*. Words I never forget." Although I wasn't a great student, I'm glad my father allowed me to finish school and be a kid.

After dinner we share a tiramisu, and both have an espresso before driving across the causeway to the Brickell area. The show is at the Flamingo Theater Bar inside the Four Ambassadors residential complex. When these buildings were erected in the 1960's it was a posh hotel, which is why the theater is located inside the lobby area. Over time it was converted to high-end apartments because the buildings are along the Miami South Channel, the body of water connected to Biscayne Bay.

When we arrive inside the lobby, Rubi and Alain are sitting on the sofas waiting for us. Alain says hello to Sol then turns to me. "*¿Qué vuelta mi hermano*?" he asks while embracing me in a hug. As Alain is telling me about this new project he's working on, I glance over at Sol and she's engrossed in conversation with Rubi.

My friends embraced Sol and I'm extremely happy they did. When I told her I wanted to introduce her to them she was worried and anxious she wouldn't fit in or they wouldn't like her. I've noticed she's critical of herself, and always quick to apologize or not say what's on her mind. I'm not quite sure why Sol's that way. She's smart, kind, and friendly, not to mention gorgeous. You'd think she would be more confident in herself than she is.

Our tickets are scanned and Sol's grasping onto my hand, our fingers interlocked, as we enter the theater. The Flamingo Theater Bar is a large room, crimson and beige walls with traditional wall paneling. The small stage at the front has a merlot-colored curtain as a backdrop and throughout the room there are small round tables with chairs. The back wall has bookshelves filled with random books and two framed pictures, one of a jester and another of a man's portrait wearing glasses with a prop nose, like the kind people wear for Halloween.

The room is more than half full and our table is near the front, second row off to the left. The show is scheduled to start in ten minutes so we made it with plenty of time. When we arrive at the table, Rubi and Sol excuse themselves to go to the bathroom.

"How's it going with *la jeva*?" Alain asks.

We're interrupted by a waiter who takes our drink order. I order a white wine for Sol, and a water for me. Alain orders himself a gin and tonic and a beer for Rubi.

"She's incredible and I want to be with her every minute of every day, but she doesn't know that yet." I shift in my seat so I can get a glimpse of Rubi and Sol when they return from the restrooms.

"Why not?"

"Something is holding her back. It's like she wants to move forward but she's always hesitant. I want to make sure she feels comfortable. I no want to push her away."

"*Bueno*, I like her, a lot. Rubi told me she spoke to her the few times you've been to my house and she really likes her too. If it's up to Rubi, you'll marry her."

"If it's up to me, I would too, bro."

Alain leans in, places his left arm across the table. "Wow, already? I haven't seen you like this since we lived in Cuba."

"I know. For the first time in a long time, I feel alive."

Carlos Varela takes the stage not long after Rubi and Sol return from the restroom. I lean back in my chair and drape my arm over Sol's shoulders, bringing her closer to me. When Varela begins singing some of the songs I've played for Sol, she sings along and my chest swells.

"You liked the show?" I ask her while we're driving across the McArthur Causeway, Star Island illuminated to our left, and the Miami Beach high-rises lighting up the night sky.

"Very much. He sounded incredible and I liked the theater because it was small. It felt like an intimate show." She turns in her seat toward me.

"It was my first time at that theater. I liked it too." We continue to drive in silence with the radio playing, Led Zeppelin's "Whole Lotta Love" streaming through the speakers.

"You want to spend the night at my place?" she asks, while at the light on Alton Road.

"What kind of a question is that?"

"Um, you don't have to if you don't want to," she responds, turning her head away from me.

"*Muñeca*, of course I want to sleep over." I reach across the console and begin drawing circles on her thigh.

Her head turns and a smile stretches across her face, lighting up her eyes.

After we find a spot to park my car we're walking hand-in-hand toward her apartment building. It's nearly midnight and it's quiet. As we approach her building, I hear footsteps behind us and turn to see where they're coming from, but don't see anyone.

"What's the matter?" Sol asks.

"I thought I heard someone walking but there's nobody there." Sol squeezes my hand a little tighter.

CHAPTER FIFTEEN

Soledad

"Ugh, that steak I had last night still feels like a rock in my stomach," Melida complains as she's walking into the kitchen.

Last night after Melida landed, we went out for Cuban food. She was in the mood for Latin food and someone from her job recommended the restaurant. I checked it out online and it's a trendy spot so I was hoping the food didn't disappoint, which is often the case with trendy places. I tried to persuade her otherwise, but I was unsuccessful.

Dinner was mediocre, at best. The service was terrible, and our food came out barely hot. Let's not forget we dropped a pretty penny for this meal, simply because we were on Ocean Drive in South Beach. I knew it would be this way but didn't want to ruin Melida's plans. It's her birthday weekend so what Melida wants, Melida gets. Thankfully dinner went by quickly, or so it seemed to me because I spent most of the time telling her about Amaury and our relationship.

"I hate to say it, but I told you so." She grimaces at my words.

"Yeah, yeah. I should've listened to you. Now I know better." Her eyes roll.

"Touristy spots are usually not good, you know that." I pull two mugs out of the cabinet and place them on the countertop. "Honestly, I'm surprised you chose that place. Trendy spots are not your usual vibe."

"A colleague told me about it, was raving how good it was." Melida works at Gemelli's Liquor Distillery as the Director of Regional Sales for the Wine Division, one of the biggest wholesale liquor distilleries in Boston. When she was in college, she started waiting tables at a wine bar and restaurant and loved learning about wine. So much so she got a job selling it. She's always raving about her job and jokes about being a professional wine taster. "When I get home, I'm gonna tell him he owes me one because it sucked." She grimaces.

"Do you want me to call Amaury and cancel our

plans for today?" I ask.

She shakes her head. "No way. I haven't ridden a jet ski in years and am wicked excited about it."

Last week when I told Amaury Melida would be in town this weekend, he offered to take us jet skiing. When I asked him if he knew someone with jet skis, he told me he'd take care of everything. Of course, I jumped on the opportunity, especially since I've never been jet skiing. When I mentioned it to Melida, she squealed in excitement.

"You sure? If you don't feel well, we can go tomorrow instead."

"Yeah, I'll take some Alka-Seltzer and will be good as new."

"Whoa, this is a nice house," Melida says as I pull into Amaury's driveway next to his Tahoe. Hitched onto the back of his SUV is a trailer with two jet skis. I didn't realize when he told me he'd handle it all he'd be the one bringing the jet skis. A smile creeps in at the thought of how generous he is.

"It totally is." I remember the first time I came over I was a little taken aback. Didn't expect him to live here, although I don't know why. I assumed as a single guy he'd live in an apartment somewhere, not a large home in this beautiful neighborhood. "And he lives by himself in this big house."

"Maybe you'll change that soon," she teases. "Let's go." Melida opens the door and then the trunk to grab her bag.

Before getting out of the driver's seat, I shoot Amaury a text letting him know we're outside.

Amaury emerges from the front door and is waiting for us as we stroll toward him, his face freshly shaven. When he shaves, he looks younger, his golden skin glows. He's wearing shorts and a snug black tank, his firm biceps on display.

"Mel, this is Amaury. Amaury, this is Melida." He leans in and kisses her on the cheek.

"Good to see you again, Melida," he says, then wraps his arms around my waist pulling me flush to his torso, kissing me.

"I missed you," he tells me.

"Me too," I respond.

As we're following Amaury into the house, Mel leans into me and whispers, "Fuck me with that accent. Rawwwwwrr." She giggles.

"Girl, don't even get me started." I squeeze her hand and she reciprocates.

When we arrive to the Florida Room, Eduardo

glances up from the cooler in front of him on the kitchen counter. "*Hola, chicas,*" he says. I didn't realize he would be here, Amaury said nothing about him joining us.

"Hi, Eduardo," I say, leaning in to kiss him on the cheek. "This is Melida, my best friend."

"Nice to meet you, Melida." He kisses her on the cheek. "Amaury told me you're beautiful and he's right." Melida smiles and then she turns toward me. I grin while shrugging.

"I only invite him for his jet ski," Amaury chimes in, chuckling.

Melida's eyes dart to meet mine and she pushes her shoulders back. I can already tell she's freaking out at having to ride with Eduardo.

"My brother owns the watersports place on Purdy Ave, we'll get two from him before going out," Eduardo says. Melida's shoulders soften at his words.

"I've never ridden a jet ski. Will I know how to do it?" I ask.

Amaury shifts his eyes toward me and says, "Yes, it's almost the same as your Vespa, except there is water."

"I rode them on a trip to Puerto Rico. They're wicked fun and easy to use," Melida says.

"Does the cooler fit on the jet skis?" I ask.

"No, but we leave it in the truck and take the two small soft coolers with us. We store it under the seats," Eduardo responds.

"And for lunch we'll find Raw Bar 2 Go. It's like a food truck *en el agua* and they sell ceviche and other things," Amaury says, his eyes meeting mine.

He knows me well, knows I always need to know about the food and where we'll be eating. "You already know that was my next question." I extend my arm out and he wraps me in his embrace.

"*Sí*, and I want to know everything about you." His lips land on mine. Kissing him when he's freshly shaven feels so different, soft and smooth skin luring me in and making me want more.

Amaury pulls into a lot on Purdy Ave. next to a park overlooking the water. Eduardo exits the Tahoe from the front seat and strides across the lot toward a small building with a window and starts talking to the man inside. Must be his brother.

"*Chicas*, I'm gonna put the jet skis *en el agua*. Why you no go with Eduardo. We need two *salvavidas*," he says, glancing at me.

"Life vests," I add, glancing over to Melida.

"It's times like this I wish my parents had taught us Spanish," Melida says. Her parents are Puerto Ricans who were born and raised in the States, so they spoke English at home, and Melida and her siblings never learned Spanish.

She opens the door and I follow her out. "Is your man trying to set me up with his buddy?" she asks.

I shrug. "Don't know. I didn't know he was coming until I saw him this morning. You okay with him joining us?"

"Yeah. Doesn't hurt that he's kinda cute. Plus, he's got an accent that makes me feel all outta sorts," she adds, wiggling her eyebrows.

"He's definitely easy on the eyes," I add, grinning.

Eduardo is a couple of inches shorter than me with dark blond hair that sits at his shoulders. He has a sandy complexion, which complements his deep ocean blue eyes with a wide flat nose, and thin lips.

"He's a nice guy, from what I know at least. I've only met him a few times but him and Amaury have been friends almost their whole lives," I tell her.

"Well, I'm not looking to get involved but am definitely here to have fun." She winks.

We cross the parking lot toward where Eduardo is talking to the man in the window. As we approach them, I notice the man is nearly identical to Eduardo except he's about three inches shorter than him.

"My brother, Luis." He gestures toward him and in Spanish Eduardo tells him who we are.

"*Hola.* Nice meeting you," the brother responds.

"Nice to meet you," both Melida and I say, in unison.

Minutes later we have life vests in hand and together with Eduardo are striding toward Amaury who's already got the jet skis in the water and tied to a dock. The sun is already warming my skin and it's only 10:00 a.m. I reach for the long sleeve shirt I brought to wear and put the eyewear retainer onto my sunglasses. After removing my shorts and tossing them into the truck, I help with unloading the soft coolers, and the other two life vests.

When Amaury returns from parking his Tahoe, we walk to the dock and Amaury begins explaining the jet ski function to me. Meanwhile, Melida is already vested up and putting her belongings onto her jet ski.

"Here is the key," he says, grasping a coiled keychain that's clipped and hanging from the life vest. "This is the *pito,*" he continues, grabbing a small red whistle between his fingers. "In case you fall, and no one is near you. This—" he points to the throttle on the right handlebar "—is how you go faster."

"Where's the brake?" I ask.

"No brake. Just release the throttle and you slow down. If you pull the key out the jet ski turns off. *Mata el motor*," he says.

"A kill switch, got it," I respond.

"Ready?" asks Melida.

"Yup, let's do this," I say.

"In this area you must go slow," adds Eduardo, pointing to the area of water in front of us. "Once we pass all the boats and are in the bay, we can go more fast."

"I'll follow you guys," I tell them.

I'm the last to push the start button and get my engine going. The low rumble of the jet ski is louder than my Vespa but has a similar feeling to it. I can feel the soft vibrations of the machine underneath my body as we slowly exit the harbor toward the bay. Melida and Eduardo are ahead of me and Amaury is slightly behind me and to my right.

"¿Todo bien, muñeca?" he asks.

I nod. "Yes, I'm good. It's like you said, like when I'm riding the moped."

As we approach the open bay, Melida and Eduardo rev their jet skis and take off, leaving Amaury and me behind.

"Ready, *para ir rápido*?" he asks.

"Yes, what's the fun of jet skiing if we can't go

fast?" I respond, and turn the throttle, jutting out, feeling the cool water splashing on my skin. Being on this jet ski gives me similar feelings of riding the Vespa, except this adds water to the mix and makes it much more exciting. The smell of the salty water mixed with the speed of the jet ski fuels my adrenaline.

Five hours later we're docking the jet skis at the same place we took off from.

"That was incredible," I say. "I've been wanting to try jet skiing for years and so glad I finally did." I climb onto the dock and start pulling my stuff from the storage compartments.

"Thank you for doing this, Amaury," Melida says.

"My pleasure," he responds from behind me.

"Yes, thank you," I add, turning to face Amaury.

He leans into me and whispers, "You can thank me later, *muñeca*," then drops a kiss on my cheek, causing a tingling sensation to run through my body.

"Should we wait here while you get the truck to load the jet skis?" asks Melida.

"No, I pick them up later. Luis will take care of them," Amaury responds.

We gather our things and collectively start walking toward the truck, which no longer has the trailer on the back. When we're all inside the car, I say, "I know we had lunch earlier but I'm already starving."

"Some things never change," Melida adds, giggling.

"*Vamos al Palacio de los Jugos*," Eduardo suggests. We can drink fresh juice and have some *chicharrones*.

"What's that?" Melida asks.

"Deep fried pork chunks that are ridiculously good," I explain.

"I may not speak Spanish, but I know what *chicharrones* are." Melida retorts. "What did he say before that?"

"Oh, the name of the place he suggested but I've never been there," I tell her.

Half an hour later we pull into the parking lot of an open-air restaurant. There are tables underneath an awning and when we walk inside, it's an open space with lots of fruits and vegetables and a counter where you can order.

There are names of things I've never heard of on the menu. "What's *mamey, maracuyá*, and *guarapo*?" I ask.

Amaury takes my hand toward the area where the fruits are displayed and picks up a large oval shaped fruit, then with his finger nicks the side of it, exposing a vibrant deep pink interior color. "*Mamey*, a tropical fruit. *Batido* with this is the best." A smoothie sounds really good right about now.

"This is *maracuyá*," he says, picking up a round yellow passion fruit.

"Oh, I've always called it *parcha*. I didn't know it had another name," I respond.

"Y *guarapo* is made from this—" he lifts a sugar cane and brings it closer to me "—*caña de azúcar*."

"What do they do with the sugar cane?" I ask.

"Put it in the machine and make juice," he responds, matter-of-factly.

"What do you add to it?" I inquire, confused.

"Nothing." He places the sugar cane back onto the shelf and we gait back to the counter where Eduardo and Melida are ordering.

"Pure sugar? That sounds super sweet!" I crinkle my nose.

"It's not that bad."

"What did you get, Mel?" I ask.

"A fresh pressed orange juice. What are you getting?"

"I want to try the passion fruit juice."

Amaury orders my juice and he orders himself a *guarapo*.

"*Guarapo* helps make you strong," Eduardo adds, and throws his head back in laughter.

I don't really understand the joke, but that's a common theme when I'm with Amaury and his friends.

"What does he mean, it makes you strong?" I ask Amaury.

His lips graze my ear and he whispers, "*En la cama*." My heartbeat quickens at his words. *What is wrong with me*?

"What'd he say? Why's it make him stronger?" Melida asks.

"Supposedly makes his manhood stronger," I respond, lifting my shoulder while smirking.

"Well, in that case, maybe you should have one too, Eduardo," Melida adds, grazing his arm.

CHAPTER SIXTEEN

Amaury

A FEW DAYS LATER

We decide to meet at my favorite *ventanita*, a window where you order and consume the coffee in many of Miami's locales, to grab a *cafecito* and *pastelitos* before heading out for the day on our scooters. Drinking Cuban coffee is an integral part of my day, with me drinking at least six or seven every day. In Cuba I didn't have the luxury of drinking coffee, mostly because my father couldn't afford it. But once in Miami, it quickly became my drink of choice.

Cuban coffee is an espresso sweetened by adding sugar to it as it's expressed through coffee grinds and brewing. The perfect *cafecito* has a thick *espumita* at the top, which is the perfect blend of the thick foam of tiny bubbles from the freshly brewed coffee and the sugar.

When Sol asked if I wanted to go for a scooter ride, I was ecstatic. Anything to spend more time with this gorgeous woman. She's not shy, yet she's reticent, doesn't talk about herself much and guards the personal details about her life.

When I pull into the spot next to Sol's scooter, she's leaning on her Vespa with her left leg extended out, the entirety of her leg taunting me from ankle to hip. She's wearing high-waisted jean capri pants, a tank top, and *chancletas* on her feet. Wearing flip-flops to ride on the scooter is extremely dangerous, but she probably doesn't know that since she's new to all of this.

"*Hola muñeca*," I say, and softly kiss her cheek, the skin smooth and warm under my lips.

"Hi." She lifts her wrist to check the time. "You're late!"

"No *chica*. I no late, I run on Miami time," I reply, and wink. After turning the engine off, I rise and approach her. She smells like cinnamon and I'm going to have to ask her what it is because *me enciende por dentro* and I want to devour her. I've never been a fan of cinnamon until meeting Sol.

"Miami time?"

"*Sí*. If someone says one, it really means one fifteen or one thirty."

She raises an eyebrow over at me. "Um, okay."

"You drink coffee?" I ask her.

"Yes. What kind of coffee do they have here?"

"Café cubano, cafecito, colada, cortadito, or café con leche," I tell her.

"Other than *café con leche*, I don't know what the others are," she responds, wrinkling her nose.

"*Cafecito* is like espresso, except the Cubans prepare it with sugar in it. A *colada* is the same thing, only it's a little bigger, for people to share. A *cortadito* is a small *café con leche*."

"Oh, well in that case I'll have a *cortadito* please."

"You tried Cuban pastries yet?" I ask her, pointing to the pastry case to my left.

"No, what kind are they?"

"Here they have *queso, guayaba,* or *guayaba con queso."*

"I don't know what *guayaba* is," she says, looking away from the pastry case and meeting my gaze.

"*Guayaba* is guava, a fruit very popular *en Cuba*."

"What's it taste like?"

"Es dulce."

"I'm not a fan of things that are too sweet so maybe I won't like it. I'll have the cheese one."

"*Está bien*. You can try mine to see if you like it." I order our coffees and pastries with the young woman behind the counter.

"So where are we going today?" Sol asks and turns to lean on the wall.

"*Por* Collins Avenue to Hollywood Beach. It's scenic and a pretty ride on the Vespa. Also, there's a nice boardwalk with restaurants, and live music."

"Sounds great. I haven't gotten that far north yet so it will be new for me."

"Sol, you can't wear *chancletas* to ride the Vespa. *Es peligroso* and you could get hurt," I tell her, pointing to her feet. I don't want her to seriously injure herself.

"Oh, really?" she asks, looking down at her feet. "Should we stop by my place so I can change?"

The young woman places our coffee and pastries before us, and I slide Sol's *cortadito* closer to her.

"*Si puedes, sí*. If you suddenly stop or something, your feet aren't protected. You should wear closed shoes, or sneakers."

"Okay. We can stop by my place, and I'll run inside real quick to change them, if that's okay."

"*Claro que sí*," I respond, nodding my head in unison.

"This is the cheese *pastelito*," I say, pointing to the long, golden brown pastry with sugar baked on top. Sol extends her fingers to grasp it, bringing it to her lips.

"Mmm," she mumbles, as she's chewing. "*Que rico*. It's warm, and cheesy with just the right amount of sugar in it."

"Wait 'til you try this one." I extend the guava pastry and bring it close to her mouth, where she opens and licks her lips. Damn, she is so sexy.

Instead of letting Sol bite into the pastry, I pull it back and lean down to swipe my lips across hers. I can't resist her mouth, especially knowing how delicious she tastes. She welcomes my kisses and kisses me back, our lips exploring. I can feel the bulge in my pants growing and reluctantly, I pull back, immediately feeling the loss of having her so close.

"What was that for?" she asks in a breathy voice.

I lean into her and whisper into her ear, "*Porque me tienes loco*."

"*Vos también*," she replies, and raises her hand to my mouth, rubbing her fingers across my lips. I want to yell out at Sol's confession that I drive her crazy too.

"Here, try the guava pastry." I rest the pastry on her lips and watch as she bites into the gooey purple jam filling the flaky outside. Some of the filling rests in the crease of her lips and I have an urge to lick it off but have to control myself.

Watching her bite into the guava pastry has me fantasizing about her mouth all over me. Sol's face scrunches and she's shaking her head with her mouth still full.

"*No te gusta*?" I ask, shocked she doesn't like it.

"No. It's too sweet. I don't know, it tastes weird."

"Weird? You the first person I ever meet *que no le gustan*." I take a bite of the pastry and it's delicious. The warm guava jam explodes in your mouth with tangy and tart flavors. The first bite is always the best and the flaky buttery crunch of the puffed pastry exterior flakes off giving way to the gooey sweetness of the guava paste.

We finish our coffee and pastries and hop onto our scooters, scooting toward Sol's house so she can swap out her shoes.

"I'll be right back," Sol exclaims, as she hops off her scooter and scurries toward her apartment. The building she lives in is traditional art deco style typical here in Miami Beach. It's a small two-story building that's vibrant mint green color with mango trim and decorative architecture adorning its rounded edges, archways, and rigid rectangular windows. I watch as she goes up the stairs, opens her door, and disappears inside.

Sol emerges from the building wearing high-top red Converse sneakers. "Better," I say, pointing to her feet.

After we strap our helmets on but before taking off, I say, "Remember, *usa el pito*," I say, pushing the horn button several times. "A lot of times cars no see scooters, which is the most dangerous thing. Be vigilant and no go too fast, and you will be okay. Ready?"

"Ready as I'll ever be," she responds, nodding swiftly.

As we cruise up Collins Ave., Sol is comfortable riding her scooter. When she told me still gets nervous when riding, I thought she didn't know how to ride well and that's why she was hesitant. I think she's underestimating herself because she's doing great.

When we arrive to Hollywood Beach, we ride into the public lot to park the Vespas. I pull my old, tattered sheet from the under-seat compartment and grab a hold of Sol's hand, curling her fingers with mine. Her hand is on fire. Each time I touch her, she's blazing hot.

"Tienes las manos hirviendo," I tell her.

"They are?" she asks, holding out her other hand and resting her palm on her cheek. "My hands don't feel hot."

"It's the same as the night we met. Your hands were

burning up. I thought maybe it was because we were dancing, but then later outside your hotel you were the same."

She shrugs. "I don't feel it."

"*Estas hecha pa' mí*, that's why," I proclaim, and glance over at her as we continue our walk to the sand. I can't hide my feelings for her as much as I try, we were made for each other.

"You think so?" she fires back, pursing her lips.

"No. I know so. You know it too, *pero te haces la difícil*." The rest of the stroll to the beach is in silence, and it's because I want Sol thinking about my last words. I want her to know I'm onto her game of playing hard to get but I'll breach her walls soon enough.

By the time we're settled on the sheet to watch the waves crash, the sun is behind us and beachgoers are starting to pack up their belongings. The band on the stage behind us is tuning their instruments getting ready to start playing their set.

"It's taken me forever to decide but I finally named my *Vespa*," she says, breaking the silence that's been lingering for the past several minutes.

"¿Qué nombre le pusiste?"

"Roxy. She's chili red and fiery, has a kick to her when I ride her, and Roxy seemed appropriate."

"I like it. *Super femenino y sexy, como su dueña*," I

tell her, winking as I extend my hand to rub my fingers across her cheek, which are turning crimson red at my words. It's true though, Roxy is a sexy feminine name, just like Sol is. "*Tienes pena*?" I ask.

"Embarrassed?" She shrugs. "Guess I'm not used to all the compliments."

"You should be complimented *todos los días*," I say, pushing her hair back from her face in an attempt to cast away her self-doubt. Sol wraps her arms around herself, staring out at the ocean in quiet contemplation. "*Muñeca, ven*," I add, scooting closer so I can wrap my arm around her and bring her close to me.

CHAPTER SEVENTEEN

Soledad

Amaury tucks me into his side, and I rest my head on his shoulder. We sit in silence, watching the people around us as they pack up their things or relax with their families. The sound of the ocean soothes me like nothing else. There's such tranquility here, despite all the people surrounding us. I don't know what it is, but each time I'm by the ocean, a sense of calm overtakes me, relaxing me. I love the beach, and it's so nice to share that with him.

His compliments are welcome yet so unfamiliar to me. Before him, I rarely received compliments so it's not something I'm used to. The night we met I thought it may have been his attempt at pick-up lines, but no matter how much time we spend together he's always saying something, causing heat to rise to my cheeks with each compliment.

"You liked it, the ride here?" he asks as he adjusts the sheet.

The ride here was incredible! Collins Ave. runs parallel to the beach. The entire three-lane stretch of road is beautifully landscaped with palm trees and other native plants and trees, lined with high-rises, hotels, shops, parks, and is buzzing with traffic, which was a bit nerve-wracking.

"I did, but because I was paying attention to the scooter, I couldn't look at our surroundings."

"Next time you can ride with me, this way you can see better," he says, winking.

"I'd like that." I bring my knees up and lean back on my elbows.

"I watched you on the scooter. You ride good," he says, wrapping his arm over my leg.

"I've been riding a little every day. Guess it's paying off."

"You only need belief in yourself."

"I tend to underestimate myself often, so I know exactly what you mean. I'm working on it."

"¿Por qué?"

"Why what?"

"Why do you not believe in yourself?"

I shrug, pull a curl between my fingers and begin wrapping it around in circles. "Not sure why." I'm not in the mood to talk about the insecurities I feel because my father abandoned me.

Unwanted.

Undesirable.

Unloved.

"*¿Todo bien*?" he asks, dropping his head so his eyes can meet mine.

I nod. "Yes, everything's fine. Why wouldn't it be?"

"You're playing with your hair." Keeping my emotions hidden gets harder the longer we know each other.

"All good, I promise."

He stares at me, his eyes fixed on mine. "People always judge and criticize so *es importante que creas en ti misma.* No let anyone else's actions or words make you change who you are." Amaury drops soft kisses along my forehead.

"My entire life I've been that way, underestimating my abilities, not believing in myself, and I'm my own worst critic. But I've been trying to be better about it." I turn away from him, the intensity of his gaze a little too much for me to handle right now.

"Hungry? There's a pizza place I like over there—" he points down the boardwalk "—maybe we can grab a slice?"

"Love pizza and haven't tried any good ones since moving to Miami." I separate from him and am graced with a smile.

"*Me encanta que* you're not shy about eating because I love to eat."

"Me too, that's why I'll never be skinny," I say, chuckling.

"I no want you skinny. *¡Tus curvas me facinan!*" he murmurs, his breath tickling my ear. I'm glad someone loves my curves.

"*Vámonos*," he exclaims, jumping to his feet and extending his hand out to help me up. He's so energetic, like electricity is coursing through his body.

Hand in hand we stroll down the boardwalk, which is busy with joggers, bicycles, families, and lovers strolling.

"It's nice here, kinda reminds me of Venice Beach in California, although it's less busy here," I say, as we're strolling toward the restaurant.

"So, you really no liked the pizza?" Amaury asks, as he

pushes the kickstand on his scooter down.

We sat at an outside table at the pizza place Amaury likes and shared a small pie. It was okay, but it's not the pizza I'm used to eating. Most of the pizza in Boston is delicious, although my favorite is Regina Pizzeria—thin crispy crust and gooey cheese cooked to perfection. Before heading back home we listened to some live music, which wasn't bad for a local band.

"No, but don't take it personal. I'm used to eating pizza in Boston, where it's good pretty much anywhere you get it." I lift the seat to grab my things.

"I visited Boston many years ago but no eat pizza when there. Maybe soon you'll take me to your favorite pizza restaurant," he says, pulling me flush to him.

"Uh, maybe," I respond, raising my eyes to his and smirking. "Before I forget—" I step back from him "—I still want to get one of those cases for the back of my scooter," I say, putting my hand at the back of the Vespa.

He pauses and rubs my arm, his gaze intensifying. "Okay, we do it in the next few days."

"Sol, *ven acá*," he says, lifting my face to his. Our lips meet, his kisses are tender, and his gentleness melts my insides. The stubble around his mouth tickles. I recall how good his lips felt on my skin and want him to explore all of me. Just the thought makes my belly stir.

"Amaury," I whisper, separating myself from him. "I should go, I have an early morning."

"I no want you to leave yet," he says, his fingers rubbing my lower back. I don't want to leave yet either and his sultry words lure me back to him. "*Dejame hacerte el amor*," he whispers, his breath tickling my ear.

Him asking to make love to me ignites me from within and I can't resist. His words have me all riled up. I tug his hand and start walking toward the entryway.

Inside my apartment we barely have the door closed and we're undressing each other. Me searching for his belt buckle, him pulling at my shirt to tug it over my head. We find ourselves at my couch and when my knees touch the cushions, I let myself fall. Amaury tugs my pants off, sliding them down my legs. I reach for him wanting to pull him closer to me, but Amaury gently nudges me back. "*Recuéstate*." I lie back and let him take the lead.

CHAPTER EIGHTEEN

Amaury

My shoulders slump as I sit back on my couch. I spoke to my father after not having spoken to him in a few weeks. Phone calls with him and the rest of my family are a mission because no one in my family has a phone. But one of the neighbors about three houses away from my father's house has one and she allows family of all of her neighbors to call and use her phone. Of course, when we send things to Cuba, we also send money or something for her to compensate for her allowing use of the telephone. Phones are rare because they're a luxury and expensive to have. Although here in the U.S. we have mobile phones and internet, most people in Cuba don't have access to those types of luxuries.

I can still hear my father's words replaying in my head, "I have to have part of my prostate removed." I'm scared beyond measure because surgery in Cuba is nothing like having surgery in the United States.

The memory of my sister flashes through my mind, how she went to the hospital because she was short of breath. Her asthma was acting up and she couldn't get it under control. After arriving at the hospital, they admitted her and wanted to give her IV fluids, except they used old needles to administer the fluids. Piercing her skin caused an infection that went undetected until it was too late. The infection spread throughout her body and killed her. Totally preventable and something that would never happen in most countries. But not in Cuba where medical supplies are scarce and medical care is subpar on the best of days.

The hospitals don't have the necessary supplies, they don't have medicine, and it's barely sanitary, at least not in the hospitals outside of the tourist areas. Tourists received top tier medical attention, while Cuban citizens are left behind, in dire need of basic medical care. Tourist Cuba and the real Cuba, two different island nations existing under the same flag. Each time I think about it and how we are negatively affected by it I get angry, so I try to block it out.

He told me he needs to wait three months before he has to be at the hospital, which gives me enough time to put together a box of necessities to send over. I asked him to speak to the doctor to ask for anything specific they need for surgery, which I can send from here. I told him I'd call him back next week at the same time to see if he had an update for me so I can start buying the supplies.

My phone rings, halting the freight train running through my head. Eduardo's name appears on the screen and my heart sinks. I was hoping it was Sol because her voice is exactly what I need to hear right now.

"*Dime*," I say, answering the call.

"*Oye*, come to the Washington Ave. store. This morning when I arrived the door was unlocked. They broke in last night."

"*¿Cómo*?" I shout. Motherfucker! As if the news about my father isn't enough, now this bullshit too. I jump to my feet and grab my keys from the table next to the front door.

I park the Tahoe in the back alley and pull the back door of the shop open. Eduardo is talking with two police officers.

As I glance around the room, everything is the same as it was last night. What did they break in to steal?

"This is my partner Amaury," Eduardo says, introducing me to the police officers.

"Detective Suarez," says the woman, black hair pulled back into a ponytail. "We're with Miami Beach PD and this is Detective Vidal." She points to the young guy standing to her left, a military style buzz cut and dark mole on his chin. "Is this the first you're seeing this?"

I nod in agreement. "I only know because he called me," I respond, gesturing to Eduardo.

"They took a few helmets, and two of the Yamaha scooters we had for sale, the black one and the dark blue one. They were searching for cash because the register is open but the safe is still locked," says Eduardo.

"What happened with the alarm?" I ask.

"Disabled," answers Detective Suarez. I push my hands through my hair frustrated at how my day has started out, and it's not even ten yet.

"Do you have surveillance cameras?" asks Detective Vidal.

"No," both Eduardo and I answer in unison.

"We need a new alarm system," I say.

"I suggest installing surveillance cameras," adds Detective Vidal.

"Anyone you can think of that would do this?" asks

Detective Suarez.

"You think it's someone we know?" asks Eduardo.

"Maybe not directly. Oftentimes it's an acquaintance of someone you know that'll commit the crime. If that's the case, the person you know may have no knowledge the crime was gonna be committed," Detective Suarez explains.

My head shakes. "I no have problems with anyone," I say.

After speaking with the officers a bit longer, I ask if they can finish up with Eduardo so I can drive to the other store to check on things. I haven't heard from my employee today, which makes me think there are no issues at the West Avenue store. When I pull up in front of the store on West Ave. everything seems normal, and David is inside sitting at the desk.

"Everything okay this morning?" I ask David as I cross the showroom.

"Yeah, why wouldn't it be?" he responds.

I update him on what happened at the other location and David tells me there was nothing out of the ordinary here, the alarm was still engaged when he arrived, and nothing was out of place.

"UPS delivered us a bunch of parts, I put the boxes in the garage," David says.

"Thank you."

In the open garage Roxy sits along the back wall, next to the entrance of the office. We brought her here yesterday so I can put on the rear case Sol's been wanting. I'm expecting the part to be inside one of the boxes that arrived today. Once I find it, I'll secure it to the back of the scooter. Sol wants to start using her scooter more but needs the case for the extra storage space. It's much easier to get around Miami Beach on a scooter than in a car. Parking is difficult and traffic is always intense. With the scooter everything is quicker and simpler.

An image of Sol sitting on the desk with no shirt flashes through my mind. The swell of her breasts in her gray and black bra, her olive skin taunting me, her scent like a drug. Stopping myself was one of the most difficult things I've ever done because exercising self-control around Sol is hard. I want everything with her, yet I know it needs to be at her pace. Although she's allowing me to love and worship her, there's still something holding her back, but she won't talk about it—not that I've asked her. I wonder if she'll ever tell me what she's so scared of. I'll have to pry the information from her on one of the days she's generous with herself and feels like sharing.

Once I locate the top case for Roxy, I begin installing it. Securing it to the moped takes me less than fifteen minutes. I had planned on taking it to Sol right away, but I'll take Roxy home to her another time. Right now, I have a surprise for her and there's nothing I want more than to see my girl.

CHAPTER NINETEEN

Soledad

My phone pings with a text message notification. When I grab it, I see Amaury's name on the screen.

Amaury: I'm outside. Get your helmet, and wear sneakers or boots. And bring something with long sleeves.

I scroll through the project I'm working on then glance at my watch. Fuck it. May as well take a break.

Soledad: Where are we going?

Before I can put my phone down, Amaury responds.

Amaury: One of my favorite places.

My heart swells. I love he just showed up and wants to take me out. In my closet, I search for my red Converse and after pulling my jeans on I lace them up. I change into a white tank top, grab a long sleeve shirt, tie it around my waist, and wrap an elastic around my long curls, securing it in a low bun so I can wear my helmet. I grab my keys off the counter and hang my purse across my chest.

As I walk down the sidewalk, I see him sitting on a motorcycle. It's black, with orange flames painted across the tank and the handlebars are raised several inches away from the body of the bike.

"Is this yours?" I ask, dragging my fingers along the paint.

He nods, wraps his arms around my waist and covers my mouth with his. As usual, his lips are warm and soft. The stubble is thicker than usual today and I'm remembering what it felt like to kiss him freshly shaven.

"*Necesitaba verte*," he says, not responding to my question.

"Needed to see me? Miss me that much, huh?" I ask, teasing him. He nods and rather than respond, his lips crash into mine again. It's like he's searching for something, and he thinks he'll find it in me.

He brings his head back and asks, "*¿Te gusta*?" responding to my earlier question about the motorcycle with his own question.

My fingers fall on my lips, feeling how swollen they are from his onslaught of kisses. “It’s badass. I love it! I didn’t know you had a motorcycle!”

“I no take it out as much as I’d like to, but now that I know *que te gusta*, we can take it out more often.”

I more than like it. It’s super sexy and sleek. “It’ll be my first time on a motorcycle. A scooter is as close as I’ve gotten.”

“You’ll love it. *Es muy diferente* from your Vespa.” He’s beaming with pride as he talks about how different his motorcycle is from the scooter. “It has loud pipes and you’ll feel the vibrations of the engine, and the ride is much smoother than the Vespa.” He stands and swings his leg over and sits, settling into the seat and then strapping his helmet on before turning the key and rolling the throttle, the roar of the pipes making themselves known.

Amaury is sexy, he exudes confidence and walks with swagger, and he knows he’s a good-looking guy because he never doubts himself. But here, sitting on this motorcycle, it’s sexiness on steroids. The sight of him straddling the bike causes my breath to quicken and my belly to stir. It makes me want to straddle him on the bike and make out with him.

Instead, I strap my helmet on and climb on behind him, wrapping my arms around his waist—his unique scent tickling my nose. It's like he said, I can feel the vibrations coursing through my body. We take off down the street, the loud pipes echoing off the surrounding buildings.

We ride down the causeway, the sun inching its way across the Miami sky. The massive cruise ships docked in the waterway to my left are a sight to see, lined up one behind the next, the people on the decks are tiny specks from a distance. The palm trees lining the median strip are still, the air stagnant from the thick humid air.

When he takes the turn onto I95 South, I tighten my arms around his torso. In all my years of driving I must've seen dozens of motorcycles on the highway and always thought how crazy the idea of riding one was, yet here I am, on the back of this gorgeous man's Harley. It's exhilarating and frightening all at the same time. Amaury speeds up as he integrates himself into the traffic lanes and as the cars pass us on the left, they're so close I can see the passengers inside and what they're doing. I take a deep breath to calm my nerves and shift my eyes back to the highway. Maybe if I keep my eyes on the road, I won't feel as nervous.

I95 ends after downtown Miami and Amaury takes

the last exit toward Rickenbacker Causeway, Key Biscayne. I've not yet been to this area of the city and I'm excited to see and explore a new part of town. As the motorcycle rolls through the tollbooth and we're taking the turn, to our left are the bayfront skyscrapers lining Brickell Avenue—it feels like I can reach out and touch them. To our right is a beach, the shoreline busy with people and dogs. The road takes us onto a high bridge, giving us a spectacular view of the Miami skyline. The bay expands as far back as the MacArthur Causeway, the water peppered with yachts and sailboats as far as the eye can see.

As we descend the bridge, there is another beach to our right, the ocean water a deep blue and calm. To our left, signs indicating there's a restaurant, a marina, and a water tour company. Buildings continue to line the left side of the island, the Miami Seaquarium to our right, an ocean front property that expanses nearly a half-mile. We cross another bridge, this one low and close to the turquoise-colored water before we see a sign welcoming us to Crandon Park. The road is lined with plants and trees on both sides, mixtures of palm trees and other tropical shrubs, the occasional small sign indicating entrances to different beach parks along the way.

Finally, we roll into the Village of Key Biscayne.

There are apartment buildings along one side of the road and a small strip mall to the right with shops and restaurants. Amaury slows the speed of the Harley as we continue to drive through the town. It's a quintessential beach town, palm trees lining the streets, golf carts alongside cars, and high-rises along the stretch of beach to the east.

When the Harley rolls to a stop, we've arrived at a gatehouse at the entrance to the Bill Baggs Cape Florida State Park. Amaury leans forward, pulls his wallet from his back pocket to pay the entrance fee and then shoves it back inside before revving and taking off. The road is narrow, one lane each way, again lined with tropical vegetation. There are no cars in front or behind us and the desolate sight causes a shiver to run up my spine, which quickly dissipates when Amaury finds a shaded parking spot inside a semi-full parking area.

Once on my feet, I remove my helmet and place it onto the seat, letting my hair loose and shaking it out a bit. "What a beautiful ride! Well, at least the part after we got off the highway," I say, as Amaury is removing his helmet.

"You were scared?" he responds while hanging his helmet off the handlebars.

I nod. "A little bit. The cars were so close, and they

were going wicked fast."

"*Ven aca chica.*" He draws me to him and wraps his arms around me, dropping kisses along my hairline. "No be afraid."

Here, wrapped in his arms I'm not. I don't want to ruin the moment with my fears, so I separate from him and ask, "What are we doing here?"

"*El Farito* is here. It's my favorite place in Miami, and the beach here is like no other beach in the city, turquoise waters *como en Cuba*."

"There's a lighthouse here? In Miami?" I ask, genuinely surprised. When I was researching Miami before moving down, I never came across any information about a lighthouse.

"*Sí*. Our last day *en el mar* we could see it. It gave us—" he stops and bites his lip, seems to be in search of a word "—*esperanza*. I no remember the word in English."

"Hope," I say, my lips curling up on one side.

"¡*Sí*! Hope, and *mucha alegría*! Finally, our time in the ocean was almost over. When the Coast Guard *nos rescató* the lighthouse was so close. After they rescued us, I stared at the lighthouse the entire time until we were far away, I couldn't see it anymore." He gives me a crooked smile as he locks the engine and removes the key.

"I can only imagine what that felt like," I say, even if I don't think I can truly imagine any of what he's been through. Not even my wildest imagination could conjure anything close to what Amaury has experienced.

"*Dale,* let's go." He grasps my hand, our fingers intertwining, and starts walking toward the far end of the lot where a blue and white sign with a lighthouse begins appearing. The sign is wedged between utility poles adorned with marine rope and sprawled across the center are the words Cape Florida Lighthouse.

We walk through the gate and as we turn the corner of the tiled pathway Amaury stops so I can take the sight in. Tall skinny palm trees line the stone walkway on each side, standing over twenty feet tall with the palm fronds swaying from the breeze coming off the ocean. At the far end is an old eloquent white stone lighthouse, the top of it black, a stark contrast to the clear blue sky surrounding it.

"Wow," I whisper. "It's incredible. I never would've imagined this great towering structure being here."

"*Ya sabes* what I felt when I saw it the first time."

I raise my eyes to meet Amaury's. "I will never know what you felt, no matter how much I would like to. You spent four days in the open water and risked your life, hoping and praying to reach land. Seeing this lighthouse after your journey is a feeling you can't replicate. No matter how you describe it, words will never do it justice."

"*A lo mejor*," he responds, a meager attempt to downplay my words.

We continue down the path toward the lighthouse and when we're standing on the bricks at the foot of it, we stop to take in the surroundings. The tall white brick structure towers over us, the Atlantic Ocean its backdrop, a jetty to the left and a walkway to the right leading to the keeper's cottage.

"Do you come here a lot?"

His shoulder rises. "I like riding my motorcycle here and sitting *en el malecón*." He points to the low sea wall. "It's no the same as *La Habana*, *pero en los días que* I miss home *y mi familia*, you find me here," he finishes, his tone softens as he tells me this is the place he comes to on the days he misses his family.

He grasps my hand again and we stroll behind a group of people. At the end of the path is the keeper's cottage and we stroll to the left, past a bench. Amaury sits on the wall, pulling his knees up to his chest so his feet can rest on the edge of the cement, and I do the same. The water beneath is relatively calm and seaweed gathers at the wall's edge.

He's quiet, lost in his surroundings and thoughts

and I don't want to intrude. He tends to do this a lot, usually when we're near the water, which seems to be often, both of us lovers of the ocean.

I can't help but think how different from Carmine he is. Carmine was impulsive, loud, and rarely listened to what I had to say. When I think back on his behavior, he was often condescending and belittled me. I still question how I was able to ignore what was in plain sight.

Amaury is forthright but his assertiveness isn't obnoxious or overwhelming. In fact, it's the complete opposite because he has a calm demeanor. He's always observing those around him, listening to what's happening and taking it all in.

"I talked with my father this morning for the first time in more than a month," Amaury says, interrupting my thoughts. "He told me he's sick, needs surgery."

"Oh." I shift to look at him. "For what? Will he be okay?"

"Remove a part of his prostate, and I hope so."

"I wanted to cheer him up so I told him about you and he's happy for me. Says he wishes he could meet you because you sound incredible." Amaury drags his finger along my cheek, sending a shiver down my spine. "When I talk with him, I miss him. Coming here I feel closer to him." His shoulders slump and he shifts to adjust how he's sitting.

My heart thumps in my chest at Amaury's confession yet I also feel sad because he can't see his family. I stretch my hand in search of his, curling my fingers with his, and squeeze. I don't know what to say to him but want him to know I'm here for him. We sit in silence, enjoying the sounds of the ocean.

"No way! *Va llover*," Amaury says, breaking the silence.

"What do you mean it's gonna rain, the skies are clear and blue," I say, looking up at the cloudless sky.

Pointing to our right, he says, "There, see those clouds? *Eso es una tormenta*, heavy rain and it's coming quick."

"How do you know it's a storm?"

He shrugs. "Here in Miami *es común* because *es un clima tropical* and there is always rain like that here." It's weird to me because where we're sitting right now there are clear blue skies but not too far from the shore the dark and ominous clouds are moving toward us. I've never experienced tropical weather, as Amaury calls it, where you watch the storm clouds move in. Quite different from the blanket rain we would get in New England.

The wind gusts and when I look up, the blue skies have mostly disappeared behind the black clouds rolling in, the rumbling of the impending storm becoming louder. "We should probably go, it's gonna rain any minute now," I say.

Amaury hops to his feet and gazes at the sky. "I no think we'll make it without getting rained on. We might have to wait until it passes."

Hand in hand, we follow the small group of people toward the exit. About halfway down the stone walkway the sky opens up, and heavy rain begins to fall. Thunder crashes as a torrent of water continues to stream from the sky. I'm soaked and starting to feel cold from being wet, my bra now visible through my white tank top.

When we're underneath the shelter at the entrance to the lighthouse, Amaury asks, "Are you cold?"

"A little." I rub my arms to try to warm up.

"I know, *tienes los pezones duros*," he whispers into my ear. My eyes drop and sure enough my nipples have hardened and are visible through my bra and tank top. I feel heat rising to my cheeks and cross my arms over my chest. Amaury wraps me in his embrace, and I rest my chin on his shoulder.

When the rain passes, we sprint to the motorcycle to gear up and ride home. The parking lot is nearly empty except for Amaury's bike and a few scattered vehicles. I unbuckle my helmet from the bike when I hear, "Sol."

I lift my head and he's no longer standing on the other side of the bike but to my right. "Yeah?"

He takes the helmet from my hands, hangs it from the handlebars, and pulls me into his arms then kisses me softly before locking gazes. "*Te amo*."

CHAPTER TWENTY

Amaury

After leaving the lighthouse, Sol asked me to drop her at home. We were both wet and cold. When we pulled up in front of her building, she was quick to dismount from the back of the bike and say goodbye. When I invited her to Alain and Rubi's for dinner because Rubi made *tamales*, she dismissed the invitation and told me she was going to shower, and she needed to finish a work project she was working on. I wonder if it's just an excuse because after I told her I loved her, her gaze dropped to the floor and her body stiffened before she wiggled herself out of my embrace. After, Sol was quiet the rest of the time we were together. Her radiant smile gone;

her eyes serious.

Sol is reticent with her emotions, and I can't figure out why. We've been dating for four months and she's still holding back. Is it possible it's too soon? That she doesn't love me back? That she doesn't want to continue this relationship and is keeping her heart locked up? I hope not because what I feel for this woman I've never felt before. I'm usually good at reading people but Sol is a mystery to me.

Before I know it, I find myself at Alain's house. I thought about staying home but need some company tonight after the day I've had. Otherwise, I'll drive myself crazy thinking about Sol and all the things I don't understand about her.

"*¿Y la jeva*?" asks Alain, as I'm strolling into the yard.

"Good to see you too, *mi hermano*," I respond. I grab a bottle of water from the fridge and sit, guzzling it in one sitting. It's a good thing I don't drink, otherwise today would be one of the days I drank a lot!

"She's not coming?" inquires Rubi. She pulls two *tamales* from the large pot on the stove and places them on a dish for me.

"No, *está trabajando*, or so she says," I tell her.

"You look like *se te murió el perro*. What happened?" asks Rubi, pointing out how miserable I look while she places the dish in front of me.

Rubi is like my sister. We've known each other since we were kids in Cuba. She's petite and blonde, with big brown eyes and pouty lips. Her and Alain dated as teens and broke up then Alain came to the United States. They each got married, had kids with their spouses, and divorced. After divorcing they got back in touch and Alain brought Rubi from Cuba with her two daughters and they've been together ever since. Alain never forgot about her, always talked about how he missed her and how they're soul mates. They're meant to be. They finish each other's sentences and adore one another. It's the kind of relationship I crave. A relationship I hope to have with Soledad, if she'll have me.

My shoulder lifts as I sit back in my chair. "Today we went to *El Farito* and before we left, I told her I loved her. After I said it *no dijo nada*. She asked to go home and said she had to finish some work."

"That's why you're like this?" she asks, her hands flailing around as she speaks. "Amaury, *esa chica* is super into you. When we were at the Varela concert, she talked about you *toda la noche*. You don't see how she looks at you?"

"*¿Tú crees*?" I ask, not sure I believe what Rubi is telling me. I reach for the bottle of tabasco on the table to add some to my *tamales*.

Tamales cubanos are one of the foods I love most to eat. They're made with ground corn and the filling changes depending on who makes them. Rubi adds pork along with red peppers. Then she stuffs the corn husks and ties them shut before boiling them. She's a pro and they're delicious! Alain invites me over when she makes them because she makes enough for the entire crew. My father used to make them in Cuba, except ours never had meat since we didn't have access to meat. He'd stuff them with different vegetables he could find.

"I don't think. I know!" she exclaims. "After *el concierto*, I told Alain you two would be married someday."

"It's true," Alain chimes in. "And you know *que Rubi es bruja*." He chuckles when he calls Rubi a witch. Rubi has the uncanny ability to predict what's going to happen in any situation and with any person. It's incredible how accurate she is. She's known as the *bruja* of our circle of friends.

"*Bueno*, I hope you're right this time too. Because *esa chica me tiene loco*. I think about her day and night and want to be with her all the time. I'm not because I no want to scare her away. She's *siempre entre el sí y el no*," I say, explaining that Sol's always teetering between yes and no.

"Invite her to *la Fiesta de los Municipios*. It's next week." The Fiesta is a yearly party held at a large hall where people from my neighborhood in Cuba get together to eat, drink, dance, and reminisce. It started several years ago with just our neighborhood, and it's grown. Now it's not only our neighborhood but a few surrounding ones too. There are other parties held around Miami for different areas of Cuba. We go nearly every year because it's the one place you can count on seeing old friends from Cuba.

"*Me gusta la idea*," I tell her, liking the idea of inviting Sol to join me. When I see her again, I will invite her, especially since she'll get to dress up and I want to see her wearing one of those dresses that accentuates all her curves.

When I finished eating, I sat to play a few rounds of dominoes with Alain, Rubi, and Roberto before heading home again. As I'm driving across the causeway, I decide to drive by Sol's house. I can't stop thinking about what Rubi told me and Sol is at the forefront of my thoughts. I missed her tonight, especially when around all my friends. She belongs there with me, enjoying the regular day to day stuff of being in a relationship. I want that with her. I want everything with her. When I pull up outside of her building, I can see the lights in her apartment are off. I glance at the clock on the radio, and it reads 22:07. It's only ten o'clock but during the week she goes to bed early so it's probably too late to call her and I don't want to wake her. I wish I had a key; I'd enter quietly, slip into bed, sidle up to her, and wrap her in my arms.

I catch a glimpse of movement to my left, across the street from Sol's building. There's a dark-haired guy sitting on the wall of the apartment building. He's wearing jeans and a light jacket, although it's not jacket weather. Not a face I recognize since coming around here. Not that I should recognize everyone but since visiting Sol's I've been paying attention to the people who come and go from this neighborhood. She's a woman living by herself and although it's relatively safe around here, I worry about her. I decide against waking Sol and put the Tahoe in drive, driving off. I glance in my side view mirror and the guy is still sitting along the wall, staring in the direction of Sol's building.

CHAPTER TWENTY-ONE

Soledad

ONE WEEK LATER

I'm working on translating documents for an attorney client who needs these contracts translated from Spanish to English. I've been deciphering them for the past week because the copies I was given are not very legible and I've been struggling through this project. Thankfully, I still have two weeks to meet my deadline. Glad I got an early start. My phone notifies me of an incoming text message and it's Amaury and I smile at the thought of him. He must know I need a break from work, and I miss him. More than I care to admit.

Amaury: *Cafecito* later?

We've barely seen each other since the day we rode his motorcycle to the lighthouse, which makes things a little weird because he told me he loved me and I've not responded to him, nor have we discussed it. I know it's my fear spilling over from Carmine and how it all went down with him. I can hear Melida's voice in my head, reminding me to not punish Amaury for Carmine's sins. I've been keeping myself busy with work and making excuses to delay the inevitable.

Soledad: Yes. Usual place & time?

Meeting Amaury for coffee has become somewhat of a ritual between us. I was never much of a coffee drinker, usually only having a small cup in the morning to get my day started. But since moving to Miami and dating Amaury, my coffee habit has changed. I now have at least one *cafecito* a day, but on average, it's between three or four of them. We usually meet at the Cuban place down on Euclid and Sixth Street when we finish work.

Amaury: *Sí.* Bring your swimsuit to go to the beach *un ratico.*

I still remember when I met Carmine, we saw each other nearly every day and became inseparable. He told me he loved me just weeks after we started dating and I responded in kind. Had I known then he'd become possessive, controlling, and violent, things would've been so different. I ignored the signs that were in my face day in and day out. His dislike for my friends, his continuous criticism of them, and his desire to isolate me. His short temper, need to control everything, and the uncanny ability to ruin a perfectly good night out by starting an unnecessary fight with random strangers. I lost count of how many times he embarrassed my friends and me in a restaurant or club, and for years I allowed it because I kept silent about it.

After placing my pockabook underneath the seat, I push the key into the ignition of my Vespa. I cruise down Meridian Ave, my favorite street here in Miami Beach. The tree lined street stretches across the heart of the city, a green spine amidst blocks of buildings. The Brazilian Beautyleaf trees provide a canopy of coveted shade from the long days of sun. The beautiful tree-lined street is what drew me to live in this neighborhood of Miami Beach.

It's a typical Miami day—hot and humid. Despite the thick humidity, riding the Vespa along Meridian Ave. gives respite from the stagnant air, the warm air blowing my hair. When I get home later, I'll regret not having tied my hair back before hopping onto the scooter, but by the time I was ready to leave I realized I had forgotten an elastic and didn't feel like going back inside to get one.

I'm at the stop sign before the Café and I see Amaury leaning on the counter, his left foot crossed over his right and laughing as he chats with the girl working behind the counter. Even from this distance, I can see how beautiful he is, his golden-brown skin slick with sweat from the sweltering Miami heat.

I park the Vespa along the curb in front of the *ventanita* serving *cafecito cubano*. The first time Amaury asked to meet for coffee I fully expected a coffee house, which is what I was used to back in Boston. Although there are traditional coffee houses in Miami, they are few and far between. Instead, the locals here prefer ordering *un cafecito* and *pastelitos* through *la ventanita* to then chat with others doing the same, often times of Cuban politics.

"*Hola, muñeca.* How are you?" Amaury asks as I approach him. When I reach him, he leans in and swipes his lips across mine, the feel of them soft and hot against my own, awakening the butterflies that reside in my stomach.

"Better now," I respond, biting my lip.

He gives me a lopsided grin. "I missed you too, *muñeca*."

"*Dos cafecitos por favor,*" Amaury says to the woman behind the counter. Each time we meet here, we each have a Cuban coffee. It's strong, rich, and has just the right amount of sugar to sweeten it up.

"*Un pastelito de queso* too, please," I add. The cheese pastries have quickly become one of my favorite things to eat.

"How was your day?" I ask and drag the tips of my fingers up his right forearm.

"Long and too hot. The air conditioner *en el trabajo* broke and we can't get it fixed until tomorrow."

"I can't even imagine what it's like to not have air conditioning all day at work with this heat. I think I would pass out." The heat here in Miami is sauna like. The air is thick and heavy with humidity, the sun scorches your skin, and sweat seeps from your pores just seconds after being outside.

"Before it no bother me because I worked outside when I fixed scooters all day. Now I mostly work inside and used to the a/c y *paso calor* more easy." He pulls from the water bottle he has in front of him.

The woman places two espresso cups before us, Amaury grabs his and lifts it to his lips, and I do the same. It's hot, a thick layer of foamy *crema* at the top of the coffee caramel colored with bubbles.

"So, I was thinking," I say, placing my cup back

onto the countertop. "You want to drive down to the Keys this weekend and stay in Islamorada?" His eyes light up and he gives me a crooked smile. Since moving here I've only driven down to the Florida Keys once. Amaury and I spent the weekend in Key West. The drive there was spectacular with the views of the ocean to one side and the gulf on the other, but we didn't stop. Since then, I've been wanting to return to Islamorada to stay at one of the resorts on the Gulf side to lounge on the beach and eat local seafood.

He shakes his head from side-to-side and my hope flattens. "Rubi told me this weekend is *La Fiesta de los Municipios*. It's a party for people from the neighborhood *en Cuba*. We usually go because we see people *del barrio*. I was gonna ask if you want to come with me."

I'm bummed about not going to the Keys but I'm excited to attend a party with him. "Sure, I'd love to," I respond, interested in learning more about his culture and life back in Cuba. What better way than attending a party with people from his town. "When is it and what should I wear?"

"*Pasado mañana* at eight," he responds. Good, the day after tomorrow gives me enough time to find something to wear, whether in my closet or at the mall. "Dress for a party. Whatever you wear you'll be beautiful," he tells me, dropping a kiss on the tip of my nose.

"Sounds good. Now let's finish up so we can go swimming. It's wicked hot today and I can't wait to cool off in the ocean."

We park the scooters on the cul-de-sac on South Pointe Drive and stroll the pathway until we reach the sand. I leave my shoes on because it's still hot and I don't want to scorch my feet. Before me stands a bright orange and yellow structure, a lifeguard stand. I haven't been to this part of the beach yet, but these lifeguard stands are sprinkled across the entire seven-mile stretch of Miami Beach, each one a unique structure. The one I can see a little farther south from us is red and white striped and resembles a miniature lighthouse—very New England.

"These lifeguard stands are one of the things I loved most about Miami Beach the first time I visited," I say. Their unique architecture makes each of the candy-colored stands a work of art and a main tourist attraction.

"*Sí, son* cool. I like them too. *En Cuba* the beaches have lifeguards too, but they were plain high structures."

Once we drop our things on the sheet Amaury spread over the sand, we peel off our clothes and scurry toward the water's edge. The cool feel of the water hitting my feet spreads through my body finally getting respite from the oppressive heat. This is a great time of day for the beach because it's hot, but not the same heat as high-noon, and the water is refreshing. Beach-goers are scattered across the sand, children playing along the shoreline with their pails and shovels, a small group of guys throwing the Frisbee amongst themselves.

Amaury dives into the water, coming up for air several feet in front of me, shaking his head when he emerges. I continue walking toward him, letting the water slowly cool my skin as I approach him. When I'm within arm's length, Amaury grasps my waist and pulls me to him, and I wrap my legs around his torso.

"*Oye, tengo ganas de singarte*," he whispers into my ear. "I no see you all week and I miss *mi jeva*." I can feel his erection pressing against me. Having sex in a public place is a line I've never crossed. Although, we're out in the water and far from any people so we can probably get away with it.

"Umm, here?" I ask, peering into his eyes brimming with lust.

"Yes." His fingers crawl along my torso until they reach the hem of my bathing suit. "You want to?" The bulge in his bathing suit presses against me.

"Yes and no. What if we get caught?" I ask, looking around to see if there is anybody watching. As my eyes wander, the water around is quiet and the closest people are along the shoreline, and they're tiny from this distance.

"We alone over here, and it no look any different than we are right now, *apretaditos*." What he's saying does make sense, I mean we are tightly embraced, the only difference is he would be inside of me. I may regret this but right now I'm burning from the inside out and I feel like pushing the envelope for once. When I'm with Amaury, I find myself wanting and doing things that aren't typical for me and I'm tired of being a rule follower. I want to start coloring outside the lines.

I reach down inside of his briefs in search of him. With my hand grasped firmly around his hardness, I slide my bathing suit bottom over with my other hand and slip him inside of me, letting him feel me. Amaury's head drops back as he eases himself inside of me, hissing as he does. His grip at my waist tightens as he glides in and out of me.

"Amaury," I mumble, the sensation of his gentle thrusts spreading throughout my body.

"*Dime muñeca*," he responds, his eyes blazing with lust and love.

"I love you too."

CHAPTER TWENTY-TWO

Amaury

Sol finally said the words I've been craving to hear. After telling her I loved her last week I've been trying to find the right moment to discuss it, discuss her feelings and what's going on with her but she's been avoiding me. I'm not usually one to shy away from conversations but with Sol I have to tread lightly. I want it to be on her terms. I'm glad I waited, even if it seemed like an eternity.

We're sprawled across my tattered beach sheet, the faded oranges and yellows nearly blending with the off-white color of the fabric. The worn material is soft against my salty skin as we soak up the last rays of the sun and enjoy the tranquility of the beach at this time of day. A few stragglers remain as dusk approaches, the pink and orange sky stretching for miles.

Sol's nose and cheeks are red, burned from too much sun. I didn't see her put any sunscreen on when we got here. "You no wear *crema de sol* today?" I ask her.

"No, why? Do I have a sunburn?" she asks.

Nodding, I say, "Your cheeks are very red."

"Really? I didn't think I needed sunscreen since we got here in the late afternoon." She pats her fingers across her cheeks and nose.

"*En Miami* the sun is too strong. You always need *crema de sol, muñeca.*" The sand between my feet is warm and I drag my foot back and forth, slowly digging.

"I think I have aloe at my apartment, I'll put some on when I get home."

"This is my favorite time of day," Sol says, stretching her legs. I'm drawing circles on her upper right thigh as I lean on my left elbow to face her.

"*¿Sí, por qué*?" I ask.

"The colors of the sky and the clouds. Resembles cotton candy. Sunsets, when you can see them, are beautiful to watch. Makes me feel so small in the grand scheme of life yet it's such a peaceful transition to experience."

"For peaceful you should try the sunrise, *es mucho mejor*." I trace the red swirl pattern on her bathing suit.

"But it's so early. You have to get out of bed while it's still dark. Eww." She giggles. I reach for her, brush a few grains of sand off her forehead.

The sand at the beach in Miami is so different than the beaches I went to growing up. Here it's thick with a palish taupe color and coarse grain. But in Cuba the white sand stretches for miles and is similar to a soft talcum powder.

"It's my favorite. I run every morning on the sand and watch the sun as a new day starts."

"Why is it your favorite?" she asks me.

"I get up early every day, ever since I was a boy. It's a fresh start and it's peaceful. I can think a lot about how I want my day to go as I run. Also, I like listening to *los pajaritos*."

"The chirping birds? Yeah, they wake me up most mornings and I usually get annoyed." She chuckles. I love seeing her so relaxed, her dark curls loose and spread out around her like a crown. Her eyes are soft, and her skin is covered in sand. Her post orgasmic haze still lingers, and I would make love to her again right now, but even I must acknowledge that although there's only a few people here, it's still too many.

"That's a good ritual to have. The only ritual I have

to start my day is drinking a good cup of coffee." She purses her lips.

"Y ahora it's *cafecito* you drink."

She nods in agreement. "Yup. I can't believe I've been missing out on Cuban coffee all these years." When I first met Sol she drank coffee brewed in a drip coffee machine. But as she drank more *cafecito*, she bought a *Bialetti* Moka Express and had me teach her how to make Cuban coffee. She told me since she's learned she barely drinks drip coffee anymore, which makes sense to me. Nothing tastes better than *un cafecito cubano.*

Sol shifts to adjust the towel she's using as a pillow and closes her eyes, her long eyelashes brushing the skin beneath her eyes. Her hair is spread out around her, and the corners of her lips are soft at their edges. She's stunning.

"You know what was one of the first things I noticed about you?" I raise my hand, rest my fingers on the tip of her nose.

"What's that?" she asks.

"Your nose ring. It's small but the light hit the stone and it was shining, it caught my attention."

She lifts her fingers, begins twirling the small stud in her right nostril. "Sometimes I forget I have it since I've had it for so long."

"Today, you made me the happiest man, *sabes*?" I ask, leaning into her and hovering over her mouth.

"How'd I do that?" Sol's eyes flutter open, brown meeting green, and she lifts her left arm resting it on my upper back.

"*Finalmente* you told me *que me amas*. I never thought you would say it *y era tortura*!" Torture was exactly what it felt like waiting for her to reciprocate my feelings.

"I didn't mean for it to torture you. Those words are hard for me." Her fingers draw circles along my skin. I caress her cheek with the back of my hand, her soft skin soothing my mine.

"¿Por qué?"

She shrugs and drops her eyes. "They just are, and I wanted to make sure of what I was feeling before I responded." I sense she isn't telling me the whole reason but have realized with Sol I can't force things with her, she needs to say and discuss things on her own terms. Otherwise, it backfires, and she recoils into herself.

"*Eso es todo*, the only reason?" I ask, even if I already know what's she's going to say to me.

She nods but her eyes won't meet mine. The air around us is thick, the humidity mixed with the awkwardness. My lips meet hers and I pull her plump bottom lip between my teeth, sucking on it. The ocean salt mixed with her sweetness.

I want to ask her to move in with me but know if I do it will be a repeat of the 'I love you' situation. She won't answer me, and it will just make things awkward with us again. She's going to think we're moving too quickly, and maybe we are, but I already know what Sol means to me.

She's the woman I love.

She's the woman I've been waiting my entire life to meet.

She's the woman I want to spend the rest of my life with.

Instead of asking her to move in with me, I say, "*Eres mi media naranja*."

Sol separates from me. "Your half orange?" Her eyebrow lifts, questioning me.

I nod. "*Sí*. I'm one half and you the other. Together, we are a whole orange." It's corny, I know but I can't help it, this is how she makes me feel. I swipe my lips to hers again.

"It's cute, I like it." A smile spreads across her face.

"*¿Nos vamos*?" I ask as the sky darkens around us. She nods and kneels, pushing her arms through the sleeves and then freeing her curls.

We're strolling back to the mopeds, and she asks, "What should we eat? I'm hungry."

"*No se*. What you want to eat?"

"I've been wanting to try La Sandwicherie. Have you ever tried it?" she says.

"No, *no me gustan los sándwiches pero* I'll try it." Anything to see her smile.

We put our things into each of our mopeds, strap our helmets on, and pull out onto Ocean Drive.

CHAPTER TWENTY-THREE

Soledad

I bought a couple different dresses at Macy's because I wasn't sure which I wanted to wear. One is a cute little black dress, and the other is a red halter dress. I don't love either of them but they're the best I could do on such short notice. As I'm walking to my car, I feel like someone is following me but when I turn around there's no one there. I take a moment to assess the area, to make sure I'm not missing something or someone. The lot is full of cars but there are no people. Must be uneasy remnants leftover from the days I would have to watch over my shoulder at every step. As soon as I get to my car, I toss my bags onto the passenger seat and quickly lock my door.

"Wow, I want to take your dress off instead of leaving the house," Amaury says, stepping into my apartment. Despite spending a few hours shopping this morning, I ended up digging through my closet and found a dress I wore only once to a cocktail party last year. Plus, it's Miami, the land of endless summer so I thought it was perfect. Hits at the knees, has the right amount of sparkle to make a statement, and hugs me in all the right places. Of course, it's fire engine red, my favorite color, so I've paired it with matching lipstick and open-toed low sandals.

"You clean up nice too," I tell him, eyeing him from head to toe. Amaury called me a few hours ago to ask what color dress I was wearing. He's wearing a black suit, fitted to his slim body and tapered at the bottom. His dark red button up shirt has three buttons open at the neckline, exposing his golden-brown chest, a smattering of chest hairs peeking out, his gold chain gleaming when the light hits it.

As we stride across the parking lot toward the entrance of the event hall, Amaury curls his fingers with mine and in doing so my jitters ease up. I'm nervous because I'm not sure what I'm walking into, and other than a few of his friends, I won't know anyone here.

"*Oye*, Sol. I told you, you pick the wrong Cuban. You should've picked me, *mi reina*," says Alain, chuckling as he kisses me hello. I wonder if I'll ever get used to him calling me different terms of endearment just to mess with Amaury—today it being, my queen. Both Amaury and Alain's girlfriend aren't even phased by anything coming out of his mouth. He must be an acquired taste.

"Hi, Alain." I pull away from him and turn to his girlfriend. "Hi, Rubi," I say, kissing her cheek.

"Love your dress. Red is definitely your color, *chica*," Rubi says, dragging her fingers along my dress.

"*Gracias*," I respond.

After dinner Amaury dragged me onto the dance floor when Willie Colon started playing, told me it was a good song for me to practice dancing to. Three songs later and I need a break and a drink. We're at the bar waiting to order when I hear a woman behind me say, "*Amaury, eres tú*?"

Amaury stiffens and his eyes widen. His lips are slack as he stands up straight from where he was leaning into the counter. I turn to the woman on my left and slightly behind me. She has long blonde hair, curls cascading down her back, and a young girl standing next to her left. The girl is young, thin with long legs.

She has the same blonde curls as the woman, but what stands out to me the most are her piercing green eyes. Familiar eyes because they're Amaury's eyes.

My body turns back to Amaury who still hasn't said anything. "Who is that?" I ask him, my voice trembling as they tumble from my lips.

"*Su esposa*," the woman responds for him lifting her chin as she steps closer to me. Her words cause a sharp pain in my chest, it's as if I've been stabbed and someone is twisting the blade in my heart.

Without acknowledging the woman or her words, I search Amaury's eyes and ask, "Your wife?" my words sharp, yet barely falling from my lips. He quickly averts his eyes from mine, and the hairs at the nape of my neck stand on edge. I'm scanning Amaury's face for an answer but he's refusing to let our eyes connect. He's gaping at the woman and his face hardens—the shock of what's unfolding registering.

I cannot believe this is happening to me right now. He's married? How is it possible we've been dating all these months and I never realized? How has he hidden it so well? The young girl must be his daughter. She has the same emerald-green eyes I fell in love with. What the fuck is happening right now?

"*¿Yanelis, qué tú haces aquí*?" he asks the woman, his voice quivering. He obviously knows her because he's calling her by name while inquiring why she's at this event.

"Amaury, you're married?" I ask again but he's still refusing to let his eyes meet mine.

The silence between us balloons.

The despair I feel intensifies.

The heavy air suffocates me.

Before walking away, I rest my hand on his arm and look at him one more time, my last attempt to get Amaury to respond to me, to stop me from leaving him, but he doesn't. Instead, he stares into my eyes for a fleeting moment before dismissing me and turns back to the woman and the girl who must be his daughter. His silence is stifling. Tears burn and threaten to fall but I cannot let them free, at least not yet.

I turn on my heel, and march straight out the door. I see a bench to my left and sit, taking a deep breath trying to calm the erratic thumping in my chest. I'm struggling to breathe and keep my cool right now. I don't want to have a meltdown here in front of all these people. With a shaky hand I grab my phone from my handbag and dial for a cab to pick me.

CHAPTER TWENTY-FOUR

Amaury

The room around me is spinning and despite the loud music and crowd of people, everything is a blur.

"Amaury, are you gonna talk to me?" Yanelis asks, breaking my trance.

"¿Qué haces aquí?"

"What am I doing here? That's all you have to say?"

"No. I have a thousand things to say, but that's the only one I can say right now." Her spine stiffens and she crosses her arms in front of her in defiance. The young girl standing to her right can only be my daughter. I have no doubt this beautiful little lady is my child. The child I never knew existed until this moment. There is no mistaking those eyes are mine, the pale emerald staring at me with confusion and hurt.

"What's your name?" I ask her, stepping a little closer to her.

"Analia," she responds, and twists her hands, one into the other.

Analia. Yanelis and I had talked about kids' names, if we ever had them, and Analia was what I'd told her I'd name our daughter. The pang in my heart increases as I take her in. She's tall, has long, skinny legs and reaches my shoulders. She may have my eyes, but her hair is blonde and curly like her mother's.

"*Hola, Analia*. It's nice to meet you, I'm Amaury." I extend my hand, not sure whether I should also lean in to kiss her as well, for fear of scaring her, or crossing a line I cannot see.

"Yes, Mima says *que eres mi papá*," she responds, extending her hand to me while looking at her mother.

"You're beautiful." She smiles a sheepish grin and drops her eyes to the floor. It's the only words I can muster right now. The shock of learning I have a daughter is one I don't know how to process. Should I be angry? But how if I'm the one who left Cuba without saying a word. Did I have any right to know about her?

"Yanelis, can we talk—" I gesture behind me "—*en privado*?" I ask.

She nods and says something to Analia before walking around me.

"Why would you tell Sol you're my wife?" I ask, as I'm trailing behind her.

"Is that all you care about?" she retorts, spinning to face me.

"Yes. No—" I say, shaking my head "—but considering everything *que está pasando* right now, it's the first thing I want to know."

She shakes her head and sighs. "*Increíble*! You learn you have a daughter *y no te importa*!"

"Of course I care." I let my head fall back and close my eyes, inhaling deeply to gain my composure. *Tengo que estar tranquilo*, I remind myself. I have to keep my cool because there's way too many people around to lose my temper right now. When I've finally calmed myself, I meet Yanelis' eyes and ask, "How old is she?"

"Twelve."

"So, you were pregnant when I left?"

She nods, acknowledging my statement.

"Why you no ever tell me? Write me, send a message with someone, or tell my parents?"

"Because I hated you for leaving me, for deserting me in Cuba. We were supposed to be together forever."

A tear escapes and glides down her right cheek. Although I'm the cause of her pain, of what she's feeling, I don't regret the choice I made. I will never regret the decision to flee Cuba for a better life, even if I lost so much because of it.

"Yanelis, you always told me you would never leave Cuba. Your parents were involved with the government, and you no want to leave. You knew I couldn't stay, wouldn't stay, and it was only a matter of time."

"But I thought you loved me." Her arms extend to rest on mine.

Yanelis and I met at a rock concert in Havana when we were twenty-one. I had just finished my three years of military service and it was my first concert after three long years of mandatory service that can only be described as torture.

We were inseparable. We'd spend nights together at my parents' house or her parents' house. But her father was a high-ranking military officer and so her family lived well, extremely different from my family, as is typical in Cuba. As our relationship grew, we talked about our future, which for me included conversations about living outside of Cuba. She never agreed, and was insistent we could get married, have children, and raise them there. But I refused to agree, didn't want to raise children under the same conditions I was raised in. I wanted to give my kids more. A lot of good that did me because in the end, my daughter was raised in Cuba without me.

"I did. But I wanted my freedom more. I couldn't continue living there, it was killing me, my soul was dying." My words hurt her, I can see the pain in her eyes as the water pools around them and glides down her cheeks leaving black streaks. She swallows, trying to regain her composure.

"I found out I was pregnant a few weeks after you left. I was so angry with you. For weeks I asked all of our friends and your parents if they knew what happened to you, if anyone had news. Finally, months after you left, someone from the neighborhood told me you were in *Guantánamo* waiting to live here in Miami."

"How long have you been in Miami?"

"Almost a year. My father passed away several years ago and then my mother and I decided to come here. He's the only reason we never left, the reason why I always told you I wouldn't leave."

"Did you plan on finding me, telling me about Analia? Or is it only because we saw each other here tonight?"

"I wanted to find you. She knows about you. I've shared pictures with her of when you were young. She's been anxious and excited to meet you." I should be happy at what she's telling me, overjoyed our daughter knows who I am and wants to get to know me. But I'm livid because I've missed out on twelve years of her life. But whose fault is that? Mine? Yanelis'? Or is this just another thing the Cuban communist regime has taken from me? I see an empty chair and pull it close to sit, dropping my head in my hands.

The old rug under my shoes is a deep red and stained, the pulls in it creating a pattern of circles. I cannot believe I have a twelve-year-old daughter. Am I capable of being a father? Better yet, can I be a good one? What if I'm terrible at it? What if she hates me?

"I want to see Analia, spend time with her. Get to know her," I say, peeking up at Yanelis standing over me.

"Claro."

"Okay," I say, and pop up to my feet.

Before I can start walking toward Analia, Yanelis grabs my arm, pulling me back to her. She stares up at me, meeting my eyes. "What about us?" she inquires, her tone soft.

"There is no us, Yanelis. Our relationship ended the day I got on the raft."

"But I still love you, I've always loved you."

"That was a long time ago," I huff, pulling my arm from her and shaking my head.

"Amaury, we should at least try, no? *Nos amábamos* and the only reason we separated was because you came here. It had nothing to do with us. Think how much Analia would love having her parents together." She steps closer to me, softens her voice.

I place my hands on her arms, bring her closer to me because she needs to listen to what I'm about to say. "*Escúchame*," I say in a low whisper. "¡*Olvídate*! We can be good parents *sin estar juntos*." Yanelis needs to understand. We loved each other a long time ago but I'm a different man than I was in Cuba and our relationship is in the past. I shake my head and step back, putting more space between us. We need to focus on being good parents in separate homes.

Before Yanelis can continue with the subject, I ask, "When I can see her, *mañana*?" Maybe asking to see Analia tomorrow is unrealistic but now that I know about her, I want to know everything. Do everything. Be everything.

"*No se*. We'll see. *De verdad, no me imagine* this conversation happening like this."

I close my hands into tight fists. "No? What did you expect? How did you imagine this conversation would end?" I retort. It's not until I see the woman a few feet from us glance at me with wide eyes do I realize I'm speaking loudly.

She lifts her shoulders and her lips twist. "Not your rejection."

"Yanelis. You can't expect to just show up and be in my life again. It's been twelve years since we've seen or spoken to each other. I have my life here. I'm in love with someone else."

"*Entonces ya,* that's it? You no want us around?"

"*No me cambies la palabras*," I retort, leaning into her as my tone continues to increase. She's twisting my words and I can already see where she is going with this. "You and I are over but I want a relationship with Analia."

"¡*Veremos*!" She storms off toward where Analia is leaning against the wall, waiting for us to return, and I scurry behind her.

"We'll see! What does that mean?" I call after her.

"¡*Vámonos*!" She snatches Analia's arm and drags her toward the exit.

"Wait." I pull my wallet from my back pocket and grab a business card, handing it to Analia. I have to do something to ensure she knows I want to see her, want to get to know her, want to be her father. I don't think her mother would prevent it, but the truth is I don't know who Yanelis is anymore and I cannot risk it. "*Este es mi número de celular*," I tell her, pointing to my number on the card. "I'll be waiting for your call.

I want to see you, *hija mía*." I embrace her, squeezing my arms tight around her so she can feel the love I have for her already. She hugs me back and my heart bursts in my chest. "*Te amo mi niña*," I tell her, before releasing her, ensuring she knows I love her already. As Analia walks away, our eyes are locked until she disappears into the crowd.

I'm not a drinker but this night makes me want to down a bottle of rum. Instead, I find a chair and sulk. This night has been a torrent of emotions. As I think about the years lost, my parents begin crowding my thoughts. They never met Analia. She doesn't know she has grandparents who love her. Aunts, uncles, and cousins who would've given anything to spend time with her. The more I think about it, the angrier I become at how much Analia missed out. At how much we, as her parents, failed her.

"*¿Oye, mi hermano, qué paso*?" Alain asks, interrupting my thoughts. He's obviously concerned at how upset I look while in the middle of a party.

"*No se*," I say. Because the truth is, I have no idea what the fuck happened. "My whole world just shattered. Everything I thought I knew suddenly changed."

"What do you mean? Where's Soledad?" he asks, looking around.

My shoulders sag in resignation. "She left when

she met Yanelis, who introduced herself as my wife." I drop my eyes to the floor as shame creeps in at the way I handled the entire situation.

"*¿Cómo*? Yanelis is here in Miami?"

I recount the night's events to Alain, whose mouth is slack as he listens to the story unfold. The incredulity of it all something to behold.

"Bro. I may be terrible at relationships and giving advice about women, but I have two kids and here's what I know. *Aqui, en la Yuma*, you can go to court and make sure you see your kid. Yanelis can't stop you from seeing her. That's not what you should be worried about." His words give me some reassurance. I hadn't thought about that, but truthfully what concerns me most is Yanelis will tell her lies about me, and Analia will believe her.

"Yanelis will poison her," I tell him. "Her lies are what I'm afraid of."

Alain stretches his hand out to rest it on my shoulder. "I'll give you the phone number of the lawyer who helped me. Call her Monday." I nod in agreement, the defeat weighing heavy.

"You need to find Sol. Make things right with her," Alain says. "*No sea come mierda, esa mujer es especial*," he scorns, reminding me how incredible of a woman Sol is and how much of a jerk I can be.

He's right. Sol is the woman I love. The first woman I've loved since being in this country.

What was I thinking, letting her walk away from me the way I did? I should've talked to her, listened to what she was saying, explained what was happening. Instead, I froze, gave her the silent treatment, and dismissed her as if she means nothing to me. Where did she go anyway? I start searching the room for her culling through the people on the dance floor, groups gathered by tables or the bar, telling old stories and laughing. There's no sight of my beautiful Sol. Of course she's not here! After the way I acted, why would she be here?

I'm zipping my car through traffic, driving as fast as I can toward Sol's apartment. I've called her phone, but it goes straight to voicemail. I hope she's home, I need to apologize to her, explain what I can. It's all overwhelming to me, but I cannot imagine what it felt like for her as she watched it unfold.

Of course, there's traffic on the causeway to the beach, it's a Saturday night. Fuck! As we're inching our way down the three-lane stretch of road, I'm antsy, nervous. With each minute that passes, it's a minute for Sol to allow negative thoughts to creep in. For her to believe I lied to her, for her to feel unloved and unwanted.

Thirty minutes later I'm out front of Sol's apartment. I don't even bother to find parking and push the hazard light, leaving the Tahoe double parked. I'll deal with it later. I sprint up the walkway and peer up at her windows. They're dark. Did she not come home? Is she asleep? I take the steps up two at a time until I'm at her door. I want to bang loudly, but also don't want to freak her out. Besides, it's late and if I'm too loud her neighbors may wake up or call the police.

"¿Sol, *estas ahí*? It's Amaury. Please, open the door." I rest my ear against the wooden door but don't hear anything. There are three glass panes across the upper middle of the door but it's dark on the other side. Either she's inside and ignoring me or she's not home. I'm hoping it's the latter because the thought of her ignoring me makes my skin crawl. But where would she have gone? I knock a few more times. "Sol, *por favor*. We need to talk, please."

My pleas are met with silence and my heart is racing. Just thinking I may lose Sol is too much to bear right now—a mixture of anger and fear coursing through my veins. I grab my phone from my pocket and shoot her a text message.

Amaury: I'm at your house. We need to talk. Where are you?

I incessantly look at my phone in hopes I somehow missed the notification of an incoming text, but she hasn't responded. After two hours of waiting in the silent darkness there's no sign of her and I call it a night. "*Pinga*," I shout, slamming my hands on the steering wheel before driving off.

CHAPTER TWENTY-FIVE

Soledad

Last night after I fled the party, I came home, changed, and took my scooter for a ride. I needed fresh air to clear my mind. After riding aimlessly around Miami Beach for over an hour, I ended up at the Big Pink for comfort food. They make killer milkshakes and bread pudding, and I needed to drown my sorrows. Plus, I couldn't be home. The short time I've lived in this apartment is filled with memories of Amaury. Turns out it was a good decision to not be home because he texted me while he was waiting for me outside my place. I can't deal with him, at least not yet.

I'm lying in bed, can't force myself to pull back the covers and wake up as my mind swirls with questions

I have no answers to. How is it possible he has a wife? What's his story going to be, some lame excuse like we don't live together anymore so it doesn't matter? I cannot imagine what he'll come up with. What is wrong with me that men find me unworthy and easy to lie to? How do I never pick up on it? I make the worst decisions when it comes to men. Must've inherited it from my mother because she's had rotten luck with them her entire life.

I often asked my mother about my father and why he didn't live with us. She never talked much about him and rarely answered my questions. I stopped asking her about him because she would get upset and we would end up arguing. I used to resent her about it, think she played a big role in my being fatherless. The older I got the more I realized that probably isn't the case, but the truth is I'll never know. I do still resent not knowing anything about him, and she refuses to talk about him. Luckily between Melida's dad and my uncle Carlo, I had father figures to show me love, but they weren't substitutes for the love I still wish I had received from my father. Despite their presence, I still felt unwanted and like I'm damaged goods. Those feelings creep in occasionally and cast shadows on my self-esteem.

My mother worked two jobs to maintain us, so I

didn't get to see her a lot and spent a lot of time at my aunts' and uncle's houses, or at Melida's house. Watching my mother work tirelessly cleaning houses during the day and waiting on tables a few nights a week taught me I have to be self-sufficient, learn how to hold my own, and work hard to do and have the things I want. Growing up with a single mom taught me to be goal oriented and mature.

I'm not sure if growing up without a father is the reason I'm unable to read through the smokescreens men put up, but I do know I have to be better at it. I cannot continue to let myself and my heart be deceived the way it has been.

Between barely sleeping and crying most of the night, I feel awful, like I've been hit by a truck. There isn't enough caffeine to snap me out of my funk this morning. After drinking three cups of coffee, I draw a bath and sink into the warm lavender scented water, yearning to shake this feeling that's overtaken me.

Deceived.

Duped.

Dejected.

I feel alone and those feelings intensify as I soak in the warm tub. How fitting, considering my name is Soledad, which means loneliness in Spanish. I've learned to be comfortable in my own skin and welcome the solitude and the peacefulness that accompanies it. For a while it seemed everything was working out with this move to Miami, but now, I'm not so sure. I miss my friends, more than I care to admit. I miss my mother, and I miss my family. Other than Dayi, the only friend I've made since moving here, I have no one, and right now the isolation is overbearing.

As I lie there, attempting to rid myself of the negative thoughts racing through my mind, loud knocks resonate through the apartment.

"Sol. *Abre le puerta*, please! I know you're home. I just want to talk, please. Open the door!" I rest my head back on the tub and feel the tears gliding down my cheeks. After a minute he starts again. "Sol, please. I deserve the chance to explain." He sounds as desperate as I feel.

The sound of his voice slices open the wound all over again, causing the tears to gush down my face. Deserve a chance to explain? After hearing he has a wife, he deserves nothing! Those words have played over repeatedly since last night, like a broken record playing the same few notes over and over. I know opening the door and listening to what he has to say is probably the right thing to do, but I've been burned one too many times and need to be emotionally ready for the conversation we will inevitably have.

Work has me in Fort Myers for the next week. I have to interpret at a federal trial, and it couldn't come at a better time. I need the distraction away from here, away from my apartment, and away from Amaury. When I get back, I'll deal with this mess. Once I hear the knocking let up, I get out of the tub, get dressed and pack my bag. It's best if I leave early this way I won't be home when Amaury comes by later, like I'm sure he will.

As I descend the stairs, he comes into my purview. Amaury is leaning against his motorcycle, head dropped. When he hears my footsteps approaching, he raises his head and removes his sunglasses, meeting my gaze. Even from a distance, I can see his eyes are red and puffy. Seems neither of us got much sleep last night.

"*Muñeca*, we need to talk." He's right, we do but I can't. I'm not ready to hear what he has to say. I need time away from him to clear my head and process the last twenty-four hours.

"Don't call me that." I lift my chin and adjust the straps of the bag on my shoulder.

"Sol, *te pido por favor*, you have to listen to me." He pushes himself up and steps closer to me, to which my response is to take two steps back.

I swallow the lump in my throat and force the

words. "Amaury, first of all, I don't have to do anything! Second, I knew—" I throw my hands up "—there was a reason I was holding back with you. I finally let my guard down and let you in and it blows up in my face. I should've known better! I don't want to see you." I step around him and scurry to my car parked across the street. "If I'm ever ready to see you, I'll let you know." I don't turn around but can hear his footsteps behind me.

"I'm sorry. I never mean to hurt you. Believe me, *por favor*." That's rich. He wants me to believe he didn't intend to cause harm, yet he lied about being married. I huff and shake my head. I can feel the anger brewing and before I say something I regret, I unlock my car, toss my bag in the back seat before opening the driver's door and climbing in. "*Al menos merezco la oportunidad de explicar*," he shouts as I'm shutting the door. Is this guy listening to himself?

After starting the engine, I open the window and yell, "You deserve? You don't deserve jack shit after what happened last night. Asshole! Spare me the lies you're about to spew and go back to your wife!" I crank the music, pull the button to close my window, and start maneuvering out of my parking spot. I don't know what song is streaming through the speakers, but it doesn't matter, I just need something to drown him out. I can see Amaury is still speaking but I'm done listening to him. As I drive down Euclid Avenue, I can see him through my rearview mirror through the tears. I turn onto Fourteenth Street and again on Meridian and then pull over until I can gain composure.

The drive across Alligator Alley was drab—little to see, no cell phone service, and somber with a deep ache in my chest.

Time. Dragged. On.

I even turned the radio off. I wallowed in the silence, let the last few months replay in an effort to see if I willingly ignored any signs—something I'm apparently good at.

After locating the courthouse, I drive to my hotel about half an hour away and overlooks the Gulf of Mexico. Last week when Lily assigned me this job at the federal courthouse who would've thought a short beachfront stay was just what I needed. To think, I almost invited Amaury to join me but never got around to it. The universe works in mysterious ways and here I am—thank you Madam Universe. I check-in, drop my things, and immediately head down to the beachfront bar.

With a margarita in hand, I mosey down to the sand and stretch my legs on the lounge chair bordering the calm waters. My free hand finds my phone. I see six text messages from Amaury and ignore them then dial Melida's number.

"What up, bitch," Melida says when she answers.

"Hi, Sol," Jestine says in the background.

"Hey, girls," I respond, closing my eyes. What I'd give to be with them right now. They'd comfort me and then help me snap out of this self-pitying spiral I feel coming on before it overwhelms me.

"I'm at Fort Myers Beach sipping on a margarita."

"Is the sexy Cuban with you?" Jestine inquires.

"Ugh, no! That's a good thing, too."

"What happened?" asks Melida.

I recount the entire happenings of last night and this morning.

"Get the fuck outta here! He's married?" Melida exclaims.

"Are you sure?" Jestine adds.

"Yup. Her exact words were, 'his wife,' but in Spanish. There is no mistaking them. He couldn't even look me in the eye when I tried to ask him about it. He ignored me! Didn't even have the balls to respond to me. If that's not an admission of guilt, nothing is!" I exclaim. "Tells me everything I need to know!"

"Wow, you get all the good ones, don't you?" Melida quips.

"Seriously, I don't know what the fuck is wrong with me." I sigh and lick some salt off the rim of my glass.

"Maybe there's some misunderstanding," Jestine chimes in.

"What misunderstanding, Jess? I heard the words. He didn't deny it in the moment and ignored me. It's like I wasn't even there. There is nothing to misunderstand! Sorry, I don't mean to snap at you, but I'm just angry and bitter about this entire situation." I lick more salt off the rim and gulp some more.

"Speaking of losers," Melida says. "Krissa said Carmine was in the hotel restaurant last week with a group of people. When he recognized her, he stood up from the table and walked over to her and said, 'I know my girl moved to Miami. Tell her I'll see her soon enough' and then he went back to his table." The hairs on my arms stand tall and a shiver runs through me, instinctively causing me to look around.

"What?"

"Well, it's not exactly a secret you moved. Plus, that news segment you were on, it was national news, played everywhere over and over for days. Someone probably saw you and told him," Melida adds.

“I told you she’d freak out and we shouldn’t have said anything yet,” Jestine says.

“Um, what do you mean you shouldn’t have said anything? Of course you had to tell me! What the fuck, Jess?”

“That’s not how I meant it. What I meant is we should’ve gotten more info before telling you because now you’re freaking out.”

“You should always tell me anything that has to do with Carmine. He’s sick and apparently looking for me so yes, I’m freaking out!” I stand from the chair and head toward the bar to get another drink. I decide to enjoy the view and have dinner from the comfort and safety of my room’s balcony instead of down here on the beach. Although I know Carmine isn’t here, just hearing he’s looking for me is enough to worry me.

“I’m sorry, of course we’d tell you. We’re just trying to get more information about what he knows,” Jestine’s voice softens.

“I know. Sorry. When it comes to Carmine, everything freaks me out. If you hear or find out anything, let me know, and thank you for telling me, now I can be extra vigilant.”

“So, let’s get back to the Cuban, what are you gonna do?” Melida changes the subject.

Inside the lobby I find a bench across from the elevators and sit, placing my drink on the ledge to my right. "I haven't thought about it. He wants to talk to me but I'm not ready to listen to what he has to say. We've been together for about six months and I saw no red flags. It's causing me to not trust myself and my instincts. First Carmine fucked with them now Amaury too?" I twirl a lock that's hanging over my shoulder while staring at the artificial plants surrounding me.

"For what it's worth, I think there's more to the story from the little I know about him. I met him when I visited you for my birthday and he seemed genuine to me. And that's a lot coming from me because you know I instantly pick up on someone's BS. Besides, I don't like many people," Melida says, chuckling.

"True. I'm glad you're my friend and not my enemy," I respond. "I have to take an elevator up to my room so I'm gonna let you go," I tell the girls.

"Love you, Sunshine," Jestine quips.

"Love you Sol, and I miss you more than you know," Melida says.

CHAPTER TWENTY-SIX

Amaury

Yesterday Sol walked away from me and I could feel my heart splintering with each step she took. Betrayal was sprawled across her gorgeous face. Her eyes puffy from lack of sleep and too many tears. All of it my fault and I wish I could turn back time and change things. I should've been honest with her from the get-go, told her the truth about my past but because my past was in Cuba, I didn't think it mattered. Never did I imagine Yanelis would show up the way she did, with my child in tow.

Despite only getting a few hours sleep, I push the sheets back as soon as the day breaks and drive down to the beach to get in my morning run, a ritual I kept after completing my three years of military service in Cuba.

A few weeks after my eighteenth birthday, I was shipped off to begin my time in the military, not that I had a choice because it was mandatory. My father had been a member of Castro's regime and believed serving in the military would make me a man, help give me guidance and purpose. I thought it was bullshit, especially since I hated the government and fighting with them went against everything I stood for.

For three long years I lived the rigid day-to-day of waking up before sunrise, making my bed to the point where my commanders could roll a coin along it, and shining my shoes every day. While enlisted I was miserable and would sneak out whenever the opportunity arose, which was at least once or twice a week. I'd leave before midnight and have to return before six in the morning for roll call, although many times I didn't make it because I'd missed a bus or was tangled up with a girl somewhere. The times I got caught, I would be punished by having to do extra guard duties, or clean-up duties. But what hurt most was when my weekend leave passes were revoked and having to serve several months beyond my original completion date. Looking back, those years taught me discipline, loyalty, and trustworthiness, because I had to learn to trust my brothers in arms as they had to learn to trust me. I also fell in love with running because it was truly the only time during my service I could be alone.

My morning run was how I channeled the hate I had for my commanding officers who treated us like vermin, and the hate I had for the government that stripped me of my freedoms. During my runs I would daydream about fleeing the island and living freely in the United States—my thoughts and dreams were the only things the Cuban government couldn't take from me.

After leaving the military service, I continued my morning runs because they set the tone for my day. In Cuba I would run along the beaches whenever I had the chance. It was much nicer than running through any neighborhood. Now in Miami Beach, I religiously pound the sand every morning and watch as the sun crests, giving life to a brand-new day. There's something about a new day breaking that soothes my soul—the smell of a new day, the crisp fresh air, and the birds chirping as they start a new day.

Once I park my car in the nearly empty lot at Forty-sixth Street, I pull my laces tight and jog at a light pace toward the sand. This morning the ocean is turbulent and the dark gray storm clouds are rolling through the sky not far from the shore. It's like Mother Nature is soothing my soul and sympathizing with me. The waves are crashing at an incessant pace, matching the erratic beating in my chest.

Typically, I find peace running parallel to the shoreline. The stillness of the early morning hours together with the sound of the birds waking, and the ocean soothe me, but not today.

The ocean rages.

The sky rumbles.

My heart thunders.

I have no one to blame but myself yet I'm so angry. My legs are burning because I'm running harder than usual. How did I get here? It's like my past life in Cuba will never cease to impact my present-day life.

Without realizing, I find myself at South Pointe Beach. The last time I was here with Sol we made love in the water, and she told me she loved me. Seems like a lifetime ago when everything was going well. I fucked up and don't know if she'll ever forgive me. Had I told her the truth since day one, we would likely be in a very different place today. I probably would've woken to her soft curls sprawled on my pillows while we slept tangled in the sheets. Looking back, I don't know why I kept it from her. I thought telling her would push her away yet never imagined she would learn it from anyone other than me and it would be worse. Lies that bind.

Eight miles later and I feel no better than I did when I woke up. I take a quick dip in the water to cool off before heading home to start the day, which I can already tell is going to be a long one.

I'm working on a vintage 1976 Vespa Rally we bought a few weeks ago at an estate sale and I started taking apart last week. Giving these classic beauties the TLC they need is usually therapeutic for me. Since my run didn't do much for me today, I'm hoping working on this red lady will. Although, seeing the red Vespa only reminds me of Sol. Dammit!

"*Oye mi hermano qué vuelta*," Eduardo shouts from across the garage. He turns the music down a notch and waltzes over to me. "Every time I see her, I'm fascinated. I can't believe we have this in our shop!" he exclaims, dragging his hand along the back fender.

I ignore him and continue what I'm doing. I'm off-kilter today and I don't want to take it out on those who have no fault.

"*¿Tienes el moño virao*?" he asks. Yes, I am in a bad fucking mood, can't he tell? I crack my neck and a grunt lets loose.

"Pass me the pliers," I say.

He hands them to me and as I'm taking them, he grasps them tightly. "What you do now? When you're like this, it's because you fucked up."

Of course he knows something's up. He's known me my entire life and hiding anything from him is impossible, especially since I wear my heart on my sleeve.

When I was seventeen, I used to date a woman named Yenifer, she was my first love. Yenifer was twenty and, in my head, I had our whole future planned out. Little did I know I was nothing but a boy toy for her. One day I wanted to surprise her and so I skipped school and showed up at her house with a bouquet of flowers I'd picked along the way. When I got there, I saw her in bed with some guy and was left speechless. Rather than confront her, I watched as she and the guy continued having sex. Yenifer told the guy the same things she'd tell me when we were together. Turns out it was her boyfriend, and I was her sidepiece. It was the first time I had my heart broken. When Eduardo saw me later that day, I tried to hide it from him but failed. That night we rode our bikes all around Havana and he didn't let up until I told him what happened.

"Yanelis is in Miami," I tell him. Normally Eduardo would've been at the party we were at when everything happened but he couldn't attend because his son had a show at school and he went to the performance.

"*¿Cómo?*" he exclaims, shocked at my words.

I recount Saturday night's events up until Sol left me standing in the middle of the street like a stray dog.

"*No puedo creerlo mi hermano*," he says, his voice a low whisper. I can't believe it either and the shock still hasn't worn off.

This new reality that's my life is something I'll need to learn how to navigate. I haven't heard from Analia or Yanelis since Saturday, and I'm worried about it. I don't want Yanelis to poison Analia with lies about me. I've called some people to see if anyone knows Yanelis' phone number or where I can find her but so far, I've not had any luck. Add Sol to the mix and it's what we Cubans call an *arroz con mango*—basically a clusterfuck!

To make matters worse, Sol has been ignoring my calls and texts. She's away for work and I don't know where she is, or I'd show up and try to make things right. All I can hope is Sol will hear me out and understand the truth, that I love her.

CHAPTER TWENTY-SEVEN

Soledad

SIX DAYS LATER

The last week has been good for my soul. Work has kept my mind occupied throughout the day and then I was able to end each day with a gorgeous sunset and the sand between my toes. If only I could also say I've come to terms with Amaury being married and he and I are no longer.

I had been guarding my heart something fierce since Carmine fucked with my head. When I moved to Miami, I was reluctant to open up to Amaury, but he schmoozed his way in with his sweet words, a thick accent that caresses my skin like a feather, and slow lovemaking, which ignites me from the core. There was no hope in escaping him or the spell he put me under until last week when a young girl with his vibrant green eyes stared at me as she stood next to his wife.

His wife. The thought of him being married crushes me.

The trial I was working on ended late last night and so I stayed an extra night. After having a late breakfast, I pack my bag and retrieve my car from the valet.

Before driving off, I decide to text Dayi and ask her to meet me for dinner.

Sol: Trial is over & I'm driving back to MIA – dinner tonight?

Almost instantly, Dayi replies.

Dayi: YES – LOTS to catch up on.

She doesn't know what happened with Amaury, so I wonder what we're catching up on.

Sol: Perfect. *Las Vacas?* I'm in the mood for steak.

Las Vacas Gordas is hands-down my favorite Argentine steakhouse in Miami Beach, although I'm usually dining with Amaury when I go. I love the name too, The Fat Cows. Even the décor of the restaurant resembles black and white cows. The steak is mouthwatering, and they make the best fries I've ever had. They don't get any fresher. A potato slicer cuts the potato into shoestring fries, and they're fried to crispy perfection. Whether you order them regular or *a la provenzal*—what Argentines call fries with fresh garlic and parsley—they're phenomenal!

Dayi: Steak and wine. Sounds like a perfect night. See you at 7ish?

I glance at my watch and it's just past noon. Even with hitting Miami traffic, I have plenty of time.

Sol: See you then. oX

It took me nearly four hours to get home. Once in South Florida, traffic was intense. It was a slow crawl until I reached the beach. I thought Boston traffic was heavy, but Miami is way worse. Plus, the drivers here are terrible!

After getting home, I unpack and relax on my couch until it's time to meet Dayi for dinner. I haven't picked up my *Twilight* book in over a week and need to know what's happening with Bella and Edward.

Two hours later and I realize I was so consumed with my book I lost track of time and now I'm gonna be late. I quickly wash up, throw on some jeans, a tank, and a jean jacket, and swipe some lipstick across my lips. After locking up I strap on my helmet before starting my Vespa. How I missed my Roxy. Twenty minutes later I park her next to a few other mopeds.

Sol: Just parked. Will get us a table & wine.

The man at the door recognizes me and seats me at a table near the window.

Dayi: See you in 15.

Here I was rushing to be on time, and Dayi is late. Should've known she runs on Miami time. When Dayi walks into the restaurant I'm already sipping my wine.

"Hey, *chica*," she says, kissing me hello.

"Sorry, it's been a rough week, and this wine was calling my name." I sip from my glass as she settles into her seat.

"Cheers." Our glasses clink and we drink up.

"So," I say. "What's this business about having lots to catch up on? What did I miss?" I inquire.

"Umm, you didn't miss out on anything. Apparently, I'm the one who missed out," she quips, sipping her wine.

I raise an eyebrow, wondering where she heard the gossip from. "What do you know?"

"What happened with Amaury?"

"How do you know something happened with

him?"

"*Chica, por favor*, don't act as if nothing happened." Her hands are flailing as she's speaking. "He came by the office Thursday asking for you. Said he hadn't seen or spoken to you since last Saturday and he was worried."

"He went by the office?" I'm surprised to hear this. I didn't think Amaury would be that guy. "Did he cause a scene? Did Lily say anything?"

I'll never forget the day Carmine showed up at my office in Boston. I was working late on a project with Mona, and he showed up unannounced, storming through the halls as if he owned the place. Luckily, I was alone with Mona. I was so embarrassed. After I calmed him down and left with him, Mona began regularly inquiring about my relationship with Carmine. I never had the courage to accept her offers of help or to tell her the whole truth.

Her head shakes. "Nah, he was chill, just asked for you. He was there for maybe five minutes. Lily didn't even see him." Thank goodness, I can't even fathom what I would do if he'd caused a scene or upset Lily. Amaury doesn't seem like a guy who would cause a scene. Then again, how much do I really know him?

"That's it?"

"About his visit, yeah. But there's more to the story, *hací que habla*! I'm waiting to hear all the *chisme*." Her enthusiasm for me to fill her in on the gossip is cute even if I'm dreading retelling having my heart ripped apart.

The waiter interrupts us to take our order, and I order our usual, *enrollado*, a one-pound skirt steak and fries for us to share with a *provoleta*, grilled provolone cheese, for us to start with.

I fill Dayi in about Saturday night's events and how I scrambled out of there with my tail between my legs.

"Wait, he's married?" she asks, her eyes wide.

"Yup. Leave it to me to find the married guy. I make the worst decisions when it comes to men."

"Is he married married, or Cuban married?" she asks, her hands animated as she's speaking.

The wine glass hovers at my lips. "Umm, what's the difference?"

"Girl, if he's married married, you're done because he's a shady ass motherfucker! If he's Cuban married, then he's not really married and there's nothing to worry about."

"I'm confused. What the heck does that even mean?" I pour us both more wine because this conversation isn't getting easier.

"*Chica*. When we're in a serious relationship, we Cubans tend to call each other *esposo* and *esposa*, even if we're not actually married." That's a first for me—couples referring to each other as husband and wife if they're not married, but it doesn't mean it doesn't happen. If I've learned anything since moving to Miami, it's that I don't know much about Latino culture outside of my own.

"What? Why?"

Her shoulders rise in uncertainty. "We just do!" she exclaims, taking a long sip of wine.

"Oh. Well, I don't know if it's his actual wife or not. He didn't deny it or even look me in the eye, which is basically a confirmation if you ask me. Besides, I didn't stick around long enough to find out, and I haven't spoken to him since then."

My phone vibrates on the table, and I flip it to see who's calling. Unknown number, again. I've been getting more of these calls, but they never leave a message. A chill runs up my spine. I silence it and place it facedown again.

"Is that him?"

I shake my head and pull from my wine glass, then run my finger back and forth along the rim. "No. Unknown number."

"You need to find out," she adds.

"Find out who the unknown number is?" I ask, raising an eyebrow.

"No. Hello! We're talking about Amaury. You okay?" she inquires, her lips twisting.

"Yeah, I'm fine. Sorry, my phone distracted me, but you're right. Last Sunday he came by my place but I was so upset I didn't want to see him. I needed space to ensure I had a clear head before having the conversation, otherwise I'd say and do things I regret. I also didn't want to be in a position to let him smooth talk his way out of it. Then I left for work, but I'll call him soon so we can finally have our conversation."

"He looked worried. He had dark circles around his eyes when I saw him."

"So, you think it's possible he wasn't legally married to this girl?"

Dayi slides her wine glass across the table. "For sure! I know more couples who are Cuban married than actually married."

"He did tell me he loved me before all this went down. I believed him too. After Saturday, I don't know what I can believe anymore."

"Look, I've only met him a handful of times, but he seems legit. My bullshit meter is strong!"

"Melida said the same thing," I tell her.

Dayi shifted the topic of conversation from my drama with Amaury to some drama in the office the other day with the people in the suite next door and how they could overhear the entire thing as it unfolded. Something about one of the employees who was caught stealing. Honestly, my head wasn't into the conversation, which is terrible of me. I don't want Dayi to think I only care about myself.

Dinner was delicious and as we're walking out, Dayi says, "Let's hit up the Purdy Lounge. Even though it's Saturday night, it's chill there." Part of me wants to call it a night but I decide to hang out for a bit longer.

"I'll go for a little while. It's been a long week." I follow her on the short ride from the restaurant to West Avenue, where we find parking and walk the two blocks to the lounge.

"I hope Oscar is working the bar tonight. I have a crush on him. I've been waiting for him to ask me out but so far, *nada*. I might have to make the first move."

"Why don't you ask him out then?"

"One of these days. I want to get to know him better before I do." Once inside, we find a spot near the far end of the bar and nestle into the vacant space.

The Purdy Lounge is a local bar and nightclub that isn't the typical South Beach vibe. It's mostly locals, with nights ranging from live music and reggae to game nights. It's Dayi's favorite bar and I can see why. The crowd is laid-back and not pretentious, a stark contrast to the rest of the nightclubs in South Beach.

"Hey, Dayi. Good to see you." Oscar's smile stretches across his face, his jet-black hair accentuating his pale skin.

"Hi Oscar, this is my friend, Sol. I'll have a margarita. Sol, whatcha drinking?"

"Ice water, please. I've had enough wine and need to get home soon."

"Water? What a buzzkill!"

"Hey, someone's gotta be responsible," I say, giving her a nudge with my shoulder. "But seriously, I have to ride my moped home and we drank two bottles of wine at dinner."

After Oscar returns with our drinks, he's chatting with Dayi and my mind wanders to Amaury. I can't stop thinking about my conversation earlier with Dayi and how maybe he isn't legally married. I grab my phone to send Amaury a text message. I type and delete numerous times, unsure of what to write him and decide to keep it simple.

Sol: Hi.

Before I can even put my phone down, his response appears on my screen.

Amaury: *Hola.* I've been waiting to hear from you. Are you OK?

Sol: Yeah. You?

Amaury: Not good. I miss you. We need to talk.

Sol: Yes, we definitely do. Are you around tomorrow?

Amaury: Yes. Time?

Sol: Early afternoon?

Amaury: Yes, I'll go over at noon.

Sol: See you *mañana*. Good night.

Amaury: It's been too long since I've seen you *muñeca*. I love you!

I don't know how to respond to Amaury's last words, so I don't. I realize that probably worries him, but I need to protect my own heart.

"Hey Dayi, I'm gonna call it a night." I slide the stool back and grab my bag from the back of it.

"Already? We just got here," she exclaims.

"I'm tired, and besides, you're here to flirt. I don't want to cramp your style." I wink. "I'll see you later." I kiss her on the cheek and make my way through the crowded area.

When I'm pulling up to my building, I see my car parked along the sidewalk has a flat tire and my heart starts racing. After parking my scooter, I approach my car and notice all four tires are flat—they've been slashed.

CHAPTER TWENTY-EIGHT

Amaury

Before driving to Sol's house, I need to drop this package off at the agency. It's a place in Hialeah I visit once a month to send necessities to my family. My usual packages include bricks of coffee, vitamins, over-the-counter meds, soap, shampoo, conditioner, and toothpaste, as well as underwear or socks. This care package also includes stuff for my father to take to the hospital for his surgery—sheets, a blanket, a pillow and pillowcase, various size needles requested by my father's physician, and some comfortable pajamas for him to wear while staying in the hospital. I'll also send some cash for him to have to buy groceries on the black market.

I often wonder how so many families survive with the scarcity on the island. Many Cubans have family in Miami and do what I do, but there are plenty of Cubans on the island that don't. They have to just live with the little they have or barter with neighbors or tourists to get necessities. I hate thinking about it because it makes me angry each time I do.

When I arrive to Sol's neighborhood, there's no parking anywhere near her apartment. No surprise since it's a Sunday. I pull into a garage near Collins and walk the four blocks to her building. As I approach the mint-colored building I see a dark-haired male walking up the stairs toward Sol's unit. I fully expect him to turn to the door across from Sol's place, but he doesn't. He knocks on her door and stops me in my tracks. What the fuck? Who is this guy?

Rather than continue, I lean against the lamppost and wait to see how this all unfolds. Sol still hasn't answered and the guy knocks again. I see the door crack open and then quickly close, Sol yelling at the man to leave. Shit! He's pushing his way into the entryway, and I can no longer hear Sol's voice. I push off the lamppost and sprint toward the building.

The guy was able to gain entry but he didn't close the door completely behind him and I push my way into her apartment, leaving the door ajar. I hear the male's voice from Sol's bedroom and hurry through the hall to get to her. She's pinned to the bed, his hands around her neck.

"You bitch! Did you think I wouldn't find you?" he's shouting. Sol is kicking her legs and she's no longer screaming, her face red from the lack of air.

I grab the dude's arm and pull him back, dragging him off the bed and turning him toward me. I reach back with a closed fist and punch him, landing just below his left eye, the area turning bright red. When he loses his balance, I push him to the ground and straddle him, and wrap my fingers around each of his biceps to hold him in place.

"*Llama al 911*, NOW!" I shout.

The guy is trying to wriggle his way out from under me and because he's restricted, spits in my face, "Fuck you!"

"*Que singao que eres*," I say to him, before landing another closed fisted punch to his nose, causing blood to spray from his nostrils. Good, maybe that'll keep him quiet for a few minutes. What kind of spineless motherfucker preys on a woman like this? If I didn't want to spend the rest of my life behind bars, I'd strangle him, in the same manner he was doing to Sol.

"I called. They said they're sending someone. The station is a few blocks away so hopefully they'll be quick." Sol is exasperated and when I glance up, her chest is heaving and her eyes are wild, with strewn curls and a red face. The guy takes the opportunity while I'm distracted and attempts to knee me in the back but because of the position we're in his effort doesn't have much strength. I again strike his face, hitting him near his eye again, which is already starting to swell.

"Who is this?" I ask her.

"He's my ex-boyfriend, Carmine," she responds, pulling a curl and wrapping it around her fingers. My heart is racing at the thought of this asshole being her ex. I want to hurt him so bad but know I shouldn't do anything else until the police arrive.

I look back at his face and it hits me. "You the guy I saw outside a couple weeks ago."

"What?" shrieks Sol.

Without removing my eyes from Carmine, I say, "The day we were at South Pointe Beach. I went to Alain's house after, and you no come with me. I drove here after *pero* you were sleeping. I saw him outside, sitting on the wall across the street."

"I'm so stupid," whispers Sol.

Thankfully, I can hear sirens in the distance. "Sol, go outside and meet the police," I command. She does as she's told and scurries out of the room.

"You lucky I no kill you, *come mierda*."

I hear voices again—Sol, a female, and a male. "My boyfriend has him pinned down in my bedroom," she says.

"Amaury, how are you involved here?" asks the male. When I turn my head, I recognize the man as Officer Joe Torres. I met him a few years ago when we had an incident at the shop on West Ave. Turns out he's from the next town over from me in Cuba and we have friends in common. We're not friends but friendly since we run into each other often here on the beach.

"I got here and saw him forcing his way in. I ran upstairs and he was strangling her on the bed. I punched him to control him," I recount.

"Miss, why don't you come with me in the other room so I can take your statement," says the petite blonde female officer to Soledad. She nods and follows her out of the bedroom.

"Amaury, please get up, I'll take it from here," Torres says. I rise and take two steps back, standing next to the window and it's when I notice blood spatter on my shirt.

"What's your name?" he asks, looking at Carmine.

"Carmine," he responds. I glare at him, the blood around his nose drying.

"Do you have a last name, Carmine?"

"Coretta." He sneers at me, curling his lip.

Joe approaches Carmine while simultaneously pulling his handcuffs from his belt. "You have the right to remain silent," Torres says, grabbing his wrist and placing a cuff around it. The officer continues to read Carmine his rights as he places his handcuffs behind his back.

"¡*No te quiero ver más por aquí, oíste*!" I exclaim. Not sure if he even understands me but I'm furious right now. If I ever see him around here again, I don't know if I'll be able to restrain myself next time.

I follow them out of the room. Torres and Carmine continue outside and I sit next to Sol, who is on the couch talking to the woman, whose name badge reads Cruz. When Sol finishes recounting the events, the officer asks her to stand up because she wants to take pictures. Sol does as she's asked and stands near the window.

It's there I see the redness of her upper arms and neck, except the neck area has redness in the form of Carmine's fingers. The area on her left cheek is bright red, much different from the faint redness on the right side of her face. Anger stirs inside of me again. What would've happened if I hadn't been here? Would he have caused serious harm? Or worse? I can't think about the what-ifs because it's just going to enrage me and me being upset solves nothing.

When Officer Cruz is finished taking pictures of Sol and Sol says her statement is complete, the Officer asks me for my statement. I retell the events as I saw them happen, and she continues to take notes as she listens.

"Remember, if you need medical attention, go to the emergency room right away," Officer Cruz says.

"Thanks, Officer. I'm okay, just rattled."

"Okay. You have my contact information should you need it. Please take care of yourself." She turns and exits the unit, pulling the door closed behind her.

When she does, I turn and find myself face to face with Sol. She wraps her arms around my neck. "Thank you, Amaury." She starts shaking, I can hear her whimpers, the tears dampening me.

"You're okay now."

"I think he wanted to kill me," she says, gasping for words through her tears.

"But, *no lo hizo*. And now he's arrested," I respond, tightening my embrace. My hands are rubbing her lower back, an attempt to calm Sol's nerves.

"I don't want to be here. Can we go to your house, please?"

"*Claro que sí*," I respond, grateful she wants to be at my house instead of staying here. This way, I can keep an eye on her. I have an alarm system at my house and surveillance cameras. I'm not sure Carmine knows where I live but I'm hoping it doesn't matter since he's behind bars.

"Okay. I need to pack some stuff, my computer, work clothes, things like that. Just for a few days. Is that okay?" She lifts her gaze to meet mine, her light brown eyes wild and red from the tears she's been crying.

"*El tiempo que necesites*," I tell her. I mean it too; she can stay as much time as she wants. If it were up to me, I'd have her move in. But first, we need to straighten out the mess from the other night with Yanelis. I caress her face, let my fingers linger at her jawline.

"Give me a few minutes." She separates from me and disappears into the hall.

"If you need help, tell me. I'll wait here," I say.

An hour later we pull into my driveway. I called a buddy of mine to have her car towed to his lot to get her tires replaced and we'll pick it up in a few days when it's ready.

As I'm unloading her suitcase from the trunk I say, "I take you to get Roxy later. This way you can get around until your car is ready."

"Thank you, Amaury. I promise I'll only be here a few days until I figure out what I'm gonna do," she says, pushing her hair behind her ears.

"*Muñeca*, you can stay as much time as you need. ¿*Oíste*?" I grasp her face between my hands and kiss her, savor her taste, the sweetness of her skin mixed with the saltiness of her tears.

She's letting me explore her mouth, kissing me back, her hands dragging up and down my biceps. Abruptly she separates from me. "Stop, please."

"Why?"

"Are you really asking me that question, Amaury?" Sol crosses her arms over her chest and steps back from me.

"*Muñeca, te amo*. I know we need to talk, *pero eso no cambia* my feelings for you." I stretch my arm out to her, but she puts more distance between us. My heart aches because she's erecting a barricade after I worked so hard to tear it down. I know she loves me, I felt it when she kissed me, in her touch.

I push my hands through my hair. "Sol, please. Tell me how to fix this."

CHAPTER TWENTY-NINE

Soledad

Fix this? "I'm not sure we can, Amaury." My heart tightens at the words.

Amaury's eyes widen. "*¿Cómo*?" He holds my stare, searching for answers.

The thumping in my heart increases. Is he for real right now? Acting surprised as if he has no idea what I'm talking about? "You lied to me. You're married. If we hadn't gone to the party, I would've never known you have a wife."

"Yanelis is no my wife," he says, his tone flat.

"Why would she say she is then? What does she have to gain from it?"

"*En Cuba*, we were together many years before I

left. We always talked about marriage, *pero* we never got married."

"So, she lied?" I purse my lips, remembering my conversation with Dayi yesterday.

He nods. "We always call each other *esposo* and *esposa*, but everyone does that, married or no." He's telling me exactly what Dayi explained.

"Why wouldn't you have told me? I asked and you ignored me!" A tear escapes from me and I swipe it away.

"Shock. *Estaba en* shock. I no understand what was happening in the moment. *Me dejó sin palabras*." Without words is right, he literally said nothing to me that night—couldn't even look at me.

I swallow, not prepared to hear the answer to the question I'm about to ask. "Do you love her?"

"No." His head is shaking. "I loved her a long time ago. I was a different person *viviendo otra vida*." His shoulders slump and the blood-spattered shirt momentarily distracts me from his words.

"I don't understand why you wouldn't tell me."

"Because when I left Cuba, I left her. It was the end of our relationship. *No sabía que* I had a daughter." His eyes meet mine and they're solemn.

"You had no idea?"

Again, he's shaking his head. "You remember

when I told you how I left Cuba? I told no one, not my parents. No one, especially not Yanelis. We no tell anyone because it was dangerous and we no want to get arrested again. Less people know it's better." I remember our conversation from our first date, and it makes sense. I don't understand it, but it makes sense.

I nod, let him know I'm listening.

"Yanelis' father was an important man in the government. When I talked about *La Yuma* and coming here, she always said no. Her family lived good in Cuba. When I saw her again last week, she told me about Analia. She was pregnant when I left, *pero yo no sabía nada*." He drags his hands down his face. "I have a daughter and I'm a stranger to her."

When I think about what I learned, it seemed impossible he'd be able to explain away what happened and that I'd forgive him. But if he was never married, is there anything to forgive? He left her not knowing she was pregnant. Left with the idea of it being the end of their relationship. What exactly should I have expected him to tell me, if in his mind it had ended all those years ago?

"*Perdóname*, Sol. I no mean to hurt you. *Créeme*." I want to believe him, but right now I'm exhausted from what happened with Carmine. Honestly, I didn't think we'd have this conversation right now.

"I'm tired, Amaury. I want to lie down and rest. Can we finish this conversation later?"

He nods. "You can sleep in my room, I no bother you."

"No, it's okay. I'll sleep in one of the spare bedrooms."

A ringing phone wakes me and when I look around, I don't recognize where I am. I rub the sleep from my eyes and my face is still throbbing from Carmine's slap. To my right, the window has dark gray curtains hanging from the black curtain rod. Light is peeking in through the part between the panels of fabric. The walls in this room are white, a picture of a palm tree lined street on one wall, and Havana's *Malecón* on another. I stretch my arms behind my neck and roll my ankles. As I awake, I recall how my day started, the incident with Carmine, and how Amaury showed up at just the right time.

The clock on the dresser reads 18:54. I don't know how to read military time. What time is it? How long have I been asleep for? I pull the covers back, rise, and make a quick bathroom stop. When I see my reflection in the mirror, I don't even recognize myself. The left side of my face is red and swollen, red marks appear on my neck, imprints from Carmine's hands. Tears leak from my eyes as I stare at the aftermath of everything I allowed Carmine to do to me over the years. *I could've been dead*, I whisper to myself.

When I exit the bedroom, the hall upstairs is quiet and empty. The white walls are covered in artwork, just like the entire first floor. The wooden floors are cool under my bare feet, creaking as I pad down the hall. When I descend the stairs, I hear Amaury's voice. He's talking to someone but his voice is low so I can't make out what he's saying. I continue to follow his voice until I see him stretched out on the couch in the Florida room, wearing a fresh blue shirt, dark jeans, his sockless feet resting on the armrest.

"*Mañana te busco a las cinco*," he says. I wonder who he's talking to? I shouldn't be eavesdropping, but my curiosity gets the best of me.

"Okay. *Te quiero*. Put your mima on." Mima. I remember that's what he calls his mother, but why would he say your mima if he's talking to his mother?

"*Sí*, I told her five. *Gracias, Yanelis*. *Chau*." After ending the call, he drops the phone on the coffee table and lets out a long sigh. His arms extend up and he places them under his head. From this angle, I catch the right side of his face, the stubble growing from days of not shaving, reminding me how the roughness of his facial hair feels as he explores me with his mouth. A tingle spreads through my body.

"Hi," I say, and shuffle toward him.

He turns and rises, a smile spreading across his weary face. It looks like he showered, the blood no longer spattered along his arms. "You sleep good?" he inquires, giving me a lopsided grin.

I nod. "Incredibly well. Almost forgot where I was." A sheepish grin creeps across my face.

"What time is it?" I ask.

He lifts his wrist to glance at his watch. "Five past seven."

Silence hovers, the unspoken words swirling in the air around us as we gaze at each other from a distance.

Amaury takes a step toward me but abruptly stops. "Sol. Talk to me, *por favor*. Tell me we'll be okay. I love you *y te necesito*!" He's beautiful, even with dark circles under his eyes from the lack of sleep.

The pang in my heart aches. I love and need him too. I want us to be okay. "No more secrets?" I ask.

His head shakes. "*Prometo*." His promise is all I need right now. He's been a man of his word and I trust he's telling me the truth.

I close the gap between us and wrap my arms around him, crashing my lips with his. They're warm, the softness of his lips a contrast to the scratchy hair growth around his mouth. He pries my mouth open, his tongue pushing its way in.

Without separating our bodies, I pull my face away from his and say, "We'll be okay." I reach for the button of his jeans and then push them down his thin waist. He's wearing black fitted briefs, the tip of him protruding from the top, glistening from his arousal. His nose drags along my neckline, inhaling my scent. I nudge him back to sit on the couch then remove my pants. I leave my panties on. I remember he once told me he loves making love to me with them on because it gives him more pleasure.

When he's seated, I straddle him, pulling him from his briefs. I rise to position myself over him, but he stops me. "*El condón*, in my jeans pocket," he says, pointing to his pants strewn across the floor.

I ignore his words and let him fill me. I drop my lips to his ear, grazing the skin, and whisper, "I love you."

CHAPTER THIRTY

Amaury

"You must be hungry," I say, pulling my jeans up. I'm not sure if Sol ate today before I went to her house and then after the Carmine incident we came here, and she fell asleep. I'm starving so I'm almost certain she is too.

She's sprawled across the couch, wearing only her underwear and bra. One of the things I love about her is she's unassuming. She wears what makes her feel comfortable. Her bra is pink, her underwear black. I don't think I've ever seen her wearing a matching set. Right now, her skin is glowing.

"I'm starving. I only had toast with my coffee this morning not expecting the day to turn out how it did." I don't think anyone expected this day to start out like it did. I'm just thankful it didn't end how Carmine wanted and I have my girl here at my house. I lean down, pull her lips between mine and suck on them. Although I made love to her and let my body show her how much she means to me, with her it's never enough. She's addictive and the more I have her, the more I want her. Her scent drives me wild. I'm like a dog in heat.

I rise again. "We can order takeout, if you want. Otherwise, I made black beans last night, we can have those with some rice, *tostones*, and grilled chicken. It won't take me long to make dinner. Your choice." I love to cook and eat in as much as possible so I'm hoping she says no takeout.

"I'd rather not order takeout. I was gone all week and have been eating out every day. A home-cooked meal is long overdue! Besides, I've never tried your black beans and you rave about them all the time." She graces me with a beautiful smile, the left side of her face still red.

"*Listo*. I start cooking now and dinner will be ready in thirty minutes." I grab my shirt from the back of the couch and pull it over my head.

Sol joins me in the kitchen about fifteen minutes later. "Can I help with anything?" she asks.

"*Sí*. Get the dishes over there." I point to the cabinet on the far end of the kitchen. "We can eat here at the counter, if you want."

"Counter is good, it's easier that way too," she responds.

We're nearly finished with dinner and I'm itching to ask her about Carmine. I thought she would've brought it up by now, but she hasn't. I'm wondering if she's trying to avoid the topic all together. Let's see if I can draw it out of her.

"I think you need classes, to learn how to protect yourself," I say.

She nods in agreement. "When I left Carmine, I had thought about taking self-defense classes but never got around to it. Then I moved to Miami and forgot about it. I assumed I had left Boston and I was safe. I hadn't realized the lengths he would go to, although I should've. Now self-defense classes seem like a great idea. I'll look into finding a class."

"My friend owns a place, I call him tomorrow. He's former military and very good."

"Thanks."

I push the stool back and rise, grabbing my plate to put it in the sink. "*Y ahora*, what happens? What did Officer Cruz tell you?"

Sol finishes chewing what's in her mouth. "She told me the State Attorney would call me because even though I gave a statement to the police, I'll have to tell the State Attorney again. I'm guessing you'll get a call too, since you saw some of what happened."

"I'll tell them everything. How much time does he stay in jail?"

Her shoulder rises in uncertainty. "I don't know. I asked the officer, but she said I needed to ask the State Attorney. What I do know, is he might be able to pay bail so he can get out of jail while the case moves forward."

I lock my gaze with hers and cross the kitchen, closing the gap between us. "I no want you staying at your house alone, Sol. Please, stay here until it's over."

"Umm, that could be a long time," she says, turning toward the window while pulling a curl between her fingers.

"Sol, *no importa*," I tell her, placing my finger at her chin to turn her gaze back to me. "I want you to live with me." Sol's eyes widen as I'm speaking but I continue to keep my eyes steady, letting her know I'm serious. I don't care how long it takes because I want to move in together.

"Let me think about it," she responds. I can see the thoughts swirling because she's quiet, her lips slightly pursed. If I had to guess, she's probably trying to convince herself things are happening way too fast but at the same time doesn't want to return to her apartment after today's incident. I know that's what I'd be thinking if I were in her shoes.

"No make a decision right away. Take your time."

"I've never been so scared in my life," she says. "When I saw Carmine's face on the other side of my door it took me by surprise. I got too comfortable, let my guard down and he knew it. He was waiting for the right moment to show up. I wasn't strong enough to push the door closed and he gained entry. Fear rushed in as he grabbed my arms and pushed me toward the bedroom. I didn't know what he wanted, why he was there. When I asked, he said, 'shut up you fucking whore, I'm the one doing the talking today' and then he slapped me." Her hand lifts, resting on the red area of her cheek. "Stupidly, I complied." She's staring blankly at the wall as she's talking.

I'm about to interject when she speaks again.

"I thought I was gonna die today. I was suffocating. If you hadn't shown up, he would've killed me."

I need to hug her, remind her she's safe. "But you're here. No think about that. Think about him being arrested."

She reciprocates and squeezes her arms around me before separating, our eyes locking on one another. "Thank you for today. For everything you've done for me."

Is she serious right now? I'd do anything for her! How does she not know this yet? "*Haría todo por ti.*" I drag my thumb across her plump bottom lip.

"Do you know why he showed up, what he wanted?"

She shakes her head. "Like I said, he's my ex-boyfriend. We were together for almost two years. In the end, he was becoming abusive and so I escaped before it became worse."

My heartbeat quickens and rage stirs inside of me. "*Cómo qué* abusive?"

She shifts in her seat and stares out the French doors overlooking my backyard. "I don't like talking about everything I lived through. Besides, I figured no one wants to hear how weak I was."

"Weak? *Muñeca*, you are no weak." I extend my hand out to touch her, feel her skin. Sol remains still, her eyes fixed on something in the backyard.

"At first, he wasn't physically abusive. He was just controlling and emotionally abusive. Would never trust what I told him. Would check my phone, interrogate me each time I got home." Her eyes are still and they're staring into nothing as the memories spill.

I swallow. Listening to her recount being with this asshole is enraging me, and she hasn't even gotten to the abuse part yet.

"When he and I started living together, I wasn't much of a cook, but he expected me to cook, and clean, basically do everything at the house. If it had been up to him, I'd have been barefoot and pregnant." Sol's index fingers draw back and forth in a slow repetitive motion along the countertop. "The first time I made a pasta dish he wanted, he took one bite, told me I was worthless as a woman, and threw the food away, dish and all. Then he screamed and insulted me the entire time I cleaned up from making dinner and when I was finished, he left to go eat something. It was the first time I experienced his rage."

As Sol is remembering, a tear slips from her eye, and she wipes it away then clears her throat. "I think he felt emboldened because after the first night he started causing scenes when we went out. If someone even glanced at me, he would start a fight with the guy. He got arrested more times than I can remember, and according to him it was always my fault."

I adjust my jaw. Listening to what she's telling me is incredible, seems surreal she had to live with such a person yet here she is telling her story.

"It got to the point my friends stopped wanting to go out with me if he was coming, which is exactly what he wanted. They kept telling me I should leave him, but I ignored all their pleas. He would call me a whore for dressing in a way that attracted men. Said I provoked them purposely for their attention." She shifts in her seat and pushes her dish back.

"The first time I thought he was gonna hurt me was when I returned home late from work. He accused me of sleeping around and when I told him I was at work late he grabbed a knife and approached me, stabbing the wall to the left of my face—inches away." Tears start streaming down her face as she remembers yet her voice remains steady, flat.

"Every time he acted out, afterward he would apologize, tell me he loved me, treat me like a queen. It was a vicious cycle of love bombing, soul crushing, love bombing, abuse, and so on. Each time the abuse happened it increased in severity from the time before. Each time I convinced myself he loved me, and he'd never hurt me."

Listening to Sol talk about her past is shocking to me. It's the first time I hear a survivor talk about what they lived through. I want to hold her and protect her, but she's not finished. I don't know if it's okay for me to embrace her. Besides, she needs to let this all out, let go of everything she's holding inside of her.

"It wasn't until he slapped me that I had a wakeup call. The day he slapped me was because we had gone out to dinner with some of his friends. He was telling a story about some mutual friends and stupidly I clarified something, which he interpreted as me correcting him and embarrassing him in front of his friends. He gave me a stern look while at the table and I knew. I knew when we got home something was gonna happen, I just didn't know what. We didn't even make it home. As soon as we got to the car, he slapped me with an open hand."

Motherfucker! To think the man I had pinned down today made her suffer like this.

"I knew I had to leave because it would never get better. I lived in fear day in and day out. Walked on eggshells. Rarely went out unless I was with him and didn't even want to work for fear of doing something wrong and not knowing it. I only spoke when spoken to and basically stopped seeing my friends and family. I was a stranger living inside my own body. I didn't recognize myself. I planned my escape every day, during every waking moment. I thought about how I would do it, when I would do it, where I would go, and what I would take."

"How long until you left?"

"158 days passed between the day I made the decision until the day I left. It was the longest 158 days of my life. Each day I woke up wondering if it would be my last."

"Soledad." I approach her, pull her into my arms, and wrap her in my love.

"The slap was the last time he hit me, although I did have to endure verbal and emotional abuse as well as his tirades, which included throwing shit at me or shaking me." Soledad is overcome by tears; she's trembling and sobbing. I don't have words to console her, so I embrace her tightly, letting her know she's safe now.

"I was one of the lucky ones."

CHAPTER THIRTY-ONE

Soledad

TWO MONTHS LATER

"I need a minute before going inside," I say. Amaury is in the driver's seat and Melida is behind him, her hand resting on my shoulder. The Tahoe is parked in the corner lot across from the Family Courthouse in downtown Miami.

"We still have time," she says. "Your hearing doesn't start for another forty minutes." After Carmine attacked me, I applied for an Injunction for Protection Against Domestic Violence after the State Attorney mentioned it was something I could look into. The State Attorney explained that although his bond was initially denied, Carmine's lawyer was filing a motion for an Arthur Hearing, which is another hearing where he would again be requesting bond. So, although Carmine was currently being detained, it was possible he would be released in the future, depending on the outcome of the second hearing. The thought of him being released terrifies me!

"*Muñeca*, breathe," Amaury says, his hand on my thigh. When I applied for the injunction, Amaury came to this courthouse with me. Based on my application, a temporary injunction was immediately entered and then a final hearing set for a couple of weeks later. I then hired a lawyer to represent me at the Final Hearing because I was too nervous and needed all the help I could get. She obtained a continuance because she said more time was needed for the Final Hearing. It was rescheduled for today.

"I'm anxious about testifying while Carmine stares at me." I pull a curl between my fingers as I stare at the tall courthouse in front of us. My lawyer explained this hearing is a little different than the criminal case, which is still pending. She told me at this hearing the burden of proof is lower than in the criminal case and we must prove I'm in imminent danger of harm, which is why an injunction is necessary. The lawyer explained she'd ask me questions about our history, about his behavior when we lived together, and about the events at my apartment in Miami.

"Sol, listen to me," Melida says. I shift in my seat, meeting her dark eyes. "Carmine has instilled fear in you for too long. You already gave your statement to the police and the State Attorney. Just think of this as doing that again." My eyes wander, land on a white piece of lint on her dress near her shoulder. I stretch my hand to remove it. "Think of this as a practice run for when you have to testify at the criminal trial. Remember, no matter what, he can't hurt you anymore. You're in a courtroom, there's a bailiff. There's a judge. You're safe." Mel's words are calm and even, she's doing her best to calm me, to get me to stop overthinking what's about to happen. "Today, you have all the power. Just remember to use your voice to wield it."

I swallow and release a deep exhale, nodding. "Okay, let's go. My lawyer said security can have a long line, and I don't want to be late." I reach for the door handle and when I climb out of the car, Amaury is there waiting for me, wrapping my hand in his. Melida is to my left, her hand holding onto my forearm. Last month when I told her about this court date, she immediately told me she'd be here to support me. She flew in the day before yesterday.

We pass through the courthouse security and take

the elevator up to the twenty-first floor. As we walk into the waiting area, I'm searching for my attorney and see her off to the left in a navy suit. Silvia Gonzalez has dark hair with dark rimmed glasses. I remember seeing her in court a few times when I was interpreting and consistently being impressed by her courtroom demeanor. "Hello, Soledad. Amaury," she says, extending her hand out first to me, then to Amaury.

"Hi, Ms. Gonzalez. This is my friend Melida. She's here for moral support."

Silvia extends her hand, meeting Melida's. "Silvia Maria Gonzalez. Pleasure to meet you, Melida."

"Likewise," responds Melida.

"Let's have a seat in here." Ms. Gonzalez is gesturing to a small room at her back. "This way, we can talk privately while we wait for our case to be called."

We all take a seat around the small table. "Amaury, you won't be able to be inside the courtroom until you're called as a witness."

My heart begins racing at her words. "Why can't he be inside?" I ask.

"He's a witness and it's almost certain Carmine's lawyer will invoke the rule of sequestration. That means any witnesses who are gonna testify are not allowed to sit inside the courtroom until it's time for their testimony. After he testifies, he can stay inside.

This prevents the witness's testimony from being influenced by what's happening in the case."

My eyes meet Amaury's. "It's okay, *muñeca*," he says, resting his hand on my shoulder. "Melida will be inside the whole time." I nod.

"The most important thing is to tell the truth," Ms. Gonzalez says. "Take your time. Really listen to the question asked and only answer the question asked. You can ask for the question to be repeated if you don't understand it. And Sol," she says, her gaze meeting mine, "don't look at Carmine at all while you're testifying. Keep your eyes on me when I'm questioning you. When his lawyer questions you, if you don't feel comfortable looking at his lawyer, look straight ahead."

"Okay." I pull a curl through my fingers, my nerves pooling in my belly.

"Remember, Carmine's lawyer will cross-examine you. Her job is to advocate for her client so her questions may not be easy to hear. Don't let her rattle you." I nod. Earlier this week I was in Silvia's office as we prepared for today's hearing. She asked me some questions as if she was cross-examining me, preparing me for the questions I may get asked.

"You're shaking," says Melida. I glance at my hand and see the tremors. "Remember, he can't hurt you anymore." She grasps my hand in hers and squeezes.

"Caruso and Coretta," a male calls out.

"That's us," Ms. Gonzalez says. "Amaury, come with us so I can let the bailiff know you're a witness and then you can have a seat in the waiting area."

Before walking through the door, Amaury pulls me to the side and grasps my face between his hands. "I love you. You are strong and everything is gonna be okay." His lips brush mine and then I turn to walk through the courtroom doors.

Inside the courtroom is small, there's approximately three rows of benches to our right behind a low wall. There are two large desks in front of the area where the judge sits, and a woman is sitting to the left behind a computer. The fixtures are all dark wood, contrasting the pale color of the walls. Above where the judge will be sitting there's a sign that reads, "We who labor here seek only the truth." The bailiff disappears through a door behind the woman. Along the right side wall there's a witness box. I'm glad we're in this courtroom where the witness box chair isn't facing forward but rather across the courtroom. This way it'll be easier to ignore Carmine when I'm testifying.

Noticeably absent from the courtroom is Carmine.

After taking a seat at the large desk closest to us, my lawyer greets Carmine's lawyer and they're making small talk. His lawyer is dressed in a black pant suit, long hair pulled back. I turn to see Melida right behind me and reach for her hand. "You got this, Sol," she mouths. "I love you."

The creaking of a door sounds, and I turn in my seat. The door at the back of the courtroom opens and a police officer walks through, followed by Carmine who's wearing ill-fitting orange scrubs, two sizes too big for his frame. Behind Carmine is another officer. But what stands out the most, are the shackles at his hands, linked to the ones around his ankles. I lift my eyes to meet his and follow him until he turns and sits in his chair. The two officers stand off to the side, each of them crossing their arms as they lean against the wall. I wasn't ready to see Carmine in shackles. I almost feel bad for him but know I shouldn't. He's where he is because of his own choices.

My job has had me inside courtrooms for years, but this is the first time I'm here for my own case and not interpreting. Despite the years of exposure, it feels like my first time in a courtroom. The nerves I feel are like no other, my stomach churns. Silvia slides a yellow pad across the table to me together with a pen. "This is for you to take notes. If you have any questions or concerns come up, write them down for me. If you hear something you want to point out to me, write it down."

"All rise," calls out the bailiff.

The female judge appears through the door, ascends the steps, and sits. "You may be seated. Madame Clerk, please call the case for the record." I swallow and my heart rate increases. I pull a curl between my fingers and twirl.

The attorneys are speaking but I can't focus right now, not understanding what they're saying. I'm thinking about my testimony, reminding myself to remain calm because Carmine can no longer hurt me.

"I'd like to call Soledad Caruso," says Silvia. My heart is thrumming as I stride across the courtroom to the witness stand. Once there, the clerk swears me in, and I take a seat. I glance over at Melida who mouths "I love you." My attorney begins asking me questions, my name, my occupation, and how I know Carmine. She's calm, her steady voice guiding me and keeping me grounded. I remember my conversation with her when she explained she would begin with basic questions, have me lay the foundation and work my way up to the reason why we're in court. Told me this is required for legal purposes but will also help ease my nerves because it will get me comfortable with testifying.

"Ms. Caruso, can you please tell us what happened that led you to file for an injunction?" I swallow and take a deep breath. This is the moment.

To speak my truth.

To face my fear.

To reclaim my power.

"Carmine knocked on my door," I say, shifting in my seat. "There's no peephole on the door at my apartment so I cracked the door open to see who it was. When he saw my face he pushed the door forward with his hand, stuck his foot on the threshold. I wasn't strong enough to push the door closed and he gained entry into my apartment."

Ms. Gonzalez takes two steps toward me and asks, "What happened once he was inside your apartment?"

My hands are shaking, and I interlock one with the other in an effort to calm them. I'm thankful they're hidden behind the witness box. "He grabbed my arms and pushed me toward the bedroom. I asked him why he was there, and he said, 'shut up you fucking whore, I'm the one doing the talking today' and then he slapped me." Tears slide down my cheeks as I recount the moment.

"What happened next?" Ms. Gonzalez asks.

I take another deep breath, swipe away the tears from my eyes and begin speaking. I describe how he pushed me onto the bed, straddled me, and wrapped his hands around my neck, putting pressure on the skin beneath his fingers. My voice quivers but I push through. I describe how my arms were pinned to my sides by his legs and I was kicking my feet. The tears steadily fall as I continue telling the judge how I was feeling short of breath. How I felt like I was suffocating, and thoughts of dying were running through my mind. I describe how Amaury pulled Carmine off of me, and I could suddenly breathe again. Watched as Amaury neutralized Carmine and made me call 911. She shows me pictures the police took, and the ones I took with my phone a couple days later when the purple bruises made their appearance.

"Was this the first time Mr. Coretta put his hands on you?" Ms. Gonzalez inquires.

My head shakes.

"Please answer yes or no, Ms. Caruso. Your response needs to be verbal so the record is clear," instructs the judge.

Shifting my gaze from my lawyer, I look over at the judge. "No, it wasn't the first time." Tears continue streaming down my cheeks.

Ms. Gonzalez asks, "Please tell us about the first time Mr. Coretta put his hands on you." I respond by telling them about the first time he slapped me when we still lived together.

Ms. Gonzalez asks questions to guide me through

the history of my relationship with Carmine, has me explain how jealous he was, how he monitored my phone calls, how he would start fights with random strangers, show up at my work, and how he would emotionally and verbally abuse me. She has me tell the court why I moved to Miami, how I tried to get away from him, how I tried to start over.

"No further questions," says Ms. Gonzalez. I swipe tears from my cheeks, take another deep breath to prepare for the questions Carmine's lawyer is going to ask me.

"Ms. Ventura, cross examination," says the judge to Carmine's lawyer.

"Ms. Caruso, do you need a moment?" asks Carmine's lawyer.

I shake my head. "No, I'm okay," I respond, lifting my chin.

"You opened the door for Mr. Coretta, correct?" asks Ms. Ventura.

"Yes, but as soon as I saw him, I tried to close it." My heart thrums loudly. Ms. Ventura asks me a few more questions before saying, "No further questions."

"Redirect, Ms. Gonzalez?" asks the judge.

"No, Your Honor," she responds.

"Ms. Caruso, you may step down." I rise and meet Melida's eyes, which are red from her tears. She has no idea how important it was for her to be here, to support me, and how much it meant that she offered to be here before I even asked her to do it. She's one of the most important people in my life and I'm not sure I've ever expressed to her how much.

When I take my seat, Melida whispers behind me, "Proud of you, Sol." Silvia grasps my hand in hers underneath the table and squeezes, before rising to her feet.

"I'd like to call Amaury Mejia," she says. The bailiff walks out from behind the woman at the desk and out to the waiting area. A minute later Amaury strolls into the courtroom, pushes the swing door open, and crosses toward the witness stand.

As soon as Amaury enters the witness box, he's sworn in and then takes a seat. His eyes meet mine and he smiles. Then his eyes shift looking toward where Carmine is sitting, and his plump lips are set in a straight line. I can see his jaw shift as he cracks his neck.

Ms. Gonzalez rises. After asking Amaury to state his name for the record, she asks, "How do you know Soledad Caruso?"

"She's my girlfriend."

"How do you know Mr. Coretta?" she asks.

"I only met him one time. It was the day I saw

him force his way into Sol's house." Amaury goes on to describe how he watched what happened from the street and then sprinted inside the house. How he saw me pinned beneath Carmine. How he neutralized and punched him thrice, spraying blood all over the place.

When Ms. Gonzalez finishes her questions, Ms. Ventura only asks two questions. When both lawyers finish, Amaury rises and crosses the courtroom, our eyes locked the entire time. I can hear him sit down behind me, next to Melida.

"No further witnesses," says Ms. Gonzalez.

"Ms. Ventura, do you have any witnesses?" the judge inquires.

"No witnesses, Your Honor," she responds. "Due to the pending criminal case, upon the advice of counsel, Mr. Coretta will be asserting his Fifth Amendment right to remain silent at this time." Of course he doesn't want to say anything, spineless coward.

"Mr. Coretta," the judge says. "I must inform you that you have the right to testify if you choose. Or you can choose to assert your Fifth Amendment right to remain silent, as represented by your attorney. However, if you choose to remain silent, the court can take it as a negative inference. Do you understand these choices?"

"Yes, Judge," Carmine says.

"Which are you choosing, Mr. Coretta?"

Carmine's eyes shift down to the paper in front of him. "On the advice of counsel, I choose to assert my Fifth Amendment right to remain silent."

"Very well, Mr. Coretta. Thank you."

The judge is reading her notes, the ruffling of her papers loud. Her pen is moving as she's reviewing the papers in front of her. The silence in the courtroom is unnerving. My heart thunders in my chest and I wonder if my lawyer can hear the thrashing. What is the judge thinking? What happens next? She lifts her head, looks over to our table. "Based on the evidence presented by the Petitioner," she says, shifting her gaze to the other table, "the Court finds the Petitioner has met her burden and I'm going to enter a permanent injunction for an indefinite period of time."

Ms. Gonzalez squeezes my hand and drops her head close to mine. "Congratulations, Sol," she whispers. "A permanent injunction for an indefinite period of time means he cannot come near you, ever. He can't contact you, send you a message directly or through a third party." My heart thumps in my chest, tears streaming from my eyes.

"You did it!" whispers Melida.

"Ms. Caruso," the judge says. I look up, meeting the judge's eyes. "We will have you leave the courthouse now. Mr. Coretta will stay behind to be served with a copy of the injunction before being taken back into custody. You're excused. Ms. Gonzalez, if you would please stay behind so we can get you a copy of the injunction, which you can then send to your client. Court is now in recess."

"Okay, Judge. Thank you." I push the chair back and rise.

"Your Honor," my attorney says, rising from her chair. "I'm going to walk my client out and will return shortly, if I may?"

"Yes, Ms. Gonzalez, no problem." Together with Melida and Amaury, we walk out to the waiting area and when we stop, Amaury pulls me into an embrace. He doesn't say anything, hugging me so tightly we're nearly one person. My tears begin to flow freely. For the first time since everything started with Carmine, I feel light.

I separate from Amaury, look over at my lawyer. "Ms. Gonzalez," I say, "thank you! There is no way I could've done this without you. Your calm demeanor throughout kept me grounded and guided me. There are no words to express my gratitude."

"You're welcome, Sol," she says, extending her hand to meet mine. I pull her in for a hug. I don't know if it's appropriate or not, but it feels right. She returns the hug, lets her hands land on my back and squeezes then pulls away.

"Okay, we'll go. I know you have to get back inside the courtroom."

"I will email you when I have a copy of the injunction. Besides that, we're done with this case. Thank you for allowing me to represent you. You did great today. Enjoy the rest of your day." She turns and disappears back inside the courtroom.

Amaury, Melida, and I walk toward the elevator and as we're waiting for a car to arrive, Melida says, "Sol, you were amazing." Both of her arms extend out, and I grasp her hands in mine. "If I'm being honest, I was worried you would get so nervous you wouldn't know what to say but you were incredible! You kept your cool, let Ms. Gonzalez guide you, and spoke your truth. Now he can never hurt you again."

"There's still the criminal case, Mel."

"True, but you already know what you need to do."

EPILOGUE

Soledad

SIX MONTHS LATER

Since being attacked by Carmine, my life has changed, much of which is attributed to my signing up at a gym called Florida Defensive Training where Amaury's friend, a former military special ops guy, runs a program centered entirely on self-defense tactics and varying defense related courses. I've been going three times per week. Not only has taking these classes shown me I was a sitting duck, waiting to become someone's victim, but it's taught me I'm much stronger than I ever imagined. The techniques I'm learning would have likely helped me when I was attacked.

"How was class today?" Amaury asks as I stroll into the kitchen. It smells good in here, when I pull the top off the pot on the stove, I see there's red beans simmering.

"Good. Today we worked on maneuvers to help escape someone attacking but with only one hand. We had to try with both our dominant and support hands. My left side needs work!!" I exclaim, and chuckle.

"*Qué*, no kiss for me?" he asks, feigning disappointment.

I lean into the counter. "Hmm, let me think about it for a minute."

He approaches me and grasps onto my hip, pulling me flush to him. "*Quiero devorarte*," he says then kisses me, fervently. He lowers his nose, landing just below my ear and traces it down my neckline to my collarbone, inhaling my scent as he does. "Mmm. *Ese olor tuyo es único*, and I can't get enough of it." Amaury is always, and I mean always, doing this, whether we're watching TV, sitting on the beach, or lying in bed. When I ask him what it is about my scent he likes or what it smells like, he can't describe it, except to say it's a little bit sweet, a little bit salty and all Soledad—whatever that means!

Another change is Carmine is still behind bars.

Even though I have the permanent injunction, I feel an extra layer of safety knowing he's locked up. He was denied bail at his second bail hearing. Before the second bail hearing, I lost a lot of sleep thinking about Carmine free with the ability to terrorize, whether it was me or someone else. Thankfully, bail was denied! Last I spoke with the State Attorney, she told me he's going to trial, which means he's risking life in prison.

He was charged with burglary with a battery, which in Florida are felonies punishable by life. He's too cocky to take a plea, although it's my understanding the State hasn't offered one. Of course, him going to trial means I have to testify again about what happened in my apartment. I'd be lying if I said I wasn't scared, even if I already did it once. I'm extremely nervous about it because the next time I testify will be in the presence of a jury. I'll have to tell my story to strangers other than the judge.

Initially, I was reluctant because I already have the permanent injunction in place. I felt bad I would testify and possibly put him behind bars for years. However, Ms. Gonzalez explained the permanent injunction would be for an indefinite period of time but in the future Carmine could seek to modify or dissolve it based on a substantial change. Also, Melida, Jestine, Krissa, Dayi, and Amaury were all quick to remind me that he's not in jail because of me, his actions and his choices are his and he's responsible for any consequences.

I've endured enough pain over the years at Carmine's hands and now I have the power to end it. To end his reign of terror. When we were discussing it, Amaury said something I'll never forget. "If he's in jail, he can't hurt anyone else. You're protecting one of his future girlfriends." Between the possibility of Carmine filing something and what Amaury said, I was convinced I had to testify.

"I have to shower; you want to join me?" I ask.

One of the biggest changes in my life is I'm finally learning to trust my instincts and to trust my relationship with Amaury. After the attack we continued living together. At first, I thought I would only stay for a few weeks. But as the days passed, I felt lighter than I had in a long time. The weight of my relationship with Carmine had been lifted after I testified at the Injunction Hearing. The night I shared my story with Amaury was the first time I'd told someone other than Mel, Jess, and Krissa. It was a crucial turning point for me. After the hearing, I decided to seek out a therapist because talking felt good. I hadn't realized how numb I'd become to the entire situation, just pushing it down and pretending it never happened was disastrous for me. The more I spoke, the more I had to say. It was cathartic. Between the hearing, therapy, and self-defense, I started feeling strong and confident, two things I hadn't ever felt at the same time.

"*Claro*. I was waiting for you so we can shower together." The bathroom in the main bedroom has a large double shower with powerful jets and incredible pressure. It's quickly become one of our favorite activities to do together.

Amaury's invitation to move in with him lingered in the air, neither of us spoke about it although I could tell it was at the forefront of his thoughts. But he was patient with me, understood my reluctance and that I needed to arrive at the decision on my own. I didn't want it to happen all at once. I've been at Amaury's since the day I was attacked but it took me three months to officially agree to move in together. "*What's the difference?*" Melida asked me when I told her about our arrangement.

The difference is for the first three months I still paid rent at my old apartment. I kept my room separate from Amaury's even if most nights we shared his bed. From an outside perspective it may look the same, but for me, it wasn't. I still had my own space, and it was important for me. Had Melida, Jess, or Krissa lived in Miami, I would've been staying with one of them and not Amaury.

"*Why don't you move back*?" my mother asked me a few weeks after the incident. I had never told her about Carmine and the way he treated me. I didn't want her to worry about me unnecessarily. And if I'm being honest, I didn't want her to judge me. After what happened in Miami, I finally opened up to her about it because I nearly died, and she wouldn't have known the truth. I vowed to be open and honest with her about everything from that point forward. "*Because Miami feels like home, even though my family and most of my friends all still live in Boston*" is the response I gave my mother. I feel like I belong in Miami, the Latin vibe of everyday life is pervasive in all aspects of the community. The Latin vibe was something I craved while living in Boston. Besides, I'm in love with Amaury and don't want to leave his side.

I turn the stove off, and we go upstairs. As we're undressing, I say, "Remember, our flight leaves for Boston tomorrow at two thirty."

Of all the changes that have happened in my life, I think the biggest one is I now have to share my time with Amaury with his daughter Analia. Initially I was worried sharing my boyfriend with a newfound daughter would change the way he loved me. Of course, that was ridiculous for me to think. Amaury changed, but not in a bad way. He was happier than I had ever seen him. His heart expanded because there's always room for more love. At the onset, Amaury started spending time with Analia but only sporadically. Yanelis was making it difficult for him, so he hired Ms. Gonzalez to help him and now he has a permanent schedule in place, which is recognized by the courts. She now spends half of the week at Amaury's house.

At first, Analia was reluctant around me, spoke very little and generally ignored me. But with time, she opened up, became more comfortable, and realized I wasn't her enemy. Analia is smart, kind, and funny and has many of her father's personality traits. They do some of the same weird things like zap their ice cream in the microwave before eating it, crinkle their nose in the same manner, and both have the same snort when they're belly laughing.

I watched Amaury grow as a father, something he was nervous about—is still nervous about. Even now he feels much guilt about missing so many years of Analia's life, but I encouraged him to be truthful with her, about how he came to the United States before he knew about her. Analia told us she knew everything her father told her because her mother had talked to her about their history, about their relationship up until Amaury left Cuba. The night Amaury learned this, he cried tears of relief and joy. He was ecstatic his daughter understood the circumstances of their separation.

I often watch Amaury and Analia from afar and the bond that's grown between them in the short time they've known each other is incredible. Analia is always asking questions about her family in Cuba, curious for knowledge about her grandparents, aunts, uncles, and cousins, as well as her heritage and her father's journey across the ocean. As is to be expected, Amaury is quick to share, to give Analia everything she asks for, and more.

"I packed my bag already," he responds.

"Good. Can't wait to eat at all my favorite restaurants with you." He chuckles at my mention of eating out. He knows how much I enjoy food, and he indulges me.

"*Estoy feliz* to just do life with you," Amaury responds.

A NOTE FROM THE AUTHOR

This should be read after reading the book as it CONTAINS SPOILERS

I was married at the young age of 19, thought I knew everything about life, and listened to no one. I didn't tell anyone I was getting married, and my parents were furious. I had met my then husband when I was 18 and fell head over heels in love. It wasn't until after we got married that our relationship began deteriorating.

Soledad's story is one similar to my own, one that I've not shared with most of the people in my life. I've kept my history with domestic abuse silent. Until now. I felt the time was right to tell this story. Domestic abuse has many layers, and it never looks the same for anyone who is a victim or survivor. It crosses all racial and socio-economic lines. It happens every day, sometimes in the most unexpected places. Yet, it's something that's rarely discussed but should be.

This story is only my perspective and my personal experience, fictionalized through Sol and Carmine's story. Their story is not meant to define domestic abuse, abusers, victims, or survivors. Instead, I decided to share my story because sharing a personal story often helps others in similar situations feel less alone and feel seen. It helps empower others to find their voice and to make a change.

After I left my abusive relationship, I lived in Boston for some time, but my ex didn't make it easy for me and it's one of the reasons I chose to leave and move to Miami. Before I moved to Miami in 2003, I visited with the intention of finding a neighborhood to live in, and to familiarize myself with the new city I'd be living in. It's during that visit that I met my now husband in a similar way Sol and Amaury met.

My husband Alexis (Alex) is Cuban, and he's a Cuban rafter. Amaury's journey across the ocean is my husband's journey. Amaury's harrowing tales of life in Cuba, are tales told by my husband, his family, and friends. My husband crossed the Florida Straits with his brother and six of their friends. They left Cuba on August 18, 1994, not knowing what their future held. On August 22, 1994, they were picked up by the U.S. Coast Guard and spent two days on a U.S. Naval Aircraft Carrier before being taken to Guantanamo Bay, Cuba to live as refugees while they waited to be processed into the United States. It was here they learned that Fidel Castro had announced, "whoever wanted to leave, could go," and that President Bill Clinton gave a news conference to address the Cuban rafter crisis. Thousands of Cubans took to the open water in search of a better life. My husband, his brother, friends, and thousands of others, risked their lives to live freely in the United States. Thankfully, Alex's raft arrived safely. However, there were many who perished in the open waters. But, as many Cuban refugees will tell you, those who died, died free.

Alex and I have been together for twenty years. Everyone we ever met (and meet) is fascinated by the tale he tells of his journey to the United States. Of how he lived in poverty in Cuba, and how the United States gave him a new chance at life, gave him freedom, the ability to work and earn a decent living, and to never want for basic necessities.

Amor in the 305 came to me during a conversation I had with my husband, and I began writing. Telling our stories of survival, each vastly different from the other. We each overcame our individual circumstances and became a stronger individual. We both understand the role our past circumstance plays in building our character and personality, and how we cannot let our past define our future. Both he and I are grateful each day.

Today I work as a lawyer and part of my law practice is dedicated to representing women survivors of domestic abuse in civil court proceedings, to obtain civil injunctions for protection against domestic violence and in family court. I work hand-in-hand with No More Tears USA, a Non-Profit organization in South Florida dedicated to saving lives of domestic abuse and human trafficking survivors. This is some of the most difficult work I do, but also the most rewarding. I never went to court to protect myself against my domestic abuser because I was too frightened. And so, I advocate for my clients the same way I would've advocated for the younger version of myself—with my entire heart.

RESOURCES

If you or someone you know is a victim or survivor of domestic abuse, there are many resources to help you.

In South Florida (Miami-Dade, Broward, and Palm Beach Counties), No More Tears USA helps survivors get to a safe location and assists with the transition, including paying for legal representation. **nomoretearsusa.org** or 1-954-324-7669

National Organizations:

National Domestic Violence Hotline: **www.thehotline.org** or 1-800-799-SAFE (7233)

National Coalition Against Domestic Violence: **ncadv.org/resources**

In addition to the above resources, oftentimes your local government has resources to help, whether it's the county or city you're located in.

To learn more about Cuban Rafters, please visit:

www.theatlantic.com/photo/2014/11/20-years-after-the-1994-cuban-raft-exodus/100852/

www.c-span.org/video/?59689-1/news-conference-cuban-refugees

balseros.miami.edu/

www.thenationalnews.com/world/the-1994-cuban-raft-exodus-1.659541

flashbackmiami.com/2014/08/13/cuban-rafter-crisis/

www.hrw.org/report/1994/10/02/cuba-repression-exodus-august-1994-and-us-response

ACKNOWLEDGMENTS

To my Alpha Readers: Janet Aznar and Akilah Harris, thank you both for your advice on the very early versions of Amor in the 305. Silvia Maria Gonzalez, where would this story be without you? Your invaluable participation, feedback, constructive criticism, and guidance on the criminal law aspect of this story was vital to its success. Although I'm a lawyer, I know little about criminal law, and you made sure the details were accurate. Thank you for being so generous with your time, your wisdom, and your experience.

To my Beta Readers: Kristie Puentes, Pamela Fero, Sarah Troxel, Diana Castrillon, and Courtney Montiero – thanks for all your feedback when reading an early version. Your insight is invaluable and I'm truly grateful for you. Love you ladies!

Getting a book published takes teamwork and I couldn't have written, published, and marketed this book without an incredible team. I started out strong and **Murphy Rae** created the stunning cover that exudes Miami Beach vibes. When work consumed me, I fell behind in my writing and putting this book into the world was delayed by a year. This resulted in me having to make a lot of last-minute changes. My initial editor was booked and so **Virginia Tesi Carey** made room in her busy schedule to accommodate me. Thank you, V! **Alyssa Garcia** with Uplifting Author Services also made room for me in her busy schedule to format the manuscript and make it beautiful for the e-readers and print. My proofreaders, Courtney DeLollis and Amy Briggs, your fresh eyes caught things so many of us missed and you helped make the final product what it is. **Kiki** and the entire team at **The Next Step PR**, thank you for your patience in waiting for me to finish this book so that you can help market and introduce it to the world. My assistant, **Jonathan**, is a Godsend. Jonathan, without you I don't know where I would be or how I would survive every day. You're incredible and I although I tell you all the time, Thank you!!!

My stories pull from the real-life experiences I've lived through, and those experiences were almost always with one or all of my life-long friends, **Jessica**, **Kristen**, **Lucia**, **Melissa**, **Jenny**, and **Donata**. I love each of you beyond measure and thanks for allowing me to fictionalize our adventures.

Life keeps me busy. Add writing fiction to the mix and it takes away time from my family, my mother, and siblings. You're all so patient with me yet encourage me beyond measure.

To my husband, **Alexis**, who sees me awake at the wee hours of the night typing away when I want to write just one more paragraph. *Gracias por tu apoyo y paciencia.* In particular, thank you for always sharing your stories of life in Cuba. Your stories, and those of **Angel Nuñez** and **Roger Acosta**, are the only reason I was able to write Amaury's story as I did. Amaury is a creation of each of your experiences. I hope I did your story justice because like Sol, I will never truly understand what you lived through, and what you felt as your rafts floated across the open ocean. *Espero que algún día Cuba sea libre y que ustedes lo puedan ver.*

Most importantly, to my readers. I'm extremely grateful! Thank you for choosing my books. There are not enough words to express my gratitude.

ABOUT THE AUTHOR

Shelly Cruz is a lawyer who runs her own law firm in Miami, Florida. She was born and raised just outside of Boston, Massachusetts by a fierce Argentinian mom and super strict Puerto Rican dad. When she's not researching and writing legal documents, she enjoys expressing her creativity by writing fiction. She's a lover of love, Carminece, and relationships, which is why she writes wicked sexy Carminece. In her free time, Shelly loves reading, traveling, and riding on the back of her husband's Harley Davidson motorcycle while enjoying the open road.

Shelly loves to hear from her readers, please send her an email to shellycruzwrites@gmail.com

Facebook
facebook.com/shellycruzwrites

Instagram
instagram.com/shellycruzwrites/

Goodreads
goodreads.com/author/show/20726422.Shelly_Cruz

Twitter
twitter.com/shellycwrites

Pinterest
pinterest.com/shellycruzwrites/

Made in the USA
Middletown, DE
20 August 2022